THE PIPIL SAGA

MILTON MANRIQUE JUÁREZ

Published by Milton Manrique Juarez
P.O. Box 32266 | Las Vegas Nevada 89133 USA
www.miltonjuarez.com

Book design copyright © 2016 by Milton Manrique Juarez. All rights reserved.
Cover design by Milton Manrique Juarez
Interior design by Milton Manrique Juarez

Published in the United States of America

DEDICATION

To my two princesses: Samantha and Sophia.

ACKNOWLEDGMENTS

I would like to thank all the people in my life that believed in me, and pushed me to be better. Special thanks to my test readers. Thank you for not losing interest in the story and always begging for the next chapter. I couldn't have done it without you. And last but not least to my editors, who were able to work and adapt to my writing style.

CONTENT

PREFACE

This is a work of fiction. Any similarity to any other work or historical events is purely coincidental, except for the chaneques, which are mythical characters that my grandparents used to tell me about when I was a child. They were beings who stole children by enchanting them with their touch. Like any other child, these legends used to scare me, but I got to an age when these fantasy stories were just that—— fantasy stories. Most of the stories my uncles and grandparents told were all make-believe. In their stories, they had been victims or witnesses of these apparitions. They never really saw these beings, let alone the Sihuanaba herself.

Still, those stories left a mark in my life, so I decided to write my own story to continue the tradition with my children. I hope this story also fills with melancholy all those who have forgotten how to be children. And to all those who still are, I hope this story will inspire you for years to come.

There are many of us who have forgotten our culture. We have coupled the change of the new era, and we have forgotten our ancestors and our roots. It seems that we only think of them when the schoolteacher requires us to study our history, but it all just stays in the classroom.

For as humble that our ancestors may have been, they also had struggles, had dreams and longing for something better for their families. We cannot and should not forget their sacrifices. Many of them had to endure great suffering to achieve their dreams——slavery, racism, opprobrium, etc. In the end all that is left is us, their hope. In this Pipil story, I found it necessary to remember them as they were. In this fictional story, I have tried to maintain and show their culture as closely as possible, but keep in mind that it is still a work of fiction.

It has really been an adventure to write this story. I hope you enjoy it as much as I have.

Let's never forget where we came from, and we'll find peace in our destiny.

——MILTON MANRIQUE JUÁREZ

INTRODUCTION

The reflection of the crescent moon shines strong in the lagoon this night. All is quiet until the water begins to boil. The vapor flows from the boiling bubbles covering the entire area as an early-morning mist. Even the fishing boats are completely enveloped.

The woman drops her comb to the ground, fixes her eyes on the water, and looks around. There is no one, not even her faithful servants. Suddenly everything has become silent. The animals have gone completely mute. Neither the crickets nor coyotes can be heard anywhere. The owls and quetzals have closed their beaks. She stands up and starts looking around, unable to see anything but the tree shadows.

The bubbles burst and began to grow stronger. *What's going on? This seems like witchcraft?* The beautiful woman thought. But in this land there are no powerful witches. At most, there are healers and seers. Even the most prestigious ones are unable to make the water boil, much less mute the animals. This has to be something more powerful.

The beautiful lady puts her hand into the warm water to test the seriousness of its heat. The water is so hot that it could melt the skin of any animal. *What's going on?* She asks herself once more.

The beautiful woman stoops down to pick up her comb, but a large snake has seized it. The snake begins to climb the rock where she had been sitting just a minute ago. The serpent wounds itself on top of the stone and fixes its gaze firmly into the woman's eyes and begins to vaporize into a growing dark steam. The snake vanishes, leaving only its steam behind it, which begins to grow and forms into a shape of a man. The vapor hardens, and a tall man with indigenous warrior armor appears in front of her. He wears a crown of feathers on his head, with leopard patches on his body and a pair of long braids.

"Tezcatlipoca!" One of the indigenous gods appears in front of her with a smile on his lips. The shocking look of surprise on her face explains everything.

"Is that how you greet your old friends, Sihuehuet?" The God comes down from the rock and takes her hands into his.

"What do you want with me?" The woman asks, being very suspicious of the jaguar god, and pulls away.

"I just came to visit you. What? I can't visit my old friends?" The god asks sarcastically.

"You have never visited me before. Have you ever even thought of me? Even when Tlaloc banished me from heaven, it didn't seem to matter to you. You didn't defend me. You didn't even defend your son."

She takes two steps back, away from her old friend. "What do you want? Have you come to torture me? Could it be that I have not paid dearly for my transgression?" The beautiful lady asks.

"I come in peace. Believe it or not, I think it's a shame what happened to you. It also saddens me to see you here— you and all your beauty. It's very sad indeed."

"You call this beautiful?" Sihuehuet interrupts him, very indignant.

Tezcatlipoca steps away from the river and starts walking deeper into the forest, leaving Sihuehuet talking to herself. As any other god, he is not here to hear complaints, let alone listen to an enraged woman.

"Do you see these trees? Your lake? And your mountains?" Sihuehuet leaves his questions hanging without an answer. She just stares at him and starts walking after him. "This is a beautiful paradise, but I'm getting bored with it. I think it would be a good place to build a monument to the gods." The god looks around and stops his gaze when he sees the woman walking near him. "This is your home. Isn't that so?" The woman just bows her head in affirmation to the god's statement. "This land is rich in minerals. Its animals are beautiful, and its plants are strong. It would be a pity to lose them. It would be a shame if this lake were to dry."

"So, you came here to brag about your strength? To teach me a lesson? To torture me?" The beautiful woman takes a pause. "Oh, I see. You think I'm happy here; a place where I'm not even a ruling queen. I am a goddess, not a simple human or beast of this rotten world." Sihuehuet pushes her hair away from her face with her delicate hands and averts her gaze away from Tezcatlipoca.

"Ha ha ha. Goddess." Tezcatlipoca sarcastically laughs. "You were never a goddess. Powers you really never had, no more than just your beauty and charms. You carry god's blood in your veins, but you're not a goddess. But I did not come here to discuss your status or social position. I came here to bring you good news." Tezcatlipoca takes a step closer to the woman.

"Good news for me, or for you?"

"For both of us." Sihuehuet fixes her gaze on the god of discord, very attentive to his next words.

"Well? I'm all ears."

"I know you've been looking for Chalchiuhtlicue's bracelet. Your excavations are not just for gold and precious stones."

"My excavations are my personal business, not yours," the beautiful lady answers.

"Do not worry, I won't tell anyone about your secret." The god slowly walks deeper into the woods. "With the bracelet, you could enter the kingdom without being noticed. But would you want to enter a kingdom where no one likes you? A place where you're not welcome? Plus, a place where you wouldn't have a good social status. Here you are a queen. You command and others obey you."

"Where are you going with all this?" Sihuehuet asks getting very impatient.

"You and I have a common enemy; a very powerful god and most worshiped by mankind."

"Tlaloc!" Sihuehuet whispers under her breath. "I didn't know you were enemies."

"Not enemies per se. It's complicated."

"Complicated? Or is it just jealousy? Maybe you're just looking for revenge."

"Never mind that. But tell me, what does Tlaloc appreciate most?" The god waits for an answer but doesn't get one, so he decides to answer it himself. "It's a very simple question—— his precious humans, of course. Of all the gods, including Quetzalcoatl, humans love him the most."

"So what's your plan? To help me find the bracelet?" Sihuehuet asks.

"No, you know I can't intervene in the affairs of this world. But I can give you useful information. The rest is up to you."

"That has never stopped you before." Sihuehuet pauses for a brief moment, waiting for a response that will never come. "Okay, so tell me what I need to do," she finally exclaims.

"You already know what you need to do. Find the bracelet. The only thing I can tell you is that you are in the right place. The bracelet is buried in the skirts of the Lamatepeque volcano."

"I already know that. You're not giving anything new."

"Yes. But what you do not know is that Itzalku is not a prisoner in the god's realm."

"Itzalku?"

"Yes. All this time I also thought he was a prisoner of Quetzalcoatl, and that he was imprisoned in the god's realm. But it is not so. Quetzalcoatl decided it was best to keep him in a prison hidden near the valley of the hammocks."

"Why are you telling me this? Doesn't this go against the code of the gods?"

"The code says that I can't help you or get involved. I'm not helping you. I'm merely giving you information about your lover."

"My lover? Or your son?"

"I have many children."

"Of course you do. But there's only one like Itzalku." Tezcatlipoca sits on a log while Sihuehuet analyzes the situation. "If Itzalku is a prisoner on earth; that means that he also has been banished from the realm. He may not return either. So, your plan is that we reign on earth."

"You were always so perceptive." The god smiles and stands up. "With the help of Itzalku, you could conquer the Pipils and banish the Spaniards from these lands. All of the land would be yours. Then you could expand your dominion to the land of the Mayans and Aztecs."

"So much is your hatred for humans?" Sihuehuet asks with a smile on her lips.

"No, I love humans. If it wasn't so, I wouldn't have protected them. What I hate is their worship for Tlaloc and their weakness to do what is necessary to survive. These Pipils are very weak. Their hearts are too noble, and they have forgotten their offerings and sacrifices to their gods. So I intend to punish them for that."

"And for that you want me to release Itzalku? You intend to use Itzalku and me to take dominion of humanity." The god doesn't answer the question but takes note of her statement.

"The bracelet of Chalchiuhtlicue has enough power to break the spell on Itzalku's prison. That is all that you'll need." The god leaps skywards. In an instant, he transforms into a big black bird and flies toward the moon.

MILTONMANRIQUEJUAREZ

ROAD TO LAKE COATEPEQUE

The wagon is very visible from high up by the cave. The gang leader decides to climb a tree for a better view. It's a human family traveling to the lake. It seems to be directed toward Coatepeque. Kumara makes a signal to his companions to rise and take a look.

The front man stops to inspect the site while the teen on the black horse guides it deeper into the woods. "This is a good place to spend the night. Get off the road and hide the wagon behind those trees. We have to set up a tent to sleep. Elena, only bring the most necessary items and food for the night, and take them a little deeper into the woods. We'll be safer there. Itzcua, take care of the animals. I will go scout the area for bandits and Lenca Indians."

"Yes, dad." The young man responds. Atecaltzin takes the black horse, as it is the only one saddled, and disappears down the road ahead.

Itzcuauhtzin parks the wagon behind the trees, hiding it from the road. Then he covers the wheel tracks.

Itzcuauhtzin, a thirteen-year-old boy knows exactly what to do and uses dust and dry leaves to hide the tracks of the wagon wheels and the horses' tracks.

Elena takes the children, and everyone helps out by carrying food and utensils for the night and then goes deeper into the woods, where the trees are thicker, to hide from the road.

Itzcuauhtzin takes the horses with him while the twins take their toys and some blankets to sleep.

By the time Atecaltzin comes back, everything is ready. The only thing left to do is set up the tent. "Xochitl, Tenoch, go get some water from the river. Fill those jars and bring them back so we can cook. We also need to water the horses, so hurry up." The kids obey immediately and head for the river, opening a breach through the bushes.

"Felipe, Sebastian, go and get some dry wood to make a fire." The twins quickly start to gather dry branches from their surroundings.

"Itzcuauhtzin, take the horses and go water them and make sure they have something to eat as well. We have less than an hour before the sun goes down."

"Yes, dad." Itzcuauhtzin takes two horses and ties them up on a tree where there is a lot of grass and lets them eat. He takes the saddle off of the black horse then takes the mare and guides them both down to the river. Since there is no easy path to the river, he follows the trail that his siblings left behind.

"The water is so good, Tenoch. It looks good for bathing."

"Yes, it does, but right now we can't. We have to take the water back. Mom is waiting for it." They hear a sound behind them, and they both turn around. But it's only Itzcuauhtzin with a couple of horses.

"Hurry up, my mom is ready for the water. She's just waiting for you to start cooking. I think she's making hot chocolate."

"Chocolate! I love chocolate," says Tenoch.

"Hurry up then."

The children quickly fill the jars and take them back. At ten years old, Tenoch has enough strength to carry one jarful of water by himself. He used to carry only half a jar, but now he's quite a little man.

Upon reaching the top of the gorge, the poor Tenoch slips on the mud but holds on to the jar, saving it from breaking. That costs him a scratch on his knee, but better a scratch on the knee than a beating from his father for breaking the jar, especially this one, which is brand new.

"Be careful, you dummy. We only have two jars." Xochitl laughs at poor Tenoch and then moves on. The scrape hurts and the poor child wants to cry, but as a man he holds the urge. Besides, his mom always says that men don't cry. So with a bit of shame, the poor boy descends back to the river to fill the jar and pour some water on his scratch to relieve the pain. Then he slowly begins his way back to camp.

Itzcuauhtzin lets the horses drink water and then takes the opportunity to splash some water on his face and shoulders. The water feels very good and refreshing, and especially after the long horseback journey from Tazumal. "Ah! This is good."

By the time the kids return to camp, Atecaltzin is already setting up the tent with some plastic sheets and dry branches that he found. "Tenoch, come here and help me hold these posts up."

"Yes, Dad." Tenoch obeys and runs over to help his father with the tent, while the twins play around with some wooden toys that their grandpa gave them while they were visiting him. Tenoch looks at them with envy; he also wants to play, especially with the wooden chariot and oxen that his grandpa made for him.

His grandpa has always been very skilled at the art of making wooden toys and wooden gods to sell at the Tazumal market. His father had bought him some wooden toys at Lake Coatepeque, but they were not as good as the ones his grandpa Ohtocani makes. These ones have a great paintjob and varnish.

Now that he's a little bigger and stronger, the poor Tenoch has to help his father and brother Itzcuauhtzin with the corn field and to gather cooking wood. But at least now he is allowed to use his bow, made for kids his age, with real arrows, not fake ones like the ones he used last year. He and his sister Xochitl practice together every time her mother allows it. Xochitl is a girl so she doesn't have enough strength to use a teenager's bow.

She uses one just like Tenoch's. Girls are not allowed to play with weapons, but Atecaltzin says that it is better for her to learn how to use them because the men will not always be around to defend them.

While Tenoch helps Atecaltzin raise the tent, Xochitl helps her mom prepare the dinner. Xochitl is now twelve years old and she can make corn tortillas, but when they travel to visit their grandparents and the Pipil family, they only warm up premade tortillas, tamales, pupusas, or simply prepare chorizo with eggs to eat. It's not the best, but on the road there are no luxuries—— that's what Elena always says—— there's nothing wrong with that.

Itzcuauhtzin finally comes back with the horses. He takes the other two horses and takes back to water them, leaving the first ones eating grass.

Further up the hill and through the trees, the gang watches the little camp, very interested in the humans. Two of them come down very carefully without making any noise. They go to the river where Itzcuauhtzin is still watering the horses and taking a dip in the little pool, while the other six climb down and head for the camp to inspect the humans more closely, each one very well trained in the art of stealth. This is not the first time that travelers pass through this place, but it is the first time someone camps so close to the cave since the chaneques took over the hill. Most Indians prefer to stay away, and travelers never camp at the foot of the mountain.

"The tent is ready. We only need to put up the plastic sheets on top in case it rains." Atecaltzin inspects the poles one more time to make sure they are secure. Once satisfied, he collects and puts away his ax and the leftover ropes.

"The food is ready," Elena announces.

"Let's wait for Itzcua. Felipe, Sebastian, go wash your hands," commands Atecaltzin. The children, full of dirt up to the face, go with their mother who helps them wash up.

"Both of you need a bath," Elena comments.

"But we took one yesterday," Felipe complains.

"Yes, but you guys take longer in taking a shower than getting dirty."

Itzcuauhtzin returns from the river with the horses shirtless, refreshed, and ready for dinner. The others are ready to start eating, just waiting for him to tie the horses and start having dinner.

"A little wet, my son?" Atecaltzin asks, although it is more of a statement than a question. It has been more than two years since the young man had traveled to train with the Pipils of Tazumal. All young Indian children from eleven to twelve years old are allowed to enter the academy of Pipil warriors to learn the military arts. This is the first year that the boy was allowed to go back with his parents for a couple of weeks in compensation for having completed his training and becoming Telpochcalli warrior, ceasing to be a Tameme.

"Yes. The water is really good."

"Sit down, let's eat."

"Dad I want to go to the river for a while. May I?" Xochitl asks.

"Okay, after you are done eating you can go, but only if Tenoch goes with you." Tenoch shakes his head indicating that he will go with her as he takes a bite out of his chorizo.

"Wonderful." Xochitl exclaims excitedly and starts eating her boiled egg and tortillas.

"Looks like it might rain tonight. We are going to have to make a fire inside the tent to keep us warm. Good thing we are far from the river, and there isn't much of a hill here to get us wet."

"Looks like a good place, but I don't like it very much. It's too dark," Elena complains. She has never traveled alone with her family. There were always more people whenever she traveled, at least a caravan of about twenty adults, and all of them armed with firearms. The roads are not safe. Today all travelers left early from Tazumal as usual. If it hadn't been for the wheel that broke off the wagon, they would have been able to leave with two other families who left a few hours before them, all bound for Coatepeque.

After finishing her meal, a very excited Xochitl and Tenoch rise and begin to walk toward the river. "Xochitl, take the water gourds and fill them with water. We're going to need them in the morning." The children take three large gourds and two canteens, and finally start their journey down to the river.

"Xochitl, look at the water, it looks good. Let's go for a swim," Tenoch suggests.

"No, we can't swim. We just ate. If you swim with a full stomach, you'll get a bad stomachache. But we can get wet without any problems."

"There must be crabs under the stones. I'm going to look for them."

"Do as you will; I'm going to fill the water gourds before you get it dirty."

While Xochitl fills up the water gourds and canteens, Tenoch gets in the water. The water is not deep by the shore, so Tenoch goes deeper into the river and discovers a pond on the other side. "There's a deeper pool over here. Xochitl, come check it out."

"Wait, I'm almost done." Tenoch submerges himself into the water and then starts to look for crabs under the rocks. Xochitl finishes with the canteens and gourds and then goes into the river with her clothes on. Girls always have to be covered; this is what every old lady always says. The Spaniards and the Mestizos believe that it's not proper for a lady to show her naked body, after she turns eleven.

"Ooh! This pool is good for swimming. Have you found anything yet?" Xochitl asks.

"No, not yet. There are no fishes here either."

"You don't say fishes; its 'fish,' you dummy."

"Do not call me a dummy. You're the dummy."

"I'm not the dummy. At least I can read Spanish, and you can't."

"I can read Spanish," answers Tenoch, a bit annoyed by his know-it-all sister.

"That's not true. You only know the vowels."

"At least I know how to track animals and hunt rabbits. You know nothing. You barely know how to make tortillas."

"You don't know how to hunt. Terry is the one with a good nose; you only have to follow the dog. Anyone can do that."

"Shut up, you're scaring the crabs," demands Tenoch while lifting a rock and putting his hand underneath to check for crabs.

Xochitl walks across the river and starts looking around. Then she walks up the slope of the river. "Tenoch, Tenoch," Xochitl shouts, calling her little brother who still hasn't found a single crab.

"What do you want?" The boy answers from the river.

"There's a mango tree here. Climb up and cut some down."

"Where?"

"Here, look." Tenoch walks up next to her and immediately climbs up the tree with great speed and simplicity. Tenoch was always very good at climbing trees, even better than Itzcuauhtzin. Immediately he starts shaking a branch to drop the mangos.

A big flash completely lights up the area followed by a loud thunder. *Trunnnnnnkkk.* "Hurry up it's going to start raining." She hadn't even finished her sentence when the water began to fall with great force. In this part of the land it always rains hard. Sometimes the storms come without a warning, it just suddenly starts raining. And sometimes the sun doesn't even have time to hide.

Tenoch moves to another branch, shakes it, and the mangos begin to fall. Xochitl starts gathering them right away to take back to camp.

Tenoch climbs down from the tree and helps her out.

"Look how big they are, and ripe." Xochitl tries one. "Mmm... they're very sweet."

"Hurry up; we have to cross the river before the current grows up too high!" Tenoch cries out with great urgency. They pick a couple dozens, but Xochitl can only carry about a dozen in the skirt of her dress. Tenoch boards about five to six mangos in his arms and chest to carry back.

The river rocks have been completely covered with water. The stream continues to grow and it doesn't look like a good place to cross. "We can't cross the stream like this. It would drag us down," Xochitl explains.

"Let's find another place to cross then. We can't stay here. My dad is going to be mad. What do we do with the mangos?"

"Let's throw them to the other side; we'll pick them up on the way back." Tenoch immediately starts throwing mangos across. Some of them barely make it to the other side, and others don't even clear the water. Xochitl is a better thrower, and all of her mangos reach the other side clear off the water.

Trunnnnkkk. A bolt of lightning falls very close. The children get scared and speed up. The river water is already reaching the gourds. Luckily, the gourds are already filled with water and don't get washed away. Tenoch starts to walk back to the mango tree to find another way. He turns to look around, but everything is a jungle and with overgrown bushes.

"Tenoch, let's walk up the river. There must be a shallower path." The children walk up through the mud and up the hill.

The scouts follow the children from a close distance, but the river has grown a lot more and they can't get to the other side, so they dedicate themselves to follow them from the other side without losing sight of them, while the rest of the gang is still scouting the camp.

"Where have those children gone to? I'll go look for them," Atecaltzin announces and gets out of the tent, covered with a plastic cloak.

"Go with your father, Itzcua," Elena orders her oldest son.

"Yes, mom." Itzcuauhtzin takes a plastic cloak and his ax. He covers himself with the hood and trails after his father. "Wait, Pa, I'm going with you." Atecaltzin keeps walking fast without showing any signs of having heard Itzcuauhtzin and loses himself in the jungle.

"Xochitl, Tenoch!" their father shouts. "Where are you? Come back. Xochitl, Tenoch!" *Trunnnnkkk*. His words are silenced by the sound of a thunder.

Itzcuauhtzin catches up with his father and they both keep calling out to the children. "Over here, Dad. This is where we filled up the jars. Look, the water gourds are still here." The gourds are almost completely covered by water.

"There's Tenoch's shirt." Atecaltzin picks up the shirt, while Itzcuauhtzin pulls the gourds out of the water and takes them to the top of the ditch.

"Do you think the current dragged them down, Pa?" Itzcuauhtzin asks.

"No!" Atecaltzin immediately begins to run down the river, dropping the shirt behind him and shouting the name of the children desperately.

Itzcuauhtzin picks up the shirt and scouts the place, trying to find traces of the children. He picks up a mango and looks around but doesn't see any mango trees.

For sure they found a mango tree and are probably waiting under it for the rain to pass. He turns to look at the path taken by his father, but he already has lost sight of him. *Trunnnnkkk.*

At thirteen, Itzcuauhtzin is already an expert tracker. The two years he lived with his grandfather Ohtocani taught him several Indian crafts. One of them is hunting and tracking, which are part of his training as a Pipil warrior. The young man looks around but doesn't find traces, but still not convinced that the current has swept the children down. Itzcuauhtzin has confidence that even though Tenoch is very bold, Xochitl would never let him swim in the river if there is danger. *They must be on the other side of the river.*

The water current is very strong, even for his age. Although he is strong enough, this current could drag even the strongest of Pipil warriors. Since his father is already on his way down the river, the right decision for Itzcuauhtzin is to begin his search upstream.

"Xochitl, Tenoch. Can you hear me?" There is no response, so the young warrior begins to walk up the river. *They must be on the other side of the river. Maybe I can find some other place to cross up there.*

Elena hears a child crying outside the tent. She comes out very happy and excited to see who it is. *Maybe it's Tenoch.* There's still a little light outside, but not enough to see who is crying. A few more steps away behind a tree, she can see a little creature curled up crying. The creature is too small to be Tenoch, and this child also has a pointy hat made of straw. Tenoch never wears hats.

Elena takes one step closer. "Are you okay, boy? Do you speak Spanish? Don't worry, I'm not going to hurt you. Are you lost?" The child just keeps crying without turning around. Elena takes another step closer for a better look. "Hello. I'm Elena. Are you lost?"

The creature stops crying and starts to laugh deliriously. "Ha ha ha ha ha. Ha ha ha ha ha. Ha ha ha ha ha." He stands up and turns around. Elena bends over to see his face, but his hat is covering it. Still laughing, the creature raises his face and looks straight into her eyes.

Elena jumps back from the fright. In front of her is a childlike creature with an old man's face and a child's body, hairy, with a big nose, with one ear bigger than the other, and his hands are large with long, crooked fingers. His legs are short, but his feet are large and hairy with thick toes.

Elena wants to scream but she is breathless and unable to find any words. The chaneque approaches her and, with a quick and subtle movement of his hand, spills a blue powder substance on her face, and Elena falls into his spell. She is paralyzed. She has forgotten that she has seen a chaneque and in front of her she sees her father, Manuel.

"Elena. Come with me."

"No, it cannot be. You're dead. I buried you."

"Don't worry about anything. Just follow me and I'll explain everything." At the sound of his delicate and compelling voice, Elena starts walking after her supposed father without a second thought, without remembering the twins or her family. Not knowing that she's walking straight into a trap.

The chaneques surround the area and two of them enter the tent.

"Aaaaaaaaaaaaaaaaaaaaah!" The twins shout when they see the chaneques. The chaneques immediately throw blue dust on their faces and the children stop screaming.

"Come with us. We have food, sweets, and chocolates for you at home." Sebastian and Felipe stare at the very-well-dressed Spaniards wearing silk clothes and shiny shoes. They seem like princes of Spain sent to protect them. They forget they've seen monsters, and they immediately stand up.

"Chocolates? Do you have candy and cake?"

"Of course we do. We have lot of sweets, fruits, and beverages."

Felipe and Sebastian look at each other. "Come on," they say simultaneously. They get out of the tent without thinking about the rain and leave with the "Spaniards."

"Mhuaahhhhh, Mhuaahhhhh!"

"Did you hear that, Tenoch? It sounds like a baby crying."

"Yes. It seems to be coming from further into the woods. Let's go see, there might be people who can help us, or at least have something to cover us from the rain. I'm very cold," Tenoch answers.

"Come." Both children step away from the river and start walking deeper into the woods.

"Mhuaahhhhh, mhuaahhhhh, mhuaahhhhh!" The cry comes from even further into woods. The children continue walking, but the more they walk, the crying sound seems to be at the same distance as the first time they heard it.

"Where are they? I don't see anyone," Tenoch asks.

"I don't know. It sounded like they were close."

"I think we should go back. I don't like this."

"Maybe the people are walking too. Maybe if we hurry, we can catch up to them," Xochitl suggests.

"I don't know. We are far from the river, and the sun has already set. I don't like being in the woods at night, and much less alone."

"Then let's go back." They both begin to walk back, but either from darkness or from evil work, when the children turn around to see where they came from, they can't remember the way back.

"Where is the river?" Xochitl asks.

"I don't know. It has to be that way," Tenoch suggests, pointing a finger at the thickest part of the woods. Xochitl, even though she's unconvinced, starts walking in that direction.

"Mhuaahhhhh, mhuaahhhhh, mhuaahhhhh!" This time the cry sounds nearby.

"They are close by. Perhaps they are coming this way," Tenoch exclaims.

"You're right. It seems they are coming in this direction. Let's go see," Xochitl suggests.

The two kids hurry up to the baby's cry sounds. On the other side of a Conacaste tree, they find two creatures sitting at the foot of an almond tree, both with pointy hats made of straw. They look like a couple of kids, about the same age as Xochitl. One of them seems to be eating green almonds.

Due to the strong Conacaste tree branches, the rain doesn't fall too hard in this place. There are only a few fat water drops that slip between the leaves. The rest of the water trickles down the trunk of the tree, forming a puddle of mud at their feet.

"Niltze," greets Tenoch. "Do you live around here?"

"Yes." A raspy and adult voice answers in Nahuatl, the language of the natives. Xochitl steps in front of

Tenoch to protect him. Not liking this at all. That voice has frightened her.

The two creatures stand up and head toward the children. At his waist, a machete like the ones farmers use hangs to the left. One of them is carrying a purse-like bag.

"We are lost and need help crossing the river. Can you help us?" Xochitl asks, speaking their native language.

"Of course," one of the chaneques answers as he approaches Xochitl who is standing closer to them. The chaneque spills blue powder on her face. Before Tenoch can react, the second chaneque grabs him by the left arm to prevent his escape and throws light-blue powder on his face.

TOBACCO FOR THE KIDS

Itzcuauhtzin found a footprint that looks human except that is very large with crooked fingers. He has never seen anything like it. *Looks like a giant's footprint, but giants don't exist.* The footprint is only of a left foot going on an upward direction. Itzcuauhtzin hurries up, takes his ax in hand and starts running, looking around for any signs of life, either giants or his siblings.

He arrives at a place where the river is a bit narrower and finds the footprints again, but this time there are more, and all are directed toward the river. Itzcuauhtzin examines them and they appear to be of two giants. The footprints disappear into the river. *The giants must have gone this way.* There are some stones in the river that still stand above the water. *If I jump hard enough, I could make it.* So he takes off his cloak and wraps it. He straps it to his belt next to the hatchet that his grandfather gave him after completing his first-level Pipil warrior training and gathers momentum. Itzcuauhtzin skips through the first two smooth rocks, but the third one is further away. *It will be impossible to jump without falling into the water with the current being so strong. I better not jump directly to the rock; I should jump up and let the current guide me to it.* With all his strength, the young warrior jumps and falls into the current. Just as he imagined it, the water drags him down, but he manages to hold on to the rock and climbs up effortlessly. From there on, there are only three more rocks left to cross, and all of them are close to each other, so Itzcuauhtzin crosses the rest of the river without any problems.

The footsteps of the giants guide him up the ditch, and then down the river where they disappear once more into the grass.

The storm began to cease. It is dark and the night has fallen. The clouds are still covering the sky, and there is no moon to help light his way. But his brother and sister could be in danger, so as every good warrior would, Itzcuauhtzin decides to start the search on this side of the river.

The children are following the "princes" very closely. Itzcuauhtzin looks in amazement at such small creatures with pointy hats. *Chaneques!* Those are mythical beings of whom his grandparents used to tell him about in their legends. *I never thought they were real. They steal children and sicken the adults.*

His warriors instincts gear into action and without thinking, Itzcuauhtzin jumps out of the bushes and throws his ax at the first chaneque. The chaneque turns to look in Itzcuauhtzin's direction just in time to receive the projectile in the chest. The chaneque immediately falls to the ground dead. The second chaneque jumps to a branch of the nearest tree. It jumped three meters in the air. Very impressive for Itzcuauhtzin, he has never seen anything like it. Humans are not able to jump that high.

After seeing the young warrior, the chaneque starts jumping from branch to branch and disappears into the woods. Itzcuauhtzin runs toward the children and yanks his ax off from the dead chaneque's chest. The creature lies dead on the floor with his mouth open. Its teeth are like the ones of piranhas—— thin, dense, and very sharp. They are not lined up like those of humans, rather it seems to have about three lines of teeth, but they're not straight. They just look like a bunch of sharp stones in its mouth.

The children look at the warrior, but they don't recognize him as Itzcuauhtzin but as a tall Pipil warrior painted with his white stripes and wearing adornments of hawk and eagle feathers on his head—— a strong and very brave man.

With closed fists, Tenoch immediately launches himself against the warrior. Itzcuauhtzin dodges the weak attack and takes Tenoch's arms. "Tenoch, it's me, Itzcua. What's wrong with you?"

Xochitl drops to the floor crying for her prince. "Why did you kill the prince? He was going to take us to his palace," she exclaims between sobbing cries.

"What prince? This is not a prince. This is a chaneque," Itzcuauhtzin answers.

"Who are you?" Tenoch asks while struggling to get loose.

"I'm Itzcua. What is wrong with you?"

Xochitl stands up. "Let go of my brother. You're not Itzcua. And tell me, why did you kill the prince?"

Itzcuauhtzin lets go of the child. "Sit," he commands. "Something is wrong with you." The children obey the order without opposing the warrior. After all, he is a very strong and skilled fighter; it wouldn't do any good to try to fight or flee. Itzcuauhtzin takes his ax and straps it to his belt. The purple chaneque's blood is still dripping because of the rain. "Here, put your shirt on Tenoch." The young man inspects the creature's body; his big hands, big feet; long, thick nose—— a very ugly monster really.

"How do you know my name?" Tenoch asks.

"Because I'm Itzcua. These creatures did something to you," the young warrior answers. *This really is a chaneque! No way. The chaneques don't exist. They are just stories from my grandparents.* Itzcuauhtzin still can't believe what he has just seen, his body still a little shaky but not from the cold.

Itzcuauhtzin collects the chaneque's machete and inspects it. Looks like an ordinary machete like the ones the Cuzcatleco farmers use. He also takes the chaneque's bag. He stands up and scans the area for traces of more creatures, but there are no signs of them. "Xochitl, do you know who I am?"

"No, but I know you're not Itzcua," Xochitl answers, launching a menacing look at the warrior.

Itzcuauhtzin inspects Xochitl's face. She looks good; Tenoch does as well. *This is a spell. Maybe they were touched by a bad spirit.* "Come with me, I will take you back to camp. These are chaneques and it seems that you are seeing illusions."

"Do you know where our camp is?" Tenoch asks.

"Yes, of course. I'm going to take you back."

"We can't trust him, Xochitl. He killed the prince."

"Chaneque," Itzcuauhtzin corrects.

Xochitl ignores the warrior. "Yes, but he is a Pipil warrior. He wouldn't hurt us." She fixes her eyes on the warrior. "We are Pipils from my dad's side. His name is Atecaltzin. Maybe you know him?"

Itzcuauhtzin decides to play along. *It's better that way till I find out how to remove the enchantment.* "Yes, of course. I know him. He is the son of Ohtocani, native of Tazumal."

"Okay. We will go with you then. But what will happen to the prince?"

"I'll come back later to bury him. For now, it is best to go back to the camp so you can dry up before you get sick."

Itzcuauhtzin takes Tenoch's hand and guides his brother and sister back to camp using his new machete to cut through the shrubbery.

Atecaltzin found no sign of the children, so he decided to return to where the water gourds were. *Maybe Itzcuauhtzin has had better luck.* But when he got there, there were still no signs of anyone. "Tenoch, Xochitl, Itzcua." No one responds. Atecaltzin collects the water gourds and returns to camp with hopes of finding good news. The fire still shines inside the tent. The shadows make it seem as if only the twins are in. "Elena," Atecaltzin calls but doesn't get an answer. He opens the entrance to the tent and crouches down to enter. Inside, he finds two chaneques eating ashes. "Niltze," greets one of them in Nahuatl. Atecaltzin falls backward in shock. A chaneque immediately launches out of the tent with blue dust in hand, ready to throw it in his prey's direction.

Atecaltzin rolls to the left dodging the first chaneque attack and stands up with the lightness of a seasoned warrior. The second chaneque jumps off the tent with great speed, machete and dust in hand. The rain continues to fall and turns the powder into blue paste in his hand as it drains down.

Atecaltzin pulls his knife from his belt and prepares to defend himself. It's been a long time since the Pipil warrior was in a battle. "By Tlaloc! What kind of demons are these?" *Chaneques. It can't be. The chaneques don't exist.*

"Grrrrr," growls one of the chaneques showing his sharp teeth and his machete in hand, while the second chaneque picks up a six-feet-tall spear adorned with indigenous drawings and obsidian head, like the ones wielded by ancient Pipil warriors, and a feather hanging from the trunk of the tip.

If only I had my rifle. "Where's my family?" the warrior asks with a demanding tone rather than a question. The chaneques don't answer but begin to move in the opposite direction to surround their victim. Atecaltzin backs up trying to seek protection for his back, but there are only trees. He knows that he has little chance of surviving against a machete and a spear with just a knife in hand.

The chaneque with the lance makes an attempt to pierce him with the tip, but Atecaltzin is very fast and moves away in time. The second chaneque takes that chance and tries to hack him with the machete. Atecaltzin drops to the ground and rolls, dodging the machete. He tries to slash at the chaneque, but the chaneque is too far. At the same time, a new attack of the second chaneque passes very close to his body, slashing his shirt with the tip of the spear. Atecaltzin stands up in time and covers his back behind a slim tree.

The chaneque with the machete jumps onto a tree branch. Atecaltzin, amazed by what he has just seen, moves away from the tree waiting for the chaneque to fall on him. The force in which the chaneque has jumped is supernatural. His heart starts beating faster, while the second chaneque closes in with his spear at the front. Atecaltzin looks around for a weapon. *Tenoch's bow.* Tenoch has left his bow lying beside a log. He catches sight of it fifteen meters away but doesn't even see a single arrow anywhere. This battle is getting more complicated for Atecaltzin.

"What do you want from me? Who are you?" Fear is indistinguishable in his trembling voice. The chaneques smile and prepare to attack once more.

Sonkkkk. Suddenly the chaneque with the spear falls to the ground with an ax embedded in his back. "Dad, look out!" is the voice of Itzcuauhtzin pointing up the tree. Atecaltzin looks up just in time to see the chaneque who jumps with machete in hand onto him. There is no time to move, so Atecaltzin pulls back trying to cover himself with his right arm, which is hacked from him with the machete. The chaneque falls on Atecaltzin and prepares for a second blow which could rip Atecaltzin's head off. But Itzcuauhtzin's speed is impressive and he is able to charge the chaneque with great force. With knife in hand, Itzcuauhtzin stabs the chaneque in the belly while still rolling in the mud. The chaneque screams with fear in his eyes. He knows he has met his end. Itzcuauhtzin spins in his last roll and stands up, kicks the machete off the chaneque's hand, and puts him to sleep with a punch in the face. He looks around ready to continue the fight with any other chaneque that may come his way, but there's no one else, only his siblings, paralyzed at seeing the violence in which the warrior has attacked the Spaniards.

"Aaaaaaa!" Atecaltzin lies kneeling on the floor covering his right arm under his left arm, frightened, confused, and dismayed. The children still don't recognize that he is their father but another wounded Pipil warrior, still not understanding why the Spanish princes are attacking the Indians. That war ended a long time ago.

"Dad, are you okay?" Itzcuauhtzin asks.

"My hand. That thing took my hand." Itzcuauhtzin takes off his shirt and wrapped it in the tip of the arm to stop the blood's flow.

"What are those things?" Atecaltzin asks.

"I think they're chaneques. They have enchantment powers and sorcery. The children are under their spell. They don't recognize me. I met two more across the river. They had captured Tenoch and Xochitl."

"Your mother and the twins are also missing. I believe they were taken by these creatures. We have to go after them."

"You are not in a position to do anything right now. Let's go into the tent. We have to stop the flow of blood, and we also must find a way to remove the spell from the kids."

"One of the chaneques tried to throw some kind of powder at me, but the rain stopped him." The children are the first to enter the tent. "In the wagon, I have tobacco. I think your mom brought mint and rue. Go get them, and also bring me my pipe."

Itzcuauhtzin takes his father's gun and puts it in his hands. "Take this, in case the chaneques return. Xochitl, start a fire while I'm gone." Then he takes a bow and some arrows. He exits the tent and picks his small ax and machete and straps them to his waist.

He quickly moved through the forest toward the wagon without letting his guard down. *There may be more chaneques here.* He finds the herbs and the pipe, takes a Spanish leather backpack and a couple of water bottles such as those used by Spanish soldiers, and runs back to camp.

The chaneque still lies unconscious on the floor, and in the tent Xochitl has already reassembled the fire for warmth and also has helped her father tie his bandages with some string. They seem to have stopped the flow of blood with slaked lime.

Tenoch is still shivering from the cold, but at least he took off his wet clothes and has covered himself with a blanket.

"Here are the herbs, Pa."

"Take some tobacco and rue and crush them well. Then put them in the pipe." Itzcuauhtzin does as his father commanded then takes a firebrand and lights the pipe. Atecaltzin inhales the smoke and then exhales into Xochitl's face. Xochitl reacts after half a minute. Only the tobacco has been able to break the spell though, but the smell of rue is what aromatizes the whole tent.

"Dad? Itzcua? What happened? How did I get here?"

"It worked," a thrilled Itzcuauhtzin interrupts. "How did you know it would work?"

Atecaltzin is still inhaling and exhaling the smoke on Tenoch's face, which seems to be falling asleep. But with the breaking of the spell, he comes back to life. A little more and he would have fallen into a deep sleep for several days.

"My mother always burned tobacco, rue, and mint to ward off evil spirits. I never thought it was to break chaneque's spells."

"Dad. Your arm! By Tlaloc! Your arm!" Xochitl exclaims, very worried. She still can't remember anything about the recent events.

"You don't remember anything, Xochitl?" Itzcuauhtzin asks. "What is the last thing you remember?"

Xochitl looks around the tent trying to place herself. "The baby. We were in the woods and a baby was crying?"

"Yes! The baby," Tenoch confirms.

"What were you doing on the other side of the river?" Atecaltzin asks.

"We found some mangos, and the rain fell so fast that we couldn't cross the river anymore. So we walked up the river to find another place to cross. We got distracted by a crying baby.

49

I remember walking into the woods to look for him, but we couldn't find him. I can't remember anything else after that," Xochitl explains.

"Don't you remember when I found you?"

"No," Xochitl answers.

"You told me that one of those chaneques was a prince."

"Chaneques? The Chaneques don't exist."

"Apparently they do. There are two of them dead outside. You can go see them if you want."

"O God! Tlaloc help us."

"And you? Do you remember anything?" he asks Tenoch.

"No, I do not remember either," the boy responds.

"We have to rescue the children and your mom. Surely there are more chaneques in the area. They must have taken them." Atecaltzin tries to stand up, but Itzcuauhtzin stops him with his left hand.

"You are not in any condition to track or rescue anyone. I'm going to track them. You stay here with the kids. I'm going alone."

"The chaneques took my mom and the twins? Wait, I'm coming with you," Xochitl suggests.

"No, you have to take care of Dad. It's very dangerous, plus those chaneques could return," Itzcuauhtzin answers.

"Tenoch can stay with him. Plus dad has his rifle."

"The rifle only fires a single shot at a time. If you are attacked by more than one chaneque, it won't help much. After firing it, he won't have time to reload it. You and Tenoch know how to use your bows. It's better that you stay with him."

"Itzcua is right, Xochitl. It's too dangerous. Itzcua, we should call the warriors from Tazumal first."

"There's no time, Pa. I must follow these chaneques now that there is still time. We don't know with what intentions they took mom and the twins. Tomorrow might be too late," Itzcuauhtzin answers.

"That's why I have to go with you. I can use the bow and I can run almost as fast as you." Xochitl turns his gaze toward her father. "Dad, you can't let Itzcua go by himself."

"Okay, let Xochitl go with you. Tenoch and I will be fine. I don't think those things will be back. Xochitl can help you. She's very smart. You two can help each other. These chaneques are very strong and tricky," Atecaltzin explains.

"Okay. But you need to go back to town and have the doctor take a look at your arm. It could get infected." Itzcuauhtzin starts filling his bag up with a rope and herbs in case he finds his family.

"There's no time. It will have to wait until tomorrow. Plus the children are at risk. Take your bows and take only the most necessary items. Be very careful."

"Don't worry, Pa. We'll be fine. I know how to take care of myself. I won't face them unless I know I can win the battle," Itzcuauhtzin answers.

"You're a good warrior, son. There's no doubt you're Pipil, but your training is not over. You have only met the first two basic phases. You still have a lot to learn."

"I know enough to track and survive in the woods, Pa. The important thing now is to find our family. Xochitl, hurry up.

Don't forget to wear your cloak. It's still raining outside."

"It will be very difficult to trace those demons at night and in the rain," Atecaltzin exclaims.

"Yes, but we have no choice, we have to leave now. Dad, if there's a tribe of chaneques in this area, someone has to tell the elders of the tribe. In your state, it would be better to leave as soon as possible. Tenoch can help with the horses. Go and warn the warriors. This is getting very dangerous. Leave everything that you don't need here. Also leave a couple of horses in case we need them," says Itzcuauhtzin while still filling his bag with food and herbs, knife and ax on his belt, and his bow slung over his shoulder. "What do you know about the chaneques, Pa? I need to know who or what I am facing."

"No one has seen them for over a hundred years. My dad says that they disappeared after the Spanish invasion. There is no one alive that has actually seen one. Many say that perhaps they migrated south. Others say they hid in the mountains, or fled in boats northward. Ancient warriors used to have confrontations with them very often. It is said that they stole children, but no one knows for what purpose.

Many say that they are the guardians of nature and others think they are good luck charms, but it is said that most people who saw them ended up crazy. They would sicken and then die after a couple of weeks. The Pipils always wore protective amulets made of hawk bones and jaguar teeth. The tobacco was used to ward off evil spirits that these chaneques left after them. That's why I used tobacco and rue to cure the children. Other than that, the rest were just stories, or so I thought."

"And where did they come from?" Xochitl asks.

"Nobody knows for sure. Some believe they were created by a very powerful sorcerer thousands of years ago, who was trying to conquer the big cities like Tenochtitlan and Chichen Itza. Others think it was an army created by Tlaloc or by Tezcatlipoca himself, sent to destroy humanity when it ceased to give their offerings and sacrifices to the gods. Nobody knows for sure, but what we do know is that they are lovers of gemstones, especially jade stones."

Xochitl fills up a small bag with food, also readies her bow and quiver with a dozen arrows, takes one of the canteens and hangs it over her shoulder. "Tenoch, stay alert; I'll leave some arrows here in case you need them. When you get to the town, tell grandpa Ohtocani that I love him. Do not be afraid. Everything will be fine. My dad has a shotgun. Itzcua and I will rescue mom and the twins." Tenoch hugs his sister before she leaves. Although the boy would never admit it and always fights with Xochitl, deep in his heart his sister is his best friend and he always tries to protect her. "Be very careful, son. Take care of your sister, and you take care of your brother, Xochitl." Atecaltzin also hugs Xochitl as good as he can since she is closer. "May Tlaloc protect you."

On leaving the tent, Itzcuauhtzin notices that one of the chaneques is gone. The young man runs to the place where the chaneque lay, checks around, and finds the giant footprints. "Xochitl, the chaneque is headed toward the hill. We have to follow him; he may lead us to mom. Come on, hurry up." But Xochitl is distracted observing the other chaneque. It's the first time she has seen one. A distant memory comes to her mind—— *the two peasant children with straw hats.*

"They are ugly."

"If you want to change your mind, this is the time. I won't blame you if you're afraid. These are real monsters."

"No, of course not. Let's go, the twins are in danger." Xochitl was always very protective of the twins, even more than Tenoch. There has always been a lot of rivalry with Tenoch, perhaps because Tenoch has always been very competitive.

The rain has diminished a bit; it no longer falls as strong as it did earlier. That's the only good thing about this weather. Sometimes the rain falls so strong and unexpected that as fast as it comes it ends, although the little that falls is still enough to form puddles of mud everywhere. That's why Xochitl adjusts her hood.

The chaneque has had to walk; due to his severe injuries, he has decided not to jump into the trees as the previous chaneque did. Itzcuauhtzin finds it easy to follow the broken leaves gap that he has left in his path.

The chaneque slowly climbs the mountain. The wound is still bleeding and has lost a lot of energy. His only hope of survival is to reach the cave and let his clan take him back to see Narib, one of the chaneques' sorcerers with healing powers.

Damned Pipil warrior. Next time I will rip your heart out. The blood is still dripping with the storm. As much as he tried to cover his wound with mud and squash leaves, the blood is still pouring out. If not for the rain and darkness, he would be leaving a very noticeable purple trail for the Pipils to follow.

The cave is very close. The chaneque can see it from here, but he doesn't believe he can make it. Unable to take another step and feeling his strength leaving him, Samoc leans against a rock and slowly slides down to the floor, just in time to let the darkness take him.

Higher up in the cave, two chaneques are still waiting for the rest of the gang. "He was a very young fighter, but very handy with his ax. He killed Soyo with one shot and then came at me at full speed. I had no choice but to flee," Sumal keeps explaining.

"You ran like a true coward. Chilco is going to serve you for dinner to the panthers," Duryi responds, angry at the excuses. "Samoc and Atura should have been back by now. They just went to get rid of the father. How hard can that be?"

"Let's go, I don't think they'll be back. If the father is as good as the son, we can take them for dead. I think three humans is a good hunting," Sumal explains.

"No, wait, something is moving down there." Both chaneques climb down hiding among rocks and trees to find out what it is. "It's Samoc. What is he doing sitting on the stone?" The chaneques approach him cautiously.

"Looks like he's hurt. We must take him to Narib quickly."

"This means that Atura is dead. Damn Pipils. I thought they were white. The others look white." The chaneques take Samoc and pick up the machete, then climb up back to the cave, unaware that from a few meters behind, Itzcuauhtzin and his sister are watching them.

The chaneques enter the cave and hide behind a crater. Sumal takes out some of his magic powder from his bag and spills it on the wall. He draws a rune with an upside down triangle and three sticks pointing down on the wall (X). The figure glows green and a door opens. The chaneques walked inside and the door closes behind them.

Itzcuauhtzin, who has followed the chaneques closely, hides behind a rock to see what happens in the cave. The cave is dark and he can't see very well, but he catches sight of a chaneque's rune and sees a bright-green light deep in the cave, which gradually begins to decline. He signals Xochitl to come up closer. She comes up as fast as she can, and both indigene kids enter the cave with weapons in their hands.

Luckily, the rune is still shining. "The chaneques entered through here. This has to be some kind of code to enter." The teenagers study the rune and memorize it. Itzcuauhtzin saw how the chaneque drew the rune on the rock. He's about to do it but Xochitl stops him.

"Wait, the chaneques just entered. If we open the door now, they would hear us, plus we don't know what's behind it. It would be better to go and report this cave to the Pipil warriors."

"Mom and the twins are inside. This rune is still active. If we don't do it now, we may not be able to do it later. We don't know how long the magic will last. We have to go after them, Xochitl. If you want, you go back and warn my dad. I will go after them."

Xochitl makes a face of disgust and disapproval, but still she readies her bow and puts an arrow on the string, ready for release in case something is behind the door. Itzcuauhtzin readies his ax and traces the rune.

The door opens and the green light appears again, discovering its secrets.

FIRST BATTLE CRY

Auuuuuu! Tenoch picks up his bow and hangs his quiver over his shoulders, adjusts his cloak, and helps his father saddle the black horse. They leave everything in the tent and get ready for their hasty trip. Tenoch locks the gun to the side of the horse, while Atecaltzin finishes adjusting a machete to his waist.

The child picks up the spear of the chaneque that Itzcuauhtzin killed. "Look, Pa. This spear is beautiful. It looks old."

"Let me see it." Atecaltzin takes it by the handle and studies it. "It's a very nice spear, but it's not old. The tip is obsidian. The pole is bathed in gold, or copper, I'm not sure. It closely resembles the spears used by the Pipil warriors before the Spanish invasion. It's very lightweight but very strong. How is it that these chaneques have such excellent weapons? I hope your brother and sister don't have to go head to head with them. Itzcua is still too young and inexperienced."

"Itzcua is already a warrior, Pa."

"Not yet. He still needs work. He has only met the basic level. There is much more to learn to be a good soldier."

"Grandpa Ohtocani says a warrior is born with instincts. That training only serves to tone your talents, and nothing more."

"My dad still lives in the past and still doesn't accept that the world is changing, that everything is not like it used to be. If the crown were to find out that there are still Pipil warriors and an academy, the oppression against our people would be even worse," he explains. The academy is nothing more than a small group of warriors who refuse to forget the traditions of their people. The Spanish oppression has been so cruel to them that they had to keep their trainings in secret. A couple of experienced warriors take a group of young students hunting, or at least that's what they use as an excuse. In that span of time, they take the opportunity to teach them the art of hunting, to use weapons and hand-to-hand combat. When a young man meets his training, he is subjected to physical and mental tests. If he successfully passes the tests, then the student graduates from the Calmecac to the Telpochcalli school level.

In ancient times, the Calmecac was a school for the children of the nobles and the Telpochcalli was a school for the peasant children, but now the Calmecac was used to teach history and war theory, as well as basic warrior training. But it was in the Telpochcalli where the cadets were really pushed to their full potential.

"Then we must hurry and trust that Itzcua has learned enough to rescue mom and the twins."

"That's all I ask of the gods."

"Can I keep the spear? I like it a lot."

"Yeah, it's fine. Let's take it with us."

Ahuuuuuu, ahuuuuuu, ahuuuuuu! The howls of coyotes can be heard now a little closer to the camp. "Coyotes! We must hurry. Sounds like a small pack. Untie the horses and let them loose, or else they will be swept by the coyotes. Leave the mare for you," Atecaltzin orders with urgency.

The child quickly unleashes the animals. The horses start running restlessly in the road's direction. Tenoch takes the spear and adjusts it to the black horse's left side.

Atecaltzin fixes his eyes on the chaneque and takes his machete. "Tenoch, bring me a satchel. We'll bring some evidence for the council." While the child runs into the tent, Atecaltzin chops off the chaneque's arm with the machete. By the time Tenoch returns, his father already has the arm in his hand. "Open the bag." The poor Tenoch makes a repulsive and disgusted face at seeing the bloody arm on his father's hand. All of a sudden he feels like vomiting.

"We have to show this to the Tazumal elders so they believe us. Hurry, we have to leave at once." Atecaltzin helps the boy climb on top of the mare. At his young age, Tenoch is already an expert rider. He has been riding alone for two years now. There's no time to saddle the mare, so the child adjusts himself as good as he can and takes the reins. Atecaltzin climbs up on the black horse and the two get on their way back to Tazumal.

Ahuuuuuu, Ahuuuuuu Ahuuuuuu! The howl of coyotes can be heard even closer now. It's a pack of six coyotes approaching from the riverside. The smell of blood has caught their attention, and they're running at full speed toward the camp.

"Hurry up, Tenoch. As soon as you reach the road, start running. Those coyotes are already too close and we can't let them catch up to us." *Tlaloc, protect the kids.* Atecaltzin's heart starts to pound harder. His fear is not so much for him but for his family—— the children in pursuit of chaneques, and his wife and twins hostages of those monsters. His eyes begin to fill up with tears. He wants to hold them back, but everything is happening too fast and is so overwhelming.

The coyotes reach the camp and immediately begin to look for food, destroying everything on their way. Two of them go into the tent while the other four scramble for some food they found by a tree in a metal pot.

The food is not enough, and the Coyotes finish with it in less than a minute. The leader of the pack begins to sniff the floor, searching for human scent. It catches the horses' scent instead, and immediately begins to run after them.

Luckily, Tenoch and Atecaltzin are already galloping on their way to Tazumal. Tenoch is on the lead and has made a good stretch. Not that the mare is faster, but Tenoch weighs much less than his father does, and unlike the black horse it doesn't have a saddle.

Atecaltzin is still having problems trying to control his horse with one hand. The howling of coyotes is getting closer. Atecaltzin turns to look, but the dense jungle and the curves of the road are on his way. The coyotes have divided into two groups—— a group that pursues through the road, and the other one cuts a shortcut through the trees of the forest.

"Ahiah!" Atecaltzin pushes his horse harder. Tenoch does the same. The coyotes are already next to them. They are very fast and in only five minutes, they have been able to catch up to the humans. The second group is still further back. Atecaltzin can hear them, but in less than a minute they'll catch up as well. "Tenoch, keep on riding, do not stop for any reason."

Tenoch turns to look back just in time to see two coyotes jump out of the trees and attack his father, trying to bite his left leg and take him down. Atecaltzin wraps the reins in his right arm. He tries to reach the spear, but a coyote bites his hand. The good thing is that it can't keep hold of him and Atecaltzin frees his hand. Atecaltzin turns the horse to the right and begins to spin his horse. The frightened horse starts to neigh and kick in the air.

Tenoch also turns his horse and stops. He draws an arrow from his quiver and readies it on his bow. From this distance he has no direct shot, unless he wants to hurt his father. The rest of the coyotes are now very close. Tenoch gallops back, taking the bow and arrow in one hand.

Atecaltzin manages to grab the spear and prepares to charge any coyote that comes close. A coyote makes an attempt to jump and throw him from the horse, but the horse spins and kicks striking the coyote directly on its chest. The coyote falls down crying out in pain and losing all interest in attacking again. It just stays on the floor groaning.

The other coyote growls as it shows its sharp teeth. Tenoch shoots an arrow but fails to hit its target. The coyote looks at him and decides to attack the boy, since he looks more vulnerable. Like a true predator it furiously runs toward the boy. Tenoch is still trying to ready the second arrow. The coyote leaps and opens his mouth going straight for the boy's neck.

Sonkkk. A spear runs the coyote through its right side. Tenoch's eyes widened, very surprised to see his father's great aim. Atecaltzin launched his spear with his left arm, and although he's not a lefty, he has managed to connect directly with his target.

"Be careful, Pa!" Tenoch shouts when he sees a coyote jumping toward his father. Atecaltzin crouches forward and the first coyote passes over him, but the other three are already in the air. Tenoch releases his second arrow. This time he gets lucky and hits one of the coyotes that were coming at his father at full speed. One of the coyotes manages to connect with his victim and throws Atecaltzin from the horse. Immediately the other two coyotes take Atecaltzin by an arm and a leg. "Aaaaaaaah!" The warrior screams in pain.

"Ay ya yay yay yay," Tenoch shouts his first battle cry, being now a little closer. He launches a third arrow, wounding another coyote. The cry distracts the two remaining coyotes which already see the child as a greater threat. Tenoch wastes no time and readies his fourth arrow. The coyotes recognize that it as a deadly weapon and turn away from Atecaltzin. They begin to surround the child, grunting and peeling their fangs to show their fury. The child begins to turn his horse to the left without losing sight of the larger coyote. Atecaltzin stands up and quickly takes his rifle. He takes a step closer to the coyotes, which have not yet noticed the warrior's advance.

Bang! The shot hits the nearest coyote on the chest. The coyote dies before he hits the ground. The second coyote panics and flees the scene at high speed. Tenoch also got startled by the shot and turns to see his father who is bleeding from his arm. The coyotes have bitten his right arm and right leg. The child quickly dismounts the mare with bow in hand.

"Tenoch, I told you not to stop for anything. You disobeyed me." Atecaltzin's voice sounds very angry and threatening.

"I'm sorry, Pa, but I couldn't bring myself to leave you alone. You're all I have left. I don't know where the others are or if they are still alive. I could not run away and leave you behind." Atecaltzin just stares at him, his eyes not revealing anything. Tenoch doesn't know whether it is anger or gratitude, what he sees in his eyes.

"Do you think there are more coyotes, Pa?"

"I don't think so. The shot must have scared them away." Tenoch yanks the spear off the coyote. He approaches another one that still lies wounded on the ground, looks at its eyes, and pierces it through the heart. The coyote the horse kicked has been trying to flee the scene, but it's unable to stand. The kick must have been overwhelming. Tenoch runs up to him and stabs him without thinking too much about it.

"Pick up the arrows, Tenoch, and let's go."

"Yes, Pa." Tenoch collects the three arrows he used, and stores them back in his quiver. "Are you okay, Pa? You think you can still ride?"

"Yes. I'm fine. They didn't bite me too hard."

"You better reload the shotgun again before we encounter more coyotes."

Atecaltzin pulls out his knife and offers it to Tenoch. "You killed three coyotes today, son. Here, go and collect your trophy. This was a fight, not a hunt. You deserve it." Tenoch takes the knife smiling and approaches the first coyote and rips one ear off, then does the same with the other two and saves them in his satchel. Warriors always cut an ear off his enemies after a battle. This rite is very important to Tenoch.

The poor man did not remember how he got to this place. He was chained and shackles gird his wrists. The room was very hot and dark. In front of him, a beautiful woman stared at him with an evil smile on her lips.

"Who are you? How did I get here?" the poor wretch asked, but his questions went unanswered. The beautiful and very attractive woman only observes him from head to toe.

As a twenty-six-year-old man, he already has known many beautiful women. They have always been his weakness. Although he is already married, he has never lacked any extra beautiful girl to love. His job as a courier gives him great opportunity to meet beautiful girls in different cities and villages. He has many girlfriends throughout the country, but he has never seen one as beautiful as the lady in the white dress in front of him.

It was just a couple of nights ago when he was on his way back home. It was a little late; but since he had a very important delivery to make, he couldn't wait till next morning.

He was passing by a nearby river when he decided to let his horse have a drink of water, since he was considering on riding it hard for a good part of the night. As he approached the river, he saw a woman bathing in the river by herself. The woman had her back to him and was completely naked. She was submerged into water right up to her navel. He couldn't see her face, but her hair was long and it fell down all the way to her waist.

The handsome gentleman could not resist her charm and beauty. He approached her and spoke softly, so as not to frighten her. "Hello there, beautiful. What are you doing here so late bathing by yourself? The sun already went down."

"I'm just refreshing myself a bit," she answered in a very sweet and gentle voice.

"Are you not afraid to be here alone? These places are not safe. There are animals, Indians, and criminals everywhere. If you want, I can keep you company for a while." The young man tried to get a bit closer, hoping to see her face, but the woman turned away from him and kept pouring water on her head with a small water container.

"No, thanks. I'm fine," she replied.

"I'm going into town. If you want, I can take you on my horse so you don't have to walk." The man lied, who in reality was on his way opposite to the village.

The beautiful lady did not answer but took two steps back, moving closer to the young conqueror. The young man tried to see her face once more, but the woman did not let him see her face still.

"So what do you say? Should we keep each other company? It would be nice to have a friend in this town. I come from far away, and to be honest places like this get me a little scared."

The woman took a step closer. The young man believed that he could touch her without getting wet if only she would take a couple of more steps toward him.

Finally the woman turned around, but to his surprise, the beautiful woman was not as attractive as she looked. She was a very ugly woman with long straight hair. She had a long face like a horse, and eyes as big as a cow. She had a flat nose and mouth of a goat. The poor man's knees became like water and he fell backward. The woman approached him and touched his face, and immediately the man falls under her spell.

"Why am I in chains?" the man asked in terror.

"Do not worry about anything. Everything will be okay." Sihuehuet approaches the man and starts chanting a spell in an ancient language, with fowl movements with her hands. This continues for a couple of minutes and then she touches him on the chest. The man feels all of his strengths leaving him in an instant—— his youth, his memories, and his wits. His hair loses all of its color and turns white. After a couple of minutes, all that is left is a witless old fragile man hanging from the chains, unable to move.

Sihuehuet takes a deep breath, feeling younger and more beautiful. "Take that man and leave him in the woods. If he is lucky, some beast of the field will put him out of his misery," she commands the guards and then disappears into the dark hallway.

FROM PURSUERS TO PURSUED

The kids enter the cave very cautiously. There's no one around. There's only a larger cave with very narrow passages. Light emanates from crystals which are stacked in line among the walls. The chaneques put them there to light up the way.

Xochitl and Itzcuauhtzin look at each other in amazement. They have never seen anything like it. They quietly start to walk deeper into the cave, without lowering their guard. They walk a little further passing a few bends and come up to a big cliff at the end of the path. The cave has stalactites hanging from the ceiling with shimmering crystals everywhere.

While Itzcuauhtzin surveys and studies his surroundings, Xochitl walks to her right. "Aaaaah!" Xochitl covers her mouth trying not to scream. Itzcuauhtzin runs up to her to see what has frightened her. In front of them lies a mummy hanging from a thick pole, with its hands tied above its head. The mummy is still a little damp and smells rotten. The kids cover their mouth and nose to avoid breathing polluted air. The mummy has no clothes, only an old white robe that covers its waist and falls down to its knees.

Xochitl averts her eyes from the mummy and walks further into the cave and finds a few drops of purple blood on the floor. "Itzcua, look, there's chaneque's blood over here." Itzcuauhtzin kneels on one leg and examines the blood.

"This way. Come."

The kids begin to walk down along the wall surrounding the precipice. They find a narrow road that descends down to a wider road along the wall. There's still no sign of the chaneques, but it's obvious that they came this way. On the floor they can see many traces of chaneques and a few human shoe steps.

"These are human shoes footprints. They must be the twins'. Look at this one, it's bigger; it could be mom's."

Xochitl nods in agreement. The kids begin to descend very quickly but cautiously. One misstep here and they may just soon discover how deep the bottom of the canyon really is.

The kids continue to walk down and find a gap between the rocks that leads in a different direction. "Look, I think they must have gone this way," Xochitl exclaims. Itzcuauhtzin inspects the road but can't find any shoe prints anywhere.

"You're right. I don't see any shoe prints down below." They both enter through the gap and find that the road is wider on this side of the wall. It's a little bit darker because there aren't many crystals as on the other side, but they can still see well enough to walk and avoid tripping. There are stalagmites ascending from the floor and stalactites descending from the ceiling. The ceiling is much lower though. Itzcuauhtzin estimates that perhaps is only about six meters from the ground.

They can hear some voices in the distance. The kids ready their bows and close in hiding among the stalagmites. Its two chaneques carrying a wounded soldier. *It's the chaneque I hurt back at camp.* Itzcuauhtzin signals Xochitl to stop and gets closer to her. "I'll take the one to the left, and you take the one to the right," he whispers. Xochitl nods and prepares her shot.

Without thinking, Itzcuauhtzin shoots the first arrow, which embeds itself on the first chaneque's skull. Xochitl also releases her arrow which runs through Sumal's torso, entering through the back and out in front through the stomach. The chaneque falls, surprised about what has just happened and takes the arrow with his hands trying to remove it. Itzcuauhtzin approaches him with his ax in hand, while Xochitl prepares a second shot and aims it at the chaneque.

Seeing the young warriors, the chaneque makes an attempt to find his strength and grab his spear, but his strength has left him. With sorrow and fury in his eyes, Sumal turns to see Itzcuauhtzin. "Sihuehuet will eat your heart out after she sacrifices you. Damned Pipil." Sumal threatens with a shakily voice.

"Where did you take my family?" Itzcuauhtzin asks with great authority and a threatening voice, always keeping his distance in case the chaneque tries something. Xochitl is still not taking the pressure of the bow string.

"Ha ha ha ha ha." The chaneque laughs with great mock. "You'll never find them. You will die here. You and your family. We are thousands and thousands. You don't have a chance of getting out of this place alive. There has never been a man who has entered this place and gotten out." Purple blood starts pouring out of the chaneque's mouth. Sumal makes another attempt to speak, but drowns in his own blood.

"What should we do now, Itzcua?"

"We have no choice. We have to keep going until we find Mom and the twins." Itzcuauhtzin takes the chaneque by the arms and drags him behind a stalagmite to hide him. "Xochitl, help me hide them. If other chaneques find them, they'll know we're here." Xochitl takes one chaneque and starts pulling him by the arms. Itzcuauhtzin takes the third and hides him as well. Then Xochitl collects the weapons and the arrows they used while Itzcuauhtzin uses his feet to cover the chaneque's blood with dirt.

"We have to be very careful. Don't speak out loud, and if we find more chaneques, we'll need to hide before they see us. Got it?"

"Yes," Xochitl answers while removing a small bag of blue magic dust from one of the chaneques and saves it in her satchel.

Itzcuauhtzin takes the lead and starts walking further into the tunnel, keeping a fast pace but without running. The road turns into another slope. The good thing is that there isn't a cliff like there was on the main road. This one has walls and looks like a tunnel with small stalagmites and stalactites. The walls are damp with some algae growing between them. The road is a bit rocky and full of bends.

After walking for more than twenty minutes, the kids encounter a detour. Itzcuauhtzin inspects both ways and finds that the detour is hardly ever used. There are very few footprints, but they are very old and nearly all covered with dust. "It's this way." Itzcuauhtzin heads off to the main road. Xochitl obediently follows him in silent. The kids walk in silence for a little while and walk down through some small steps. The road gets even narrower and the roof is lower. A bit further ahead, they can hear voices and noises from laboring people. They seem to be breaking stones and hammering metal. The kids hurry up with their bows and arrows in hand, ready for any situation.

Before going through the next turn, Itzcuauhtzin signals Xochitl to a halt. He cautiously gets close to the wall on his right and begins scouting his surroundings. The sound becomes much stronger and there may be many more chaneques. Itzcuauhtzin can't see anyone, but he sees a much stronger light protruding from the end of the road. "It's clear, come." Itzcuauhtzin signals Xochitl to come closer. The two crouch down and walk toward the end of the tunnel and come up to a much larger cave; that goes up very high and very wide, with shimmering crystals everywhere, illuminating the entire area.

The kids hide behind a stalagmite and begin to scan the area. At the distance, the kids can see many chaneques with spears, all in a formed a line observing workers. Itzcuauhtzin still can't see the workers from their position, only the guards, so they decide to get a little closer.

The road bends to the right and drops down even deeper. Itzcuauhtzin drops to the floor and crawls toward the cliff in front of him. Xochitl follows his example and drops down on her belly. At the bottom of the cliff, they can see a lot of humans working. There are children and adults working in what seems to be a gold mine and precious stones. There are people hanging on the walls digging with pick axes. On the sides, there are people removing dirt in sacks and wheelbarrows.

"My God! What are they doing?" Xochitl whispers.

"It seems like they are looking for treasure. Maybe gold or diamonds."

"This must be why they kidnapped mom and the children—— to make them work as slaves in this mine."

"So it seems," Itzcuauhtzin answers. "We better go back and bring the Pipil warriors. We can't do anything. There are too many chaneques."

"And what about mom and the children? We can't leave them here."

"No, but I don't see them anywhere. Do you?" Xochitl gets a little closer to the edge of the cliff for a better look. The land supporting Xochitl crumbles and she falls off the cliff, sliding straight into the precipice. She rolls a little and manages to stop right before falling completely into the abyss. The two closest guards turn to see in her direction and see the girl trying to climb up. Itzcuauhtzin holds out a hand and starts pulling her out.

"What's going on there?" A chaneque shouts from the other side of the cave. "What are you doing?"

Itzcuauhtzin pulls Xochitl completely out to the top. "Let's go." The two kids start running back to the road where they came from.

"Intruders!" shouts one of the guards. Immediately a patrol of eight chaneques start the chase, armed with obsidian spears and metal-covered helmets.

Itzcuauhtzin decides to let Xochitl take the lead and go up the stairs.

"Itzcua, the gate will be closed. Should we take the narrow path we found instead?"

"Good idea. Hurry up, they're getting close. These dwarfs are very fast."

Xochitl takes the narrow road. The road has some bends and there are places where they can't run freely.

A little further inside, the path becomes a small crack and the kids have to pass sideways. The ceiling is high and dark. There are no crystals, and the little light that reaches this place comes from the main road.

Outside the petrol keeps running upward toward the main exit, but half a dozen chaneques have been left behind to investigate the narrow path and are heading this way.

"Xochitl, wait. We can climb up using the walls to support ourselves and hide on the ceiling." Xochitl immediately hangs her bow over her shoulder and starts climbing up supporting herself with her legs and hands between the two walls in an X-shaped position. The kids reach the top. It was easy for Itzcuauhtzin because he has longer legs, but not for Xochitl. She is doing a great effort to hold on to the walls. The worst thing is that there is nothing else to hold on to but the slippery and damp walls.

The chaneques arrive at the dark pit and they pull out a green and long crystal to illuminate the area. Luckily they did not look up and just continue running along the path. They go in deeper and make a turn on another bend ahead.

"Itzcua, I can't hold on much longer," Xochitl whispers, making a great effort to keep from falling. "I'm going to climb down."

"Okay." Both kids carefully climb down. Itzcuauhtzin takes his bow and prepares a shot. "Come, we must follow them. We cannot return to the main road. There are too many guards out there. I only counted six on this side. Maybe we'll find a better hiding place ahead." Xochitl prepares her bow and follows Itzcuauhtzin very closely.

After taking the next corner, the kids can see a light coming from the end of the tunnel. The good thing is that there are stalagmites that can be used for cover. The kids get closer and find that it's only another bend. They approach it slowly. At the end of it is a chaneque with a spear facing to his left. There are no signs of the rest of them anywhere. Itzcuauhtzin stops behind a stalagmite and watches the guard for a moment. He signals Xochitl to come closer. "There's no sign of the other chaneques. Maybe they left him behind to guard the pass."

"We can't stay here. The others will come back and there's no place to hide here," Xochitl whispers.

Itzcuauhtzin stands up and shoots an arrow that spears right through the chaneque's neck. The chaneque quietly falls to the ground. The arrow has pierced his vocal cords and cut his windpipe. The chaneque shakes on the ground and dies. The young warriors get closer looking around everywhere for the rest of the patrol. Itzcuauhtzin drags the chaneque toward the roadside and picks up the spear, then he inspects the site and the ceiling one more time.

There's an even bigger tunnel inside. The light emanates from the crystals on the walls. There are very few of them, but in the darkness they are in, it's good enough to be able to walk without issues.

The kids decide to go in walking very slowly with their bows at the ready. Itzcuauhtzin gets closer to the wall. He doesn't want to be surprised in the middle of the path by a chaneques' attack. Xochitl follows suit and closes in to the wall on her right. There are many stalagmites in this place, which makes this site a perfect place for an ambush.

The kids zigzag through the stalagmites. When they reach the next corner, they notice that there are no crystals illuminating the area. The cave is dark and they can't see the ceiling. There is still no sign of the other five chaneques. The kids walk deeper inside. Suddenly they hear a noise of people running. The kids immediately hide among the stalagmites on the side.

The chaneques run past them very hastily, they seem to be fleeing from something or someone. A loud noise is heard coming from inside the tunnel. The kids keep hiding waiting to see what is. A big monster with a ram's head and horns appears along the way, with a body built like a bull. It keeps running at great speed on all fours. It's too dark to see well, but the bull destroys everything in its path. The chaneques pass through the illuminated cave and enter the tunnel back to the main road, not realizing that the guard that they had left at the entrance is gone.

"What was that?" Xochitl asks.

"I don't know. It looked like a ram-headed bull. I could not see it very well in the dark, but those horns bent backward seemed like a ram's."

"The chaneques fled from him. Perhaps that's why this path is not frequented."

"Maybe. What should we do? Do we go forward or back?"

"We're trapped. If we return to the road, the chaneques will be waiting. If we stay here, that monster will overtake us. I don't think those chaneques will stop to fight it. You saw how scared they were? I think it's better to move on. Maybe we'll find another way, or a better place to hide for a while," Itzcuauhtzin suggests.

"Okay. Let's go, but it's very dark. We should take a crystal from the wall."

"That's a very good idea. Come before the monster returns." Itzcuauhtzin quickly climbs a stalagmite using his feet to rest on the wall. He reaches a crystal and tries to pull it out, but it is in too deep, so he takes his knife and starts digging. Xochitl keeps a lookout at the end of the tunnel, just in case the monster or the chaneques return.

"I got it. Let's go." The young warriors start running through the tunnel with a bright crystal in hand. The crystal is not strong enough to light up the cave, but it's enough to light the way.

The kids take a couple of bends and finally reach the end of the tunnel. The path turns into a larger cavern, with a ravine in front, and it forks into two roads in opposite directions. At least these roads are wider and they both spread downhill.

"You hear that? It sounds like a river." Itzcuauhtzin feels a light wind passing through and cooling him a bit. He gets close to the edge to try to see the bottom of the cliff. "There's a bit of light down there, but I can't see the bottom." Xochitl carefully gets closer to the edge, not wanting to repeat her previous cliff incident. This cliff is a straight fall. Not like the previous one which had a slope prior to the direct fall.

"Yes, it sounds like a river. There's also some wind. That means there must be some other exit around here," she says.

"We cannot leave without mom and the twins." Itzcuauhtzin kneels on one leg and begins to inspect the floor.

"I'm not saying we're going to leave them. What I'm saying is that we need to find that exit. We will need it for sure. They must have sealed the other exit by now. Also, someone needs to tell the tribe about all this. There are a lot of people trapped here."

"Okay. Let's go look and then we'll come back to find mom and the twins." Itzcuauhtzin keeps on inspecting the ground with his new crystal. "I can't find any traces of chaneques anywhere. These large footprints look like they are from the monster. They come from that side." Itzcuauhtzin points to his right and starts walking to his left. "Let's go down this way."

"Do you think there are more monsters like that in this place?"

"I hope not. But be ready just in case. I would not want to face one of those. I don't even know what it was. His footprints seemed as that of a big goat or a bull. I've never heard of such a thing." Itzcuauhtzin takes the spear that he took from the chaneque and inspects it. "Look, this is a very nice spear. It seems like made of gold or something. The tip is not metal but obsidian. Pipil warriors used spears like this one back in the days before the invasion."

"Let me see." Xochitl takes the spear in her hands. "It's very light. I hope it's tough enough. Do you know how to use it?"

"Of course. Teutli taught me how to use them. He says I'm a natural for the ax and spears. He taught me how to defend myself and to attack with them." The more they walk, the floor becomes a bit rockier and the weather gets warmer.

"Where do you think they brought all those laboring people from?"

"I don't know. They have to be slaves that these chaneques have brought from neighboring villages. Or travelers like us," Itzcuauhtzin answers.

The kids hear a noise behind them. It is still far away and seems to be coming from the tunnel where they came from. The kids quickly start running down to put some distance between themselves and their pursuers.

A GREAT DISCOVERY

Itzcuauhtzin and Xochitl finally come to a crossroad, one that leads deeper into the cave and the other goes around and down the crater wall. "I think we left the monster behind," Xochitl says while trying to catch her breath.

"I think we'd better get to the bottom of this road," Itzcuauhtzin suggests and starts walking slowly, leaving the detour behind him.

"I feel very hot. The more we walk down, the hotter it gets," Xochitl complains.

"It's probably because we were running."

"I don't think so. The air is warmer. Perhaps there's lava in this cave."

"Lava? What do you know about lava?" Itzcuauhtzin asks.

"The teacher says that it is a form of liquid fire coming out of volcanoes. It seems to come from the center of the earth, and when it gets very hot the lava rises and fills the volcano, just like a water well. And then due to the heat and steam that forms up, the volcanoes erupt. She has a picture book where you can see a volcano that is shooting lava from the top."

"The teacher teaches you all that? I thought she only taught you how to read and write."

"Don't be dumb. That is only for first grade. We learn more things."

"What kind of things?"

"She teaches us how to work with numbers, history, manners, and how to behave like ladies from Spain."

"Ha ha ha. Like the ladies from Spain?" To Itzcuauhtzin this is very amusing.

"What's wrong with that?" Xochitl asks, very upset by Itzcuauhtzin mocking laughter.

"Nothing. Only that we are Indians, not whites."

"We are Mestizos."

"Our mom is *mixed*; we are *Indians*."

"Yes, but if my mom has Spanish blood, then so do we," Xochitl exclaims in a stronger and agitated tone of voice.

"My mom has half Spanish blood. If you're so good with numbers, you should know that half of a half is very little."

"Half of half is a quarter, dummy. And it's not little; it's still a lot," she replies, a little annoyed.

"A fourth, a third, bah, I don't understand any of it. The only thing I know is that it is very little. Besides, why do you want to be like those snooty ladies?"

"I'm not a snooty lady," Xochitl responds, a little louder and very angry.

"I didn't say you were a snooty lady. I asked why you want to be like one of them."

"I don't want to be like one of them. I just want to learn how to be a proper lady." Itzcuauhtzin stops to scout the way and a small opening on the wall. "What is it? Why did you stop?" Xochitl asks.

"This wall is wet."

"So?"

"So! That means that there is water between the walls. There may be water passing through the ceiling. We could be very close to the exit."

"I just want to rest. I'm getting sleepy and I think we're lost. We have been walking for hours and we are stuck in this huge cavern. We should find a place to sleep for a while."

"Okay, let's move on. Maybe there's something safer down there." Itzcuauhtzin begins his way down.

"Wait. Look there is a light in there."

"Leave it alone. I don't think that will lead us anywhere." Itzcuauhtzin keeps moving on without stopping.

"No, wait. We should go investigate, it may be another passage." Xochitl draws her bow and readies an arrow; very slowly begins to enter the opening without waiting for Itzcuauhtzin.

"What are you doing?" Xochitl ignores Itzcuauhtzin and keeps moving on. Itzcuauhtzin has no other choice but to go after her with his ax drawn.

The two kids take a couple of very narrow bends and enter a small cave with very little light. It has another outlet to the side but it is very small for adult people. "Look, Itzcua, it's another way."

"Yes, but it is very small. We would barely fit through there."

"It must be a passage for chaneques," Xochitl comments. "If you want, I'll go investigate. It may be a bigger cavern in there." Without waiting for an answer, Xochitl takes her satchel off and puts it on the floor then starts to walk in with her bow ready.

"Xochitl." Seeing that it is a hopeless case, Itzcuauhtzin looks around as if looking for something he lost. He approaches a crystal and starts to dig it out with the tip of his ax.

"Itzcua, come here. There is another way here but it's too dark and I can't see very well." Itzcuauhtzin takes Xochitl's bag and goes in sideways through the crack.

"Here, I pulled another crystal out for you." Xochitl takes her bag and crystal from his hands. The two kids reach the end of the crack and find another way. Itzcuauhtzin inspects the floor, as usual. "This is a road frequented by animals. There are footsteps of horses or cows, I'm not sure; and some other animal, maybe jaguars or tigers."

"Monsters as the ram we saw before," Xochitl adds. Itzcuauhtzin stands up and looks in front of him. There's another big cliff.

"Xochitl, I think this was a very bad idea. These footprints are fresh. It wouldn't surprise me if a monster lives here. Or worse, what if there are more of them?"

"Then let's go," Xochitl suggests and starts walking back to the cave opening.

Itzcuauhtzin stops. "Wait, I hear a river down below."

"Yeah, me too. Have you noticed yet that is not as hot as the other side?"

"It's true. It's cooler."

"We should at least go to the river and fill the canteens with water," Xochitl suggests and takes the opportunity to drink some water.

"Okay, but let's stay alert. This place could be more dangerous than the other." Both kids start to walk down the new path toward the river. The road expands gradually until it becomes a huge cave with a dimmed light.

"The river should be right here. I can hear it, but I don't see it," says Xochitl.

Itzcuauhtzin looks around and walks up to one of the walls. He gets between the stalagmites. "I found the vast river. Come here."

"What?" Xochitl runs to Itzcuauhtzin's side. Opposite to her is a trickle of water falling from the wall in a very small pool deposit. The water runs along the edge of the wall and then hides among the stalagmites and disappears.

"Well, what are you waiting for? Let's fill the canteens," Itzcuauhtzin orders. Xochitl gives him a sly look and dips her hand in the water to test it.

"It's cold." She immediately begins to fill the canteens.

Itzcuauhtzin takes a look around the site. The ceiling is very high and it is hard to see, but Itzcuauhtzin catches sight of a clearing near the ceiling on the right side of the road. "Xochitl, there is a place up there where we could sleep. We can climb up through here. Xochitl hands him one of the canteens back. "Good. Let's climb. We have to sleep for a while and then we'll continue the search." Xochitl begins to climb up while Itzcuauhtzin waits at the bottom.

A stampede of cattle can be heard coming from up the road. "Itzcua, climb up quick," Xochitl, who's almost at the top, exclaims. Wasting no time, Itzcuauhtzin begins to climb. The stampede of animals is now closer. Itzcuauhtzin reaches the top and Xochitl holds out a hand to help him up, just in time before the animal stampede runs into the cave. The kids lie down on the ground waiting to see the animals.

"Hide the crystal, Xochitl; they might see us."

A group of five rams enter the area in full stampede. Behind them is a group of chaneques mounted on panthers with long heads and long snouts like wolves, or at least that's how they seem in the dark.

Two chaneques shoot one of the rams with their spears. The ram falls to the ground still alive and kicking in pain. A chaneque closes in and spears it once again through the neck. The rest of the chaneques continue their pursuit without stopping. The last chaneque that speared the ram pulls out his spear and follows the others, leaving two chaneques behind to collect their prey.

"Ah! What an aim!" One of the chaneques exclaims and gets off his panther. "How are we going to take this ram back? We will need a cart." The chaneque approaches the ram and draws his spear.

"Leave it here. We'll send for it when we return. We can send a group of humans to help out." The chaneque pulls the second spear from the animal and hands it over to his companion.

"Let me cut the horns. I'll catch up in just a moment."

"Okay." The chaneque takes the reins of his panther and leaves after the horde.

Xochitl gets ready and silently puts an arrow on her bowstring. Itzcuauhtzin shakes his head signaling to stop. Xochitl looks at him straight in the eyes, trying to ask him why, but there is no answer. Itzcuauhtzin just shakes his head.

The chaneque starts to cut the first horn with a small saw blade. The panther looks around and turns to look up. The kids quickly hide their heads above the cliff. Itzcuauhtzin takes an arrow and gets ready like Xochitl and freezes, waiting for the panther to jump and discover them. Xochitl's heart starts pounding harder as if it wants to get out of her chest. The girl begins to lose control.

"Grrrrr," the panther hectically roars.

"What's wrong?" The chaneque asks as if awaiting a response and without taking his eyes off his work. The horn is harder than he thought and still has not even cut half through it.

The panther growls louder and jumps up the wall, but it is impossible for it to climb that high. "What's going on?" the chaneque asks while standing up. The panther falls back to the ground and then hops, roaring louder. "What are you about, dear? Is there something up there?"

The anxiety starts taking control of Xochitl and she tries to stand up, but Itzcuauhtzin stops her, bringing his finger to his mouth, making a silence sign. Xochitl stops but keeps her arrow ready in her bow.

The panther is still trying to climb, while the chaneque readies his spear. "Calm down. Calm down, beautiful. Leave it to me." The chaneque jumps up. With his powerful legs, he covers half of the wall's distance in a single leap. He holds on to a stone with one hand and gets ready to thrust whatever is hiding up the cliff.

Hearing the words of the chaneque, Xochitl can't stand her despair and decides to take a peek, just in time to see the chaneque holding on to a stone. "Itzcua!" she shouts, revealing their hiding place. Xochitl looses an arrow. The chaneque jumps, dodging the shot, which passes very close to him without causing any damage.

Itzcuauhtzin stands up just in time to see the chaneque land very close to them. Itzcuauhtzin shoots his arrow toward the chaneque. This one jumps back into the air with his spear at the ready, but Itzcuauhtzin's arrow pierces his leg and the chaneque falls to the ground hurt.

At the bottom of the cliff, the panther keeps roaring wildly. Xochitl gets ready to release another arrow in the chaneque's direction, but Itzcuauhtzin is already on his way to the chaneque with ax in hand. The chaneque gets up, but Itzcuauhtzin is very fast and he hits him on the head with the back of his ax. The chaneque falls to the ground unconscious.

Xochitl turns her full attention to the panther, which is still trying to climb, jumping hard on the wall without any success. Xochitl shoots her arrow at the panther, hurting it on the neck. The panther falls to the ground groaning in pain and rises slowly. Xochitl shoots a second arrow which pierces the panther through the chest. The panther falls to the ground, still alive and trying to survive, but the wound is deadly and there is nothing else it can do. The panther is well aware and closes its eyes, resigned to its cruel reality.

"We have to get out of here before the other chaneques return," Xochitl suggests, her heart still pounding with adrenaline and terror.

"Okay. Let's collect our things and go." Itzcuauhtzin collects his bag and bow, then looks at the chaneque lying on the ground. "Xochitl, this chaneque is still alive. He can give us information about mom," Itzcuauhtzin suggests.

"We have no time, Itzcua. We have to go."

"Let's take him with us then."

"And how are we going to carry him? We don't even have a horse. Don't tell me you're going to carry him?"

"Maybe there's something down there that we could use to pull him."

"It's a very bad idea. He's hurt and will leave a very visible trail for other chaneques to follow. It's very risky. Also, we don't have time. Leave him. Now let's go, please," Xochitl begs while preparing to climb down the wall.

"Okay, let's go." Itzcuauhtzin lets Xochitl go down first while he checks the chaneque. He collects the chaneque's knife and inspects the spear. The spear is the same as the first one he took from the other chaneque, so he leaves it alone and climbs down after Xochitl.

Xochitl checks the panther's cargo and finds a hunting net and a macana made with obsidian stones. She collects the net and a rope. Itzcuauhtzin finally descends. "Look, Itzcua, a very strong rope and a net. Let's take them."

"That's good. Is that all?"

"Yes, he looks like a hunter, not a warrior. Oh, and he also carried a macana. Look, it's very heavy." Xochitl responds, handing the macana over, then tries to draw her arrows from the panther, but they're buried deep, and one of them is broken.

"Yeah, it is heavy. Let's go. We have to go back where we came from and find a better place to hide." Itzcuauhtzin drops the macana and both kids start running upward toward the crack through which they entered.

Itzcuauhtzin stops at the crack. "Xochitl wait. I think it would be better if we continue up further. Maybe there's a safer place."

"What if there are more chaneques?"

"I doubt it. This is not a place frequented by them. There aren't many traces here other than animals. Surely these chaneques only came here because they were following those rams. I doubt there is more than one group of them around here." Xochitl doesn't seem very convinced but agrees anyway, and the kids continue their way up.

They haven't walked even ten minutes when they find a larger canyon on the right. It's dark, but Itzcuauhtzin inspects it and manages to see a crack between two walls of the canyon. "Look, Xochitl, there's a crack down there. It may be a cave or some other pathway."

"Yes, but there's no easy way to get down there. It's too far."

"We can climb down. It's not too far. If other chaneques come looking for us, it'll be very difficult for them to find us. If you want, I can go investigate."

"Okay, I'll wait here." Itzcuauhtzin immediately begins to climb between the two walls of the ravine. Once he gets down, he realizes that the crack is very narrow, and there is no trace or any signs of anyone. He immediately uses his crystal to signal Xochitl to come down.

"The road is even narrower than I thought. But I think it will be a little safer for us to rest. The panthers won't fit in here. It gives us an advantage in case the chaneques come looking for us," Itzcuauhtzin explains once Xochitl reaches him.

"Let's go then," Xochitl answers. Itzcuauhtzin takes the lead and enters the pathway. The path is very dark with damp walls. There are places where they have to cross sideways and others where they have to crouch to pass. Occasionally it extends a bit, but most of the path is still narrow. Finally the kids reach the end of the path. There is only one wall that covers the entire cave. From their position, they can't see if it has a ceiling, since the cave is too dark and the crystals' light do not reach that far.

"Looks like we ran out of road," Itzcuauhtzin states.

"You think it's too high to climb?" Xochitl asks.

"I don't know, but it looks too dangerous. This land is wet and looks a little loose." Itzcuauhtzin inspects the wall, and it actually is wet but solid.

"Let's eat something then and get some sleep. I'm very tired," Xochitl exclaims.

"You go to sleep; I'll keep watch for a while in case any of those chaneques decide to follow us." Xochitl pulls some sweet corn tamales from her satchel and gives one to her brother.

"Where did you get tamales from?"

"Before we left the camp, I packed several in my bag, just in case. Oh, look, I also brought some candy. I bought these at the market in Tazumal. I forgot that I hid them here."

"You're smart. That's very good." Itzcuauhtzin sits next to his sister as they both eat their tamales quietly. Itzcuauhtzin looks up with curiosity to find out if there is another outlet up top.

Xochitl finishes eating and leans back, putting her bag as a pillow and falls asleep almost immediately. Itzcuauhtzin watches her for a moment and begins to examine his new razor. After a while of doing nothing, his tiredness begins to gain advantage, and he falls asleep.

A couple of hunters come back by the road after a glorious hunt. Upon entering the cave, they find the dead panther lying close to the ram. "What happened here?" one of them asks. Where is Kamilo?" The two chaneques dismount and start inspecting the dead panther.

"Look, Pipil arrows," says one of them.

"Can't be. Pipils have never entered this place. Are you sure?"

"These are Pipil arrows. I'm sure. Whoever killed this panther had Pipil arrows." The chaneque examines the soil. "Look, some human footsteps. They are of a small shoe. They must be teenagers, about twelve to fifteen years old, at most."

"We have to notify Chilco," the second chaneque suggests.

"Wait, we have to follow these tracks. The strange thing is that I do not see Kamilo's trail. Look, more footprints, but Kamilo's end here. It seems like we have two intruders."

"So where is Kamilo? Do you think he was kidnapped?" the second chaneque asks.

"Or maybe they killed him and hid him. But I don't see blood anywhere but the 'animals'," the tracker adds and follows the tracks to the small stream and then returns. "They were heading up. Come on."

Itzcuauhtzin abruptly wakes up thinking he slept for almost an eternity. In reality, it has only been a couple of hours. He stands up and looks around. Xochitl is still asleep. No sign of the chaneques and everything is very quiet. He grabs the rope they took from the chaneque and fastens it to his shoulders. He studies the wall and finds a safer and solid area to climb. He tries to climb up on rock and slides down. He tries again, and once again he slips. He takes his knife and the one he took from the chaneque and uses them to stab the wall for support and starts climbing. Luckily, the two knives are very strong and he doesn't weigh that much. It takes him almost three minutes to climb to the top.

Up top, he finds another path, but it is very narrow. From the top, he can see Xochitl's crystal illuminating the area. Xochitl is sleeping very peacefully, so Itzcuauhtzin decides to inspect the site.

The road ends immediately to his right. It seems to have been blocked by a landslide. The ceiling is so low that he could touch it in a small jump. The road continues on the left but it is too dark to see its distance. Itzcuauhtzin walks a little and notices that the cliff extends in front of him more and more as he walks. There is a small curve and he takes it being very careful not to fall into the ravine, since there's barely enough room to put his feet. Just past the curve, Itzcuauhtzin finds a small tunnel. The precipice also ends there.

Itzcuauhtzin enters the tunnel and finds the end of the road. It's a wide room but very low. The only light is the one he has brought. The walls are full of very ancient hieroglyphics. Itzcuauhtzin doesn't know much about these things, but he does recognize several animal drawings, like birds, deer, and even guanacos. There are also drawings of weapons such as the bow, shields, blowguns, and Macuahuitles.

Itzcuauhtzin studies them for a moment and finding no way out, he decides to return to Xochitl, lest the chaneques have returned. So he rapidly returns to the place where he climbed up. Xochitl is still asleep. Itzcuauhtzin decides to tie the rope to a strong rock and uses it to climb down.

"Xochitl. Xochitl, wake up."

"What is it? What happened?" Xochitl asks, still very tired.

"I found a safer place up there. It's a cave with many figure drawings on the walls."

Xochitl sits up and straightens. "Hieroglyphics?" she asks between yawns.

"Hiro-what?" Itzcuauhtzin asks. It seems like he has never heard the word.

"Hieroglyphics. Those figures you found. That's what they are called."

"I don't know. But come and see. I tied a rope so you can climb up. You can go first and I'll hand you the bags."

Xochitl stands and inspects the rope. "Is it safe?"

"Sure. I tied it to a rock and just came down on it."

Xochitl pulls the rope to test it, and once convinced of its safety, she begins to climb. Once Xochitl is up, Itzcuauhtzin ties the bags to the rope for Xochitl to pull them up, then she throws the rope back down for Itzcuauhtzin to climb. Once at the top, Itzcuauhtzin unties the rope and fastens it back to his shoulder. He has no intention of leaving it there.

The two kids walk to their left and enter the cave. "It's dark in here," Xochitl says and begins to study the hieroglyphics but doesn't understand anything about them, except for a large hieroglyph in the center of the wall. The hieroglyph is a lot like a symbol that she has seen at Grandpa Ohtocani's house. "Quetzalcoatl," Xochitl whispers.

"Quetzalcoatl," Itzcuauhtzin repeats. "Why did I not see it before? It's as clear as day." Itzcuauhtzin begins to study the cave looking for more clues. "Look, here are some prints. These are not from the chaneques; they are too old. No one has come here in a long time."

"How strange." Xochitl whispers.

"Not so much. This is a very old path. The walls have collapsed and therefore no one has been here in years."

"And how do you explain the crack down there?"

"This crack must have been opened with the earthquakes, or perhaps the same earthquake that closed this road opened that crack," Itzcuauhtzin explains.

"That's a good theory. I think we're lost. We have to go back where we came from. There is no exit here, but it is a good place to sleep," Xochitl suggests, still feeling very tired.

"Yes, but wait a minute. These footprints disappear in this wall." Itzcuauhtzin tries to push the wall but nothing happens; checks the wall and it seems very solid, made of stone. "There is no way anyone ever climbed this. The ceiling is very low here. This must be a door."

"I know." Xochitl opens her bag and starts searching for something. "Help me with some light, I need to see."

"What are you looking for?" Itzcuauhtzin approaches her, very curious to see what Xochitl is looking for.

"The magic dust bag that I took from the chaneque."

"Oh, I see."

"Here it is. Do you think it is harmful if touched?"

"I don't think so. I touched it when I opened the door at the entrance. It did nothing to me, but just in case, use very little and be careful not to inhale it."

Xochitl dips her right index finger and draws the same symbol used in the first entrance. They wait for a moment but nothing happens.

"Maybe it's not a door?" says Xochitl.

"It has to be a door. There is no other explanation for these tracks. Maybe it's not made by chaneques. Obviously this is an Indian cave. Maybe it needs Pipil magic or it has some other way to open."

"Pipil magic? That doesn't exist. Nobody has magic. Those are just stories."

"That's what we thought about the chaneques, and here they are."

"Okay, perhaps it can only be opened from the inside," Xochitl suggests.

"Maybe. Or maybe it was sealed from inside."

"No. If it had been sealed from the inside, then who drew these hieroglyphics?" Xochitl asks.

"I don't know. Maybe it was people who came here after it was sealed."

"Then we are at a dead end. Let's get some sleep. You have not rested, you need to sleep. I'll keep watch this time if you want," Xochitl proposes.

"I don't think it's necessary. No one will bother us here. We're going to take a nap and then we'll leave."

Xochitl keeps studying the graph of Quetzalcoatl. "Look at the Quetzalcoatl's bow, it's separated."

"How do you know that?" Itzcuauhtzin asks while sitting next to the wall, ready to rest.

"Grandpa has a painting of Quetzalcoatl, and he always has the bow in his hand."

"So? Each person draws it as they like, or as they can."

"Yes, but there is something very strange about this one. There is a man being sacrificed here." Xochitl traces the blood with her finger following it to where it lands. "Look, the Mayan calendar. The blood of this man is falling on the calendar."

"Perhaps this cave was made by Mayans. They have always gotten along with the Pipils." Itzcuauhtzin answers.

"Yes, but remember that many of the Pipils are Maya descendants." *Maybe it doesn't need Pipil magic. Maybe what it needs is Mayan blood,* Xochitl thinks then takes her knife and cuts the tip of her left index finger and lets two drops of blood fall on the calendar. The center of the calendar moves in, and a weak and tiny light turns on from inside the calendar. "Ah!" Xochitl exhales.

"What was that?" Itzcuauhtzin asks starting to doze off.

"The calendar is shining."

Itzcuauhtzin stands up and walks over, next to his sister. "How did you do it?"

"I just touched it and moved inward."

"With magic dust?"

"No. I touched it with a few drops of blood."

"Are there any other parts moving?" Itzcuauhtzin asks.

Xochitl approaches the graph of Quetzalcoatl and tries to move the bow, trying to place it in the correct position. When tracing the image, an image of light moves with her fingers and the snake moves as if by magic. The whole image of Quetzalcoatl fills up with an immense light like fire. The rest of the hieroglyphs turn on with a big and bright light, illuminating the entire cave. The stones start moving and a block slides to the right. Much dust falls from the ceiling and the door opens revealing a bigger and very dark cave.

THE BEAUTIFUL WOMAN

Chilco was examining a new map that his chaneques had brought him, where they had traced the new and old passages of the cavern, when one soldier approaches him. "General, I need to talk to you urgently."

"What is it?"

"My lord, I have good news and bad news," the chaneque announces.

"You always bring bad news. Even if you bring good news, they are accompanied by bad news." The General observes his lieutenant for a while and finally sighs sarcastically and sits on his bronze chair. "Okay, give me the good news first."

"The first patrol returned from patrolling the north side of the mountain. They found a Pipil family and captured three of them—— two brats and one woman, I think it's a mother."

"Whose mother?" the general asks.

"The mother. Of her own brats of hers."

"What?" Chilco asks, very confused.

"Yes, the brats' mom."

"Ah, I see. So where are they?"

"We took them to Narib for inspection."

"How big are the brats?"

"I don't know, maybe seven or eight years old. They can help to remove dirt from the wells. The mother looks very strong. She looks to be of good family. Maybe she's Spanish?"

"Very good job, but for sure My Beloved will want the children for herself. So what's the bad news?"

"The bad news is that a family member is a Pipil warrior. Very large and very brave. He killed a scout and escaped."

"A Pipil warrior! These are very bad news. We need to find him immediately before he notifies the Pipil warriors and they come looking for them," Chilco orders.

"That's not all my lord," the chaneque adds.

"What else is there?"

"It was a patrol of eight, and only three have returned, plus one who died in the hands of the Pipil. There are still four more that have not returned yet."

"And where are they?"

"Kumara said they went to get the father, but they should have returned by now."

"Is the father of the family the warrior?" asks Chilco more urgently.

"No, sir. The warrior is much younger, and much more agile."

"Send two more patrols of five to look for them. I want them to bring me the father and the warrior. Dead or alive."

"Yes, sir." The chaneque exits the cave and another guard enters.

"Lord Chilco. We have a little incident at mine number thirteen."

"What kind of incident?"

"A couple of brats escaped."

"Who? How?" Chilco is beginning to lose his patience.

"We don't know who they were. But it seems that the brats were hiding among the rocks, and when they got discovered, they fled. I sent a dozen guards after them."

"All right, keep me informed and find out who they were." Chilco rises from his chair, very irritated. The last thing he needs is for someone to escape from the mine and go get help.

"Yes sir. With your permission."

The room was hot, with crystals everywhere illuminating the entire cave. The beautiful woman was combing her straight and long hair. She watched herself in the mirror, appreciating each and every one of her beautiful features. "There's no other woman more beautiful than you on the face of the earth," her lover had told her. That had cost her the fall from the gods' realm.

Now all she has is her chaneques and her treasures. Her only hope is to find Chalchiuhtlicue's bracelet. They say it was lost during a fight between her and her husband Tlaloc. Legend has it that Tlaloc and his wife had a fight over six centuries ago. Nobody remembers the reason why they were arguing. But it is said that in her anger, Chalchiuhtlicue took her bracelet off and threw it at her husband, but he moved and the bracelet fell to the earth. When that bracelet fell on earth, there was a great earthquake, such as which has never been since the creation of the world. The bracelet got buried under the Lamatepeque volcano, forming the valley of the hammocks, and it was never found. Sihuehuet, being part goddess, found out what had happened and began her search among the volcanoes of the Cuzcatleca lands, without any luck at all. Instead of the bracelet, she struck gold, diamonds, and precious stones. Like any other woman, she fell in love with her new wealth and began to gather her treasures.

At first it was very difficult because she had no one to help her. She began to lure men with her beauty and enchantments to do her job, but men did not last for long. The powers of her charms were too strong for them, and they only managed to live for a week or two. With children and women, her powers functioned in different ways because they did not fall in love with her as the men did. Instead, they lived in a world of fantasy and imagination. The charms only lasted until they fell asleep. Women awoke faster than children, while the children slept for a whole week and then woke up to a terrifying reality.

That was the reason why Sihuehuet traveled to the northern parts of the Mayan lands and allied herself with the chaneques. These creatures loved treasure and cared very little for the human issues. The beauty of Sihuehuet and her powers of enchantment had very little to do in convincing them. The chaneques agreed to help her with her search as long as they shared the treasures they found. Sihuehuet accepted their conditions, and that's how they came to the Cuzcatleca lands and began their reign in the volcanoes caverns.

The chaneques brought with them their wizards and clerics. They also brought people of war, but the biggest problem was that among them, there was no one with talent to melt and bend metals. That's why their weapons are human weapons. They were made by abducted blacksmiths from nearby villages. With these abductions also came laboring people. Thus began the war against the Pipils.

Ever since the Spanish invasion, her treasures started to wane. The Indians from these regions had never shown interest in her treasures. They didn't care for any of that. They only cared for the land, from which they got their sustenance. Now everything has changed. The whites stole the land from the Indians, and the beautiful woman's treasures have kept on waning.

Years ago, the beautiful woman and the Pipils had the whites as a common enemy, but the Pipils lost the war against the whites. *Maybe if the chaneques had assisted the Pipils, my treasures wouldn't have lessened.* Sihuehuet thought in many occasions. After so much time she still laments not assisting her enemies. Almost all of her treasures have been sent across the sea to very far lands.

The war between chaneques and indigenous had never been for her treasures, but only for the lands. Their war was very small compared to the one that the Pipils waged against the Spaniards. Everyone lost in that war. The land suffered even more. The chaneques were forced to withdraw completely from the surface and seal their caves.

Now Sihuehuet's only hope is to free Itzalku and retake the land. And once the land has been taken then she can take revenge against Tlaloc. The only thing that's intriguing for her is Tezcatlipoca. *Of course his jealousy toward Tlaloc is big, but to destroy humanity, that is very cruel, even for him.*

"Sarnik, come here." Immediately the most fearsome bodyguard of the chaneques enters the beautiful lady's room.

"At your service, My Beloved."

"Where is Chilco? I need to talk to him."

"I don't know, My Beloved. The last time I saw him, he was on his way to inspect some new hostages with a group of hunters."

"New hostages?" Sihuehuet asks.

"Yes, a couple of brats and a white woman."

"Send for him. I need to talk to him immediately."

"I'll send for him immediately, My Beloved." The bodyguard hits his chest twice and exits the chamber closing the door behind him.

Shortly after, Chilco enters the room. "You sent for me, My Beloved?" Chilco asks, bowing his head.

"Yes. I need to know if you have found anything new in the new mines."

"Not yet, My Beloved. But I got the new map with the newfound passages. There are no mines on any of them, at least not yet," Chilco reports.

"What about the new hostages?"

"The new hostages are only a couple of brats and very small, and a white woman. The brats are still asleep but she already woke up and keeps talking about her father."

"Where are they?"

"They are here, in one of the empty cells."

"Very good. Now listen carefully. I felt the presence of Pipil magic here in the cave."

"Pipil magic?" Chilco asks, very amazed.

"Yes. Maybe it has something to do with the new hostages. Or it may just be some ancient spell that got activated. We need to find out. I want to see these new hostages immediately."

"Then come with me, My Beloved. Do you want me to alert Notchím?" Chilco asks while walking alongside the lovely lady to the door.

"No. Leave that old sorcerer alone. When I need him, I'll send for him." The beautiful lady closes the door and they walk toward the prisons.

Most of the cells are very large, with guards everywhere all armed with spears and machetes guarding the prisoners. A group of thirty humans seem to be coming back from a hard day's work. Most are youngsters between twelve to eighteen years old, very few adults. Most of them are Mestizos and Indians from different tribes, perhaps two or three whites. Who really knows? In the dark you can't see very well.

Chilco and "My Beloved" come to the prison where Elena is imprisoned with her two children. "Where is my father?" Elena asks. "He said he would return immediately and he hasn't returned yet."

Chilco starts burning tobacco and incense in a small bowl with two pipes. Chilco blows through one pipe of the vessel and lets the smoke rise over Elena's face. Elena reacts slowly and awakens to a frightening reality.

"Aaaaaaa!" Elena screams with fear. In front of her is an old, small and ugly man. She immediately backs away from the bars. She trips and falls on the floor next to the twins. Elena, very confused, looks at the twins and slowly begins to regain her memory.

The beautiful lady approaches the cell bars and stares at her as if studying her. "Where are you from?" Sihuehuet asks.

"Who are you?" Elena asks shakily, ignoring the beautiful lady's question.

"I am the lady of the water and queen of nature," answers Sihuehuet. "I asked you a question, and I expect an answer."

"From Lake Coatepeque." Elena looks around. It is a narrow prison with thick bars of wood. The twins lie asleep on the floor. "What is wrong with my children?"

"They're just asleep. Do not worry, nothing has happened to them." Chilco answers in a raspy voice.

Elena tries to wake them up but they don't react. "Do not bother, dear. They are dreaming of a very beautiful paradise. They will be asleep for a while. Let them sleep. You and I need to talk. Chilco, bring her to the main salon. I want to talk to her," orders Sihuehuet.

"Immediately, My Beloved," Chilco responds. "You two, take this woman to the main salon." Both guards quickly opened the gates and take the woman by the arms. She's taller so they let her walk in front of them, pushing her with the peak of their spears. Elena has no choice but to obey.

Elena enters a very spacious cave adorned with gold and precious stones in the doorframes. A water fountain lies in the middle of the room. There's a huge wooden table to her left side where many scrolls lie. At the end of the room lies a silver chair adorned with feathers and bones where the most beautiful woman Elena has ever seen in her life sits, with a dazzling white dress that goes all the way down to her feet. The woman does not wear any shoes, yet her delicate feet are kept clean and soft.

The closer she gets to the beautiful lady, the woman's beautiful face begins to dull. Her face is not completely ugly, but it's not as beautiful as it looked from afar.

"Here is the woman you asked us to bring you by your own mandate, My Beloved," one of the guards announces.

She ignores the chaneque and stands up. She walks over to inspect Elena as if she were about to buy a horse. She walks around her looking at her from head to toe. "What's your name, dear?" Sihuehuet asks with a very firm and yet soft voice.

"E-Elena," the frightened woman responds, trembling from fear.

"And what is your descent?"

"I'm mixed."

"Mestiza? So you're half Spanish and half Indian?"

"Yes, ma'am."

"My Beloved. I am Sihuehuet. Everyone calls me 'My Beloved.' You will as well."

"Yes, ma'am, I mean...My Beloved. Why am I here? What do you want from me?" Elena asks, almost crying from fear.

"I'll ask the questions here," Sihuehuet responds with a very soft and calm voice. "You're Pipil?"

"No. I am part Maya."

"Maya? What is a Mayan doing here so far?"

"I live here with my family."

"So your family is Maya?"

"No, My Beloved. My husband is Pipil. My children are part Pipil and part Maya."

"With a bit of Spanish blood," Sihuehuet adds.

"Yes."

"And where is your husband now?"

"I don't know. The last time I saw him it was at camp. But I don't remember anything else. I don't even know how I got here."

"How many more are in your family?"

"We are seven." Elena answers, very concerned about the others.

"Seven? So that is *you*, your husband, and two twins. There are still three more which you still have not told me anything about. Are they Pipil warriors?"

"No, ma'am. We are peasants," a chaneque slaps her hard, drawing blood from her bottom lip.

"*My Beloved!*" the chaneque reminds her very angry.

"Sorry. My Beloved," Elena responds, covering her mouth in pain.

"Your other children... What age are they?"

"One is almost fourteen years old and my girl is only twelve, and then there is Tenoch who is only ten," Elena responds.

"Two boys and a girl."

"That's right."

Chilco enters the room. "My Beloved, I need to talk to you immediately." Sihuehuet and Chilco step away from the white woman to talk in private. "My Beloved, there are Pipil warriors in the caves," Chilco whispers.

"What?"

"Some hunters were hunting rams in the lower plains and found some Pipil arrows. Apparently, the Pipils killed a panther, and the panther's owner is missing."

"How many Pipils?"

"We don't know yet. It might be only a couple of them. The trackers only found traces of a couple of them. They hid in the caves below. I sent three patrols to look for them," Chilco answers.

"They may be this woman's family."

"I think so, My Beloved. The chaneques who brought her informed me that a giant and very brave warrior is with them. He's very good with weapons. They say his hands were so big that he could break a chaneque's skull with one hand. He killed several of our troops, and there are others missing."

Sihuehuet can't believe it and immediately returns to Elena. "Who is this warrior who travels with you? Is this perhaps your son?"

"Warrior? We have no warrior," answers a very confused Elena.

Sihuehuet slaps Elena again, leaving a pink mark on your cheek. "You're lying. Is it your husband? My chaneques say he killed several of my warriors."

"No, I assure you, My Beloved. No… no warrior travels with us. We're just farmers."

"Take her," Sihuehuet commands her guards.

Chilco gets closer to Sihuehuet. "My Beloved, don't worry. It's only a few warriors. We will find them and bring you their heads."

"Chilco, make sure all the entrances are sealed. I also want you to send guards to guard all the exits. I do not want anyone to escape from this place. And find out how these Pipils entered my territory," a very angry Sihuehuet commands.

"Immediately, My Beloved. But there are many other places where they could have entered. The hill is very large and there are many mazes and crannies that we don't know about," explains Chilco.

"I don't want to hear any excuses. If your chaneques had done their job from the beginning, we wouldn't have this problem. This woman has to be very important for there to be warriors looking for her. Put her in the main cell but do not send her to work; I want to keep her close."

"As you command, My Beloved." Chilco takes Elena by her arm and guides her directly to the main cell.

Sihuehuet leaves the room and goes straight to Notchím's cave, the main chaneque sorcerer. Notchím has knowledge of witchcraft, but his real talent is to make magic potions and enchantment. He also professes to have powers of divination, but they never work as he wants. In fact, they are only tricks with horses' knee bones which he calls Tabas.

"Notchím, we have a problem."

"Yes, My Beloved, my chaneques already reported it to me. Don't worry. Chilco will take care of them."

"I'm not talking about the Pipil warriors," Sihuehuet exclaims.

"So, what are you talking about, My Beloved?"

"There's Pipil magic here in the caves. Someone very powerful has entered the cave. I felt that the cave itself became alive. Half an hour ago I felt the walls moving."

"Walls, My Beloved? How so? I haven't felt anything. Not even an earthquake."

"I don't know. These Pipils did something. I felt my powers diminishing. I almost lost all of my strength when it happened. I need you to throw the Tabas and tell me what you see."

"Yes My Beloved." Notchím takes two Tabas off a shelf. He rubs them with corn oil and throws them on the table. The bones roll for a moment and then stop. Notchím studies them for a while.

"What do you see?" Sihuehuet asks impatiently.

"My Beloved, I see a feathered serpent with bright sapphire eyes," Notchím explains.

"The feathered serpent is the symbol of Quetzalcoatl. What does that mean?" The fair lady asks.

"I don't know My Beloved, but wait. The snake is coming out of a hole in the ground and is very angry. There's also a black patched jaguar along with the snake. The two fight together against their enemies."

"Describe the enemies," Sihuehuet commands.

"They are just faceless black shadows, My Beloved, but all of them are fleeing."

"Is that all?"

"No. Wait, there's another being that looks even more dangerous. It seems to be a god."

"Which god? Tlaloc? Tezcatlipoca?"

"No. I don't recognize him, but it has two heads."

"Is that all?"

"Yes, My Beloved, that is all."

Sihuehuet immediately exits Notchím's room and quickly heads over to the General's cave where Chilco just finished issuing orders to his captains.

"Chilco. Assemble the army and get ready for war. We have bigger problems than we thought."

"Bigger, My Beloved?"

"Yes. Quetzalcoatl has sent his warriors against us. Powerful warriors. Lock all the slaves and assemble the whole army. Our second war has just begun."

THE PIPIL COUNCIL

The Tazumal was very dark by the time Atecaltzin and Tenoch arrive. You can only hear the barking of dogs. The pair of survivors leaves the main road behind and takes a small trail before getting into the city. It is a narrow trail with enough room for a single horse. It is a shortcut to Ohtocani's house which is almost ten minutes away from the Tazumal on horse. Tenoch walks in front pulling the black horse where Atecaltzin lies fainted. His blood had continued to drip, and it's been over an hour since he passed out.

After their confrontation with the coyotes, the two riders started running the horses until they left the forest. Once on the esplanade they let the horses relax and continued their journey at a slow pace, until Atecaltzin fell asleep and Tenoch had to take charge and lead back to the Tazumal. On any other day, this trip would have taken only three hours and a half to four hours, if they had raced the horses. But in Atecaltzin state, they have had to slow down as if they were pulling a wagon, and have lost at least one hour worth of advantage.

Ohtocani's house is situated on the hill. It consists of four houses made of adobe, plastered with lime. It was built in the form of a staple, leaving a large patio in the midst of the construction. It has stables on the sides and a water well in the yard with a dishwashing pila to the side of the well.

There are only two roads leading to the house—— the small road leading to the city center and the trail that goes through the river. The trail is rocky and narrow. It's only used to go to the river or to take a shortcut to the main road. But Tenoch rather avoid meeting more people on the way, especially the Spaniards and Mestizos who have taken over the ruins.

At the top of the hill, Tenoch can see two men with rifles in their hands. The men don't seem to have any intention of hiding. The dogs have been unstable since they felt the unexpected visit approaching, and Ohtocani's sons got up to investigate.

"Uncle, it's me, Tenoch. My dad is hurt," Tenoch cries out. When they hear their nephew's voice, the two men immediately run down the hill to meet Tenoch. A couple of dogs run behind them.

"What happened? Where are the others?" Aquetzalli asks.

"We were attacked by chaneques, and my dad lost a hand. After that a few coyotes attacked us on the road," the boy explains between sobs.

"Quick, let's get him inside." Both men lead the horses up to the house and untie Atecaltzin. When Atecaltzin fainted, he almost fell from the horse. Tenoch had to tie him to the chair to prevent further accidents.

"Dad, Dad, Mom!" Aquetzalli shouts.

"What's going on? What's the big fuss?" Asks a very sleepy Ohtocani.

"Atecaltzin is hurt. Tenoch is here," Atlanezi responds.

"What? How did this happen?" Ohtocani asks.

"What's going on here?" Grandmother Iztacxochitl asks. "Oh my God! What happened to Atecaltzin?"

"He lost a hand and was bitten by a coyote," Atlanezi responds.

"Good God! Wake up the women. We need alcohol. Ahhh, Holy God!" Iztacxochitl cries of sadness when she uncovers his arm and sees the yellowish paste that has formed at the tip of his arm.

"Acalli, prepare some cypress water and mix it with lemon leaves and salt to wash the wounds. We will also need chamomile tea to calm his nerves if he wakes up. Xicali, bring some alcohol and some bandages."

"Come on, everyone, we have to let the women do their work." Ohtocani gets everyone out of the room. "Aquetzalli, bring something to drink for the child. He must be very tired."

"Yes, Dad." The rest of the children begin to enter the room, curious to see what happens with Tenoch.

"Sit down, Tenoch." The poor child still has coyote blood on his face and on his hands. The boy sits down on a wooden chair and gets surrounded by his uncles, grandfather, and three cousins who have woken up from her grandmother's screams. "Okay, tell me what happened? Where are Elena and the rest of the kids?" Ohtocani asks.

"We were going through the woods at the foot of Cuntetepeque when it started to get dark. We stopped for the night since it was going to start raining. When it was starting to get dark, some chaneques appeared. I didn't know what they were because they bewitched me and Xóchitl. I don't know how, but I don't remember anything else, until my dad blew some tobacco smoke on our faces to take away the charm. He told me that Itzcua rescued us and took us back to camp. When we arrived, my mom and the twins were gone. It was just my dad, and he was fighting with two chaneques. That's when one of them cut his hand with a machete. Itzcua killed one and wounded the other one."

"Chaneques! The chaneques don't exist," Aquetzalli interrupts while giving him a glass of water.

"Let him finish telling the story," Ohtocani commands. "Okay, child. Continue." Tenoch's cousins look at each other, very surprised and concerned with his story. Tina, the youngest girl, turns pale from fear and embraces her rag doll.

"Itzcua said he was going to rescue mother and the twins. Xóchitl went with him. We came to ask for help from the warriors.

Dad said that these chaneques are very dangerous and they have powers of enchantment. When we were on our way, half a dozen coyotes chased us and tried to bite dad. We had to fight them off. I killed three with my bow and dad killed two— one with a spear and the other one with the shotgun. The last coyote ran away among the trees of the forest."

"Chaneques? Coyotes? Are you sure you did not imagine the chaneques?" Aquetzalli asks.

"No. Of course not. I brought some evidence in my satchel. Yanixté, can you go get them? On the horses there are three bags; please bring them over. There is also a spear in my dad's horse." Yanixté, Aquetzalli's son, runs out to get the items.

"If what you say is true, this is very serious. No one that's alive has ever seen those monsters. It is said that they disappeared since the Spanish invasion. We have to form an expedition with the Pipil warriors. You will have to come with us."

"Here they are," Yanixté announces putting the bags on the floor but holds on to the spear. Everyone in the room shift their gaze to the spear.

"What a beautiful spear!" Aquetzalli exclaims.

"Let me see it." Ohtocani takes the spear.

"That spear is one of the chaneques'," says Tenoch.

"It's an ancient spear. Seems like Toltec descent. Very similar to ours. Is obsidian. Nobody does them that way anymore. Everything is made of iron or steel nowadays. These snake figures resemble Quetzalcoatl's symbol," Ohtocani explains.

Tenoch takes the arm from the bag and puts it on the table, with much urgency to get rid of it. After carrying it all night, the poor child still gets a bit of anxiety touching the dead and bloodied member. "This is an arm that Dad cut off a chaneque to submit as evidence to the council."

"Ahhh!" Everyone in the room sighs at the same time.

"Get the children out of here," Ohtocani commands.

Aquetzalli gets all the children out except for Yanixté. The boy is fourteen years old now and has already completed the first phase of his Pipil warrior training along with Itzcuauhtzin. That gives him the right to be at the meeting with the rest of them.

"No word of this must get out of here. We don't want the Spaniards to get involved in these matters. This is about the tribe not theirs. The last thing we need is for the royal crown of Spain to try to get involved in our affairs. This is a war we have had since the creation of man and it is our responsibility as Pipils.

Make sure the children keep this a secret. Atlanezi, go get Teutli. Tell him what is happening and have him prepare a group of volunteer warriors. We'll have to make an expedition to Cuntetepeque then come back here and wait for the council orders.

Aquetzalli, I need you to go and inform Pacotli. Make him aware of what has happened tonight and tell him we need to meet with the council immediately. Hurry up, we need to act soon. This is not just a family affair any more. If there are chaneques in the mountain of Cuntetepeque and are kidnapping people, we will need the warriors."

"Yes, Dad." Aquetzalli heads for the door and stops to talk to his eldest son. "Yanixté."

"Yes, Dad?"

"Take care of the horses. Take them to the barn and give them water and something to eat. Take your brother to help you."

"Yes, Dad," Yanixté responds and quickly goes to comply with the command.

Ohtocani is still entertained with the spear. He is amazed with the quality of work. He inspects the tip and traces the pole figures with his finger. "So, you killed three coyotes?" he asks Tenoch.

"Yeah, look." Tenoch draws the three ears and shows him.

Ohtocani smiles and gives him a hug. "That's my grandson, a true Pipil. I think you're ready to begin your training."

"But I'm only ten years old. Only twelve-year-olds can start the training."

"Yes, but in your case we will make an exception. You had your first battle and came out victorious. That is a virtue. It's in your blood. Until now you had only training with the bow. Is this true?"

"Yes. Xóchitl and I always practice together."

"And how good is your aim?"

"It's okay. Against wolves I only failed once. I hit the other ones just fine."

"Excellent. Then it's decided. When this is over, you'll stay here in the Tazumal and will learn with the other Tamemes."

"As you say, Grandpa."

"Now go and get some sleep. When the council is ready I will send for you."

"I'm not sleepy. I am too worried about mom and the others."

"Don't worry; I'm sure Itzcua will find them in time. He is an excellent tracker and very good with the ax. I myself administered the tests, and I can assure you he is very skilled."

"Grandpa, I really don't remember what happened. When I woke up, I was already inside the tent."

"Do not worry. When your dad wakes up, he will explain everything. Go and lie down in Yanixté's bed. It's almost dawn and it won't be used." The child obeys and goes to bed. He falls asleep right away. The poor child was more tired than he thought.

"Chaneques! In our time? The chaneques disappeared more than a hundred years ago. How could there be chaneques at Cuntetepeque?" a very dismayed Pacotli asks.

"There hasn't been a chaneque appearance in over a hundred years. Why would they come out of hiding now?" Tlaltonal, one of the eldest advisors of the tribe, asks. Tlaltonal has lived in this region for over fifty years. He is a descendant of the great Pipil warrior Atonal, who it is said to have injured Don Pedro de Alvarado. By inheritance, he should be the new chief of the tribe, but the invasion put an end to most indigenous traditions. Now there is only the elder's council, where the eldest is the leader and spokesman of the group called Tlahtoani.

"I don't know. But my son and his family found them. Luckily, with the help of Tlaloc, Atecaltzin and Tenoch were able to escape alive. We do not know if the others are still alive," Ohtocani answers.

"And based on this fairy tale of your grandson, you want to invoke the warriors?" sarcastically asks Pacotli, the speaker of the council.

"I think it's necessary. We must form a group of warriors and go look for them. My grandson Tenoch says he saw at least one of them. When Atecaltzin wakes up, we'll know more about what happened. This arm should be proof enough. We also have this spear. It is gold plated, with figures of snakes and obsidian point, a key symbol of Quetzalcóatl," Ohtocani adds.

"I agree with Ohtocani. We cannot just idly sit by," adds Tlacaelel, who has been very quiet during the entire meeting.

"Where is Teutli?" Pacotli asks.

"He is with Atlanezi. Atlanezi is catching him up with what happened," Ohtocani responds.

"Very will then. Send for him. We will send a group of warriors right away."

"I'll go get them," Aquetzalli offers immediately.

"Leave the spear with us Aquetzalli. We want to inspect it."

"Yes, of course." Aquetzalli gives the spear to Tlayolotl and leaves the place in a hurry.

"Ohtocani, we need to talk to Atecaltzin as soon as possible," Pacotli demands.

"He's very badly injured and unconscious. When he wakes up, we can question him."

Acohuatl stands up. "The question we're all forgetting is... what do the Chaneques want with these people? What is the purpose of these kidnappings? If they just wanted to kill the humans, they would have done it at the camp. They wouldn't have taken the trouble to kidnap them." He takes the spear from Tlayolotl's hand and examines it. "It's very impressive. I doubt that it has been stolen. This must have been made by an expert in gold and copper melting. This spear is not old. If it was, the copper would have mold." He looks at his surroundings. Each one of the elders stares at him, very attentive to his words.

Acohuatl is one of the newest members of the council. He has only been a member for a couple of years. He is the youngest, but also one of the wisest and most prudent. That's why he was elected to serve on the council. It is said that he has studied under the cover of a Catholic priest in Cuscatlán when he was young. He can read and write in Spanish, as well as Nahuatl.

"A couple of years ago, I was visiting Tikal with my family. When we were traveling back home, we stopped at Ouija. There, I heard troubling news of missing people. All this time, we all believed that the perpetrators could have been enslavers. I have heard similar stories from the surrounding villages. But now, I'm starting to believe that this may well be the work of chaneques." A big murmur explodes in the room.

"Tikal. What were you doing in Tikal?" Tlayolotl asks.

"I have relatives who live there on my mother's side. As a kid, we always traveled once a year to visit. I go every five years now. The roads are very dangerous these days, so I don't understand how Atecaltzin decided to leave so late to Coatepeque." He shifts his gaze to Ohtocani.

Although it is not a direct question, Ohtocani decides to respond. "Atecaltzin left early, but he had trouble with a wheel which caused him a delay. He must have thought he still had enough time to make the trip, but for sure he must have had more problems down the road."

"Then it is decided. We'll send a dozen warriors to Cuntetepeque to investigate. When we know more about these chaneques, then we will prepare better," Pacotli decides.

"Only a dozen warriors?" Ohtocani asks, very upset with Pacotli's poor decision.

"Yes, for the moment. If we send an army, the Spaniards may start to get suspicious. Right now we know nothing. A dozen warriors are sufficient to track the chaneques and that will also be enough to raise suspicion. Are we all agreed?" Pacotli asks aloud.

All elders bow their heads in agreement, except Ohtocani, who still thinks it's too few warriors.

By the time Aquetzalli gets home, Atlanezi and Teutli are waiting, with horses and weapons ready, and a dozen warriors at their side. "Teutli, the council wants to talk to you. They say they will send a group of warriors to investigate, but they need to make preparations first."

"I'm on my way," Teutli answers.

"Atlanezi, go with him. The council wants to talk to both of you. I'm heading for Cuntetepeque right away. I'm not going to stay and wait for the elders to reach an agreement. Besides, they will have a lot to prepare. The new sun has already come out and we have lost a lot of time already." Aquetzalli looks at the warriors, all of good reputation, and Pipils to the bone. "I need a few volunteers to come with me." Four warriors raise their hands.

"Thank you, brothers. Teutli, with your permission."

"The elderly are not going to be happy if you leave without their permission," Teutli exclaims. "But seeing the circumstances, I would do the same. Tlaloc be with you. I'll catch up later."

"Thanks, brother. Yanixté, saddle my horse and bring it right away."

"Yes, Dad. I'm going with you," Yanixté answers.

"No. I need you to stay here and help your grandfather. There is a lot to do here, and this expedition is very dangerous."

"But I'm a warrior. I have the right to go."

"You are not a warrior yet. You need much more to be a warrior. This is not child's play."

"But Dad..."

"Not another word. You stay here until it's over. Go get my horse." Yanixté leaves, more angry than sad about not being able to go on the expedition.

"The boy just wants to help, Aquetzalli. You should not be so hard on him," Teutli comments.

"This is very dangerous, Teutli. I cannot expose him to this kind of danger. These chaneques are very treacherous."

"He's your son, not mine. But if he were mine, I see no better time to let him show his knowledge and let him season. Itzcua had the same training and is out there looking for his family. He fought against several chaneques and came out victorious. How do you think your son is going to feel if you do not let him show his talents?"

"Fine, but you will have to take him. I'm on a great hurry. Now listen closely, I will begin the search at the foot of the Cuntetepeque hills by the road to Coatepeque. Tenoch said they hid the wagon there. The coyotes they killed were left beside the road. We will leave traces so that you can follow us."

Aquetzalli goes into his home and prepares for a long and dangerous journey.

Yanixté wakes Tenoch up around eight o'clock in the morning. Tenoch rises. "What's up?"

"We have to go, Tenoch. The warriors are already here. They're waiting. My dad already left with four Pipil warriors."

"Where to?"

"To Cuntetepeque, to find my aunt Elena and the others."

"How does he know where to look?"

"I don't know, but he is a very good tracker. He said he would look for the dead coyotes at the foot of the hills of Cuntetepeque, by the main road, and would begin from there. He thinks the chaneques must have hidden caves on the hill."

"What about my dad?"

"He is still unconscious." Tenoch quickly rises from the bed and leaves the room.

"Where's Grandpa?"

"He's still talking to the Pipil council. They have spent more than two hours in the meeting. Pacotli wants to talk to you. Go on and wash your face; you still have it full of dried blood."

"It must be from the coyotes. I had to spear them to make sure they were dead."

"It must have been a very good fight. Were you afraid?"

"Of course, very, especially when one of them came at me. If it hadn't been for my dad, that coyote would have bitten me and perhaps killed me." In fact, the poor child peed himself but he wasn't going to admit to that.

"Tlaloc must have been with you." Tenoch reaches the pila and washes his face. Then the two boys get into the living room where half a dozen warriors are waiting for him, including Teutli.

At seeing Tenoch, the warriors stand up and give a war cry. "Ay ay ay ay ay!" The cry is to celebrate and congratulate Tenoch's great feat. The child feels a little embarrassed and flattered at the same time. The warriors are celebrating him as a hero.

"Very well done, Tenoch. That's a real Pipil warrior," announces Teutli aloud for all to hear.

"Ay ay ay ay ay!" the warriors respond. Yanixté, very excited, slaps him on the shoulder.

"Thank you," Tenoch responds with a little humility and great reverence.

"Do not worry, Tenoch. We are going to find your family," Teutli promises.

"Thank you."

"Tenoch, my son," Grandma Iztacxochitl greets him. "Come child, you have to eat something before you go."

"Before I go?"

"Yes, the warriors need you to show them the way. We will go with them to Cuntetepeque where you guys camped and then we'll return to Tazumal," Yanixté explains.

"You're also coming with us?"

"Yes. Teutli said it would be very good training for me. Also I was put on as your bodyguard, so you can't even go pee without me. Ha ha ha," Yanixté laughs at his own joke.

"That's good. Who else is coming with us?"

"From our family, only uncle Atlanezi, you and me, and about ten more warriors."

"Only ten?"

"Yes. The council only gave permission for twelve, but my dad took four more. The elderly still don't know about that, so Teutli is going to take nine others with us."

"That's good. But I thought Pacotli wanted to talk to me."

"Yes. When you finished eating we'll go see him."

"Okay."

133

"Well, I'll leave you alone so you can eat. I will go prepare the horses."

THE HIDDEN MAGIC

Very carefully, Itzcuauhtzin enters the cave. Xóchitl follows closely with bow and arrow in hand. It is a very large room with no lights. The kids walk in and the door closes behind them. The hieroglyphs on the walls and ceiling lit up like torches all around the room. The presence of the kids and their Pipil blood have activated an ancient spell.

At the end of the room there is a skeleton sitting on a throne made of solid stone. The skeleton has a couple of rings on his fingers and a necklace made of small pieces of wood adorned with jade stones that covers its entire chest.

On the wall immediately behind the skeleton is a giant Mayan calendar made of gold that covers most of the wall. It distills a bluish brightness throughout its lines. A thick layer of dust covers most of the objects. Near the walls they can see many ceramic pots full of jewels and precious stones. There are also many skeletons sitting on common chairs lined up before the throne. They seem to be offering tribute to a king.

"This is a hidden treasure!" Xóchitl exclaims.

"The Pipil treasure," Itzcuauhtzin responds.

"This must have been a king or a chief. But why was he buried here?"

"I don't know. It seems that they were buried a long time ago. Someone must have put them in this way. It seems as if the rest of them were offering a tribute," Itzcuauhtzin explains.

"That door was sealed with magic," Xóchitl assures. "It was surely meant to keep intruders out."

"Or maybe just to hide the treasure from the Spaniards," Itzcuauhtzin adds.

"Maybe. Do you think this salon was the king's throne room?" Xóchitl asks.

"No, of course not. This is a grave. All these symbols are Pipil symbols. But Pipils do not live in caves but outdoors. I think he may have been put here after his death. These people could have been his family or perhaps other chiefs."

"There were also Mayan symbols outside, and many others that I've never seen," Xóchitl answers.

Itzcuauhtzin continues to inspect the place. "Look, here are more hiroglifs. Do you understand them?"

"Hieroglyphics," corrects Xóchitl and comes over to see them better. "They are weird. Perhaps they are just decoration drawings." Xóchitl inspects behind the throne's chair. "Look, Itzcua, a shield. It is very well preserved. A little dusty, but it hasn't deteriorated."

Xóchitl shakes up the shield to drop the dust. "It's very light and very strong."

Itzcuauhtzin comes over and takes the shield. "That's nice. It is very common among Pipils. It's a Māhuizzoh Chimalli."

"What?" Xóchitl asks very confused.

"A Māhuizzoh Chimalli. Teutli has several at home. They are called like that because they can be decorated with many different things like feathers, flowers, and even gold. This one seems to be made of wood, gold, and feathers. It's very strong. It also has Indian symbols. You're right. After so much time, it should already have been damaged, especially the feathers."

"I bet it has seen many battles."

"Surely it belonged to this chief." Itzcuauhtzin puts his arm on the handle of the shield, and though his arm is still very small for the shield, the probes easily adjust to him by themselves. "Aaaaah!" Itzcuauhtzin sighs of wonder.

"What happened?"

"The shield adjusted to my arm by itself."

"How so?"

"I don't know. I stuck my arm, and then they adjusted by themselves as if by magic."

"By magic?"

"Yes. Like the door." Itzcuauhtzin attempts to pull the shield off, and the shield loosens up so Itzcuauhtzin can easily remove it. "Look how easy it came off." Itzcuauhtzin exclaims and puts the shield back on, and again it adjusts itself to his arm. Itzcuauhtzin makes several movements and some war defense moves and the shield feels really good. "It is very light and it makes me feel refreshed. I don't feel tired anymore."

"Magic. It must be magic. There's no other explanation. This shield must be the king's. It must have been blessed by some very powerful shaman."

"Or maybe by Quetzalcoatl himself," Itzcuauhtzin adds, very excited.

"Do you think it is a celestial weapon?" Xóchitl asks.

"Could be. Why not? Remember that the gods often visited the humans in the past ages."

"Those are only legends. They cannot be taken as history or accurate information."

"You know more about legends than me. And you know that many things that legends talk about have much truth in them. If not, just look at the way we discovered this magic cave."

"Maybe. But I still find it hard to believe that all this is true. But if it is magical, why was it buried here with him? They could have used it themselves. Or at least, it could have been given to his heirs."

"For the same reason they hid the treasure—— to hide it from the invading Europeans, or someone else. Perhaps at that time they had a lot of respect for the other's things," Itzcuauhtzin answers. "I really like it. Do you think the king would be angry if I take it?"

"Apparently, you do not have the same respect. But I do not think the king will need it. It's also a warrior's shield. Whoever made it, made it for war. I think it's only fair that a warrior wields it again. And what better time than this?"

"You're right. You think there are more magical things in this cave?" Itzcuauhtzin asks.

"Maybe," Xóchitl answers and starts searching among the pots, but only finds jewelry and household utensils.

Itzcuauhtzin looks around the king's throne, as if seeking for his spear or macuahuitl, but does not find any more weapons until he looks up and on the wall sees a short spear stuck in a pair of wooden hangers. "The spear!" Itzcuauhtzin exclaims; he can hardly contain his joy. Right away he pushes a skeleton off its chair and uses it to climb and reach the spear.

"Have more respect for the dead, Itzcua, or they'll come at night and scare you," Xóchitl yells, but the young warrior is already on top and has the spear in his hand.

"Look, it resembles the one we took from the chaneque. Except that this one is made of much better materials."

"Let me see it." Xóchitl takes the spear and inspects it. "Again, the feathered serpent. No doubt these people were followers of the god Quetzalcoatl." Xóchitl hands the spear back to Itzcuauhtzin who's is trying to place the skeleton back on its chair, but most of the bones have broken and are all bunched up.

"And what are you doing now?" Xóchitl asks.

"I'm putting this skeleton back in its chair. I do not want them to be mad at me."

"Leave it, you already blew it. What can you do?" Itzcuauhtzin puts all the bones on the chair as best as he can and places the skull on top.

"Here, I'll keep looking. Maybe I'll find something for me." Xóchitl gives the spear back and searches through the pots of gold while Itzcuauhtzin plays with his new spear. "Itzcua, look, here is a chest but is sealed. Maybe there's something inside."

Itzcuauhtzin removes his shield and puts it aside with his bag and his new spear, then begins to inspect the chest. It's a chest made of copper and iron. It doesn't have any locks nor handles to open. "It is completely sealed," Itzcuauhtzin explains. He hits it several times with his fist to see if it is hollow. "It's very solid. I don't think we can break it. Do you understand these figures? Maybe it needs a little of your magic."

"What magic? I have no magic," Xóchitl responds.

"The one you used to open the door. Or how do you explain that?"

"That was not magic. That simply was the blood. And I only did it because one of the figures was bleeding. There is nothing here that indicates blood."

"Even so. Do you want to try it again?"

"No, that hurts." Xóchitl begins to read the inscriptions. But there are no recognizable symbols. Only a bird that looks like a quetzal because of its long feathers. "How strange," says Xóchitl.

"What?"

"This is a quetzal. There are no quetzals in this land. They are mostly found farther to the north in the Mayan lands, Escuintla mostly. It also has a feathered serpent."

"How do you know that?" Itzcuauhtzin asks but quickly retracts. "Don't tell me your teacher told you," he answers himself with a little sarcasm.

"Of course."

"So you think you can open it?"

"I don't know yet. There might be some kind of key around here or something."

"Use a little blood and move it like you did with the image of Quetzalcoatl."

"Ce Topiltzin Ácatl Quetzalcoatl!" Xóchitl exclaims. "This is a quetzal. The quetzals must have been named after him or him after the quetzals. In either way, they are related."

"Ce Ácatl Topiltzin? The King?" Itzcuauhtzin asks, very interested.

"Chief," Xóchitl corrects him. "The legend says that Ce Ácatl Topiltzin disappeared at sea after he turned into a bird. But there are also other legends that say the he migrated to the south. Perhaps this is his grave."

"So the one sitting on the throne is Ce Ácatl Topiltzin Quetzalcoatl?"

"I don't know. I'm not sure. It could also be Topiltzin Axcitl Quetzalcoatl II. Remember that he was the founder of these cities. I think this might be either one's tomb. But that spear is very ancient and magical. Almost

141

everything here, including that spear, bears the symbol of Quetzalcoatl. That tells me that this guy was a chief, and one of the most important ones."

"Maybe is not Ce Ácatl. Why would he be here? Wasn't he a leader of Tula? Or 'Huey Tlahtoani' as the Aztecs called their leaders." Itzcua raises his eyebrows to show Xóchitl that he also knows about history. But the girl just ignores his jest.

"Yes, but legend has it that after being deceived by Tezcatlipoca, he left his kingdom and migrated southward with many of his followers. Who would say that he didn't make it all the way here? Maybe his servants buried him here with all of his belongings, including his weapons."

"Yes, but Topiltzin Acxitl was the one who founded the city of Tecupan Ishatcu."

"Maybe so. I do not know. I don't think there's a sure way of knowing."

"Do you think his weapons were magical?"

"I don't know, I've never read it anywhere, and no one has ever mentioned it. But the feathered serpent is the symbol of Ce Ácatl. That's why he is also called Quetzalcoatl."

"How interesting. So what does this mean? That only a quetzal or a snake can open it, or what?"

"Maybe. Or it could mean that only he has the key," Xóchitl explains and rises rapidly as one who has just received a revelation. She immediately begins to check the chief's jewelry, starting with the extravagant necklace. The symbols on the wood don't tell her anything, nor the precious gems. There are two rings on his hands, one on each side. The first one has the face of a feathered serpent. The ring itself is formed by the feathered serpent's tail. The other ring is made in the form of a jaguar's head. Xóchitl takes them in her hand and notices that they distill a very low yellowish light and then turn off. She quickly returns to the chest. "What's that?" she asks Itzcuauhtzin when she sees him busy putting on a necklace.

"It's a necklace of teeth or claws, I'm not sure, but it looks good on me," Itzcuauhtzin answers with a big smile on his lips.

"We are not here to take everything that we like, let alone steal the treasure from a Cacique like Ce Ácatl. Stop messing around and help me open this box," Xóchitl orders.

"We don't know what's in there. Leave it alone. We're just wasting our time."

"There is something very important in there, and I want to find out. Look at these rings." Xóchitl gives Itzcuauhtzin one ring for to inspect it.

"Looks like a jaguar."

"Yes, but when I touched it, it distilled a yellowish light. Very slightly, but it did."

"Why isn't it shining now?"

"Who knows?" Xóchitl put on the feathered serpent ring on her left hand ring finger. The ring shines once more and it perfectly adjusts itself to her finger. "Oh!"

the girl sighs. Itzcuauhtzin opens his mouth, very surprised. "Works just like the shield," Xóchitl exclaims.

Itzcuauhtzin immediately puts on the jaguar ring, and the same magic gets activated. "It's really amazing," Itzcuauhtzin says.

"Unbelievable. This really is magical. Now I understand what you said about feeling renewed. I feel very alert and full of strength." Xóchitl approaches the chest and touches it with her ring, with hopes that this is the key to open it, but nothing happens. "It didn't work."

"I don't think these are keys," Itzcuauhtzin says. "Maybe they are just for protection or to give you energy."

"No. it's not that. These utensils are magical for a good reason. Maybe there is some charm or keyword we have to recite to make them work."

"Magic words? Now those really are fairy tales."

Open up. The box emits a blue light and then opens up. The kids look at each other, very surprised.

"How'd you do it?" asks Itzcuauhtzin.

"I just thought of the word 'open' and it opened," Xóchitl explains.

"It's definitely magical. This is extraordinary."

"Now you believe me, right?"

"I think so."

The two kids look within the chest and find some warrior costumes. Xóchitl takes the garments and puts them aside. At the bottom of the chest she finds a bow and quiver. "Look, Itzcua, they are beautiful."

"That bow is wonderful. It looks like Quetzalcoatl's bow." The bow was made in the form of a snake with the head down. The material appears to be bathed in pure gold or some other finer material. It is not arched like a normal indigenous bow. This one has a dent in the middle, designed to support your hand and room for an arrow. It has many hieroglyphs like runes along. The cord is a little thicker than normal and transparent like a nylon guitar string.

The quiver is an ordinary quiver like the ones used by indigenous warriors. It is yellow and has the same arc inscriptions as the bow, except that the feathered serpent image is large. It is made of a very soft snakeskin and adorned with leather strips on the bottom and sides.

It also has a dozen obsidian-tipped arrows and feathers in the trunk. The arrow rods are the straightest rods the kids have ever seen in their life. "What an excellent job," Itzcuauhtzin says, taking an arrow in his hand.

"It's beautiful," Xóchitl agrees. "I think it has been waiting for me." Xóchitl takes off his quiver and puts the new one in its place. "It almost has no weight."

"It looks very good on you. You know what would look great with your new weapons?" Itzcuauhtzin asks.

"What?"

"This indigenous dress. Look how pretty it is. The skin is very thin, and it has other hiroglifs."

"Hieroglyphics," Xóchitl corrects him again. "And yes, it is very nice."

"You should try it."

"No. It is also very old and very large. Leave it alone."

"I bet it belonged to a princess, and I don't think it's that big," Itzcuauhtzin responds.

"Is there anything else in the chest?"

Itzcuauhtzin shoves his hand to the bottom of the chest and starts looking. "Only one scroll, and one Indian armor."

"Let me see the scroll." Xóchitl takes the scroll and unrolls it while Itzcuauhtzin wastes no time in trying on the armor. "Just more hieroglyphics and ancient designs."

"How do I look?" Itzcuauhtzin asks, modeling his new Ichcahuipilli.

"Like all great warriors."

"Perfect. I feel invincible. I'll take it."

"Itzcua, we cannot take everything we find."

"I believe that these weapons and these clothes are gifts from the gods. Like you said before, they were made for war and it's only just for another warrior to reuse them."

"Okay, let's put back what we don't need, and then we have to go. It's getting late and we still don't know where they have taken Mom."

"Okay. Let's put this stuff back. We will come back when we have more time. I don't think there will be a problem if we take these weapons and rings." The kids put the parchment and other rare utensils found in the chest, including a very thick arm bracelet with a large jade stone in the middle, incrusted with the face of a snake and a pair of women earrings and several necklaces.

Xóchitl closes the hood and this one seals itself, with a very strong light bouncing around the slits. The satisfied kids get ready to go and start to pick up their things.

"Look, we forgot to put away the dress."

"Let me see it." Xóchitl takes the dress and holds it up over her chest.

"I think it fits."

"Perhaps, but I'm not going to put it on." Xóchitl opens the chest one more time and saves it. She takes her old arrows from the old quiver and put them in the new one. The quiver emits a faint blue light and the arrows turn into new obsidian-tipped arrows, with a very straight rod like the others.

"Awesome!" Exclaims Itzcuauhtzin who has seen quivers effect.

"What happened?"

"The arrows you just put in the quiver have turned new. They look like the others." Itzcuauhtzin takes one and hands it to her.

"This is awesome."

"Well, now we know why it was sealed. It's magical."

"I can't wait to try the bow," Xóchitl excitedly exclaims.

"You better not try it here. We do not know how powerful it may be."

"Fine. Well, I'm ready. Let's go." The kids open the cave's door with their new rings and exit with their new weapons ready for battle.

ROAD WITHOUT AN ENTRANCE

The sky is dressed in black and full of vultures circling the area, a clear sign for the warriors that there is death in the road. At seeing the birds, the warriors rush their horses. Upon their arrival they find dozens of vultures feasting on the dead coyote's bodies.

"This is the place that Tenoch told us about. Atecaltzin's camp and his wagon must be close by," Aquetzalli assures them. The warriors follow the road leaving the vultures behind to enjoy their feast in peace.

Aquetzalli finds the wagon's tracks and then they disappear.

"The wagon tracks end here. The camp must be here somewhere."

"There's the wagon," Ocoyatl points out. The warriors go into the forest and continue farther into the woods, leaving the wagon behind. The tent is still standing, but everything seems to have been turned over by the coyotes. The warriors get down from their horses and begin to inspect the area.

"There is a river nearby." Ucatl, a warrior of maximum rank, points out His head shaved and his long braid identifies him as one of the elite warriors of the Pipil tribe. He is one of the few who have had hand-to-hand combats. He is an expert hunter and an excellent weapon master, second only to Teutli of the Pipil militia.

The chaneque lies still on the ground with a few ants about it. "It's really ugly," says Aquetzalli as he inspects him.

"Why haven't the animals touched it?" Acatlel asks.

"It smells really bad. Perhaps it is so repulsive that even the animals don't want him," Ucatl answers. "If I was a coyote, I wouldn't want to try their meat either. It is gray and has purple blood. What kind of monster is this?"

"It's a chaneque. Just like Tenoch described it," Aquetzalli answers while walking in the tent's direction with ax in hand.

"Maybe it just looks that way because it's dead. Alive it may have a different color," Acatlel adds.

"The skin, maybe, but I don't think their blood does," Ucatl responds.

"I found some rare tracks. They must be the second chaneques. There are other human footprints as well. Surely they are Itzcuauhtzin's and his sister's," Ocotlel expresses.

"Let's follow them," Ucatl orders.

"Wait a minute." Aquetzalli announces from the tent and then exits with a pipe in his right hand. "There is nothing here. The forest is very dense. It would be better to leave the horses and walk."

"Sounds good, we'll tie them up here so the other warriors can find them and they can follow," Ucatl exclaims.

The warriors dismount their horses and take their most necessary items like their weapons, canteens, and satchels. They tie the horses and all run in row following the kids' trail.

Ocoyatl finds chaneque blood on a rock. "This blood is not human, but they came through here that's for sure. At least one chaneque must be injured," he reports.

"Are you sure it isn't human blood?" Aquetzalli asks.

"I'm sure. This blood is purple and it smells very bad."

"All blood smells bad," Ucatl says.

"Yes, but this one is not human, that's for sure," Ocoyatl answers.

"There's a cave here," Acatlel cries out from further up the hill. The warriors immediately rush to his side.

It is a dark cave with trash everywhere. There are pans, dishes, crates, and a couple of broken water gourds. Everything is covered in ashes, and it even seems as if someone burned old clothes.

"The footprints end on the wall at the end of the cave. This is solid rock," Ocoyatl says. "There is no way that the kids went through here, but the tracks end here.

They only go in one direction, and there is no sign of them leaving this cave."

"It has to be a door. We must find a way to open it," Aquetzalli exclaims. "They couldn't have just vanished in midair."

"Or maybe they did," Acatlel adds. "The chaneques are beings from another world. Maybe they were transported to another dimension."

"That's not possible," Aquetzalli exclaims, a little hectic. "That being down there, it's real. Itzcuauhtzin killed it. They *can* be killed. That means they are from this world."

"Okay, maybe it is a door. Then we just have to open it," Ucatl says. "But how?"

"I don't know, but if this is a door. That means that my nephews are inside this mountain. There must be some other way in. Maybe there's another hidden cave or a hole in the ground. We just have to find it."

"This place seems to be sealed. We should split into two groups and look around," Acatlel suggests.

"Very well then. Acatlel, you stay here and wait for the others and also in case this door opens up. Make a smoke signal to call us if necessary. Three by two blows will be the call signal, and two by one to find our position. We will do the same to contact you."

"Sounds good," Acatlel answers.

"Aquetzalli, it will be better that you and Ocoyatl go together and look up the hill. Ocotlel and I will go down and look by the river. No more than two hours.

Whoever doesn't find anything will immediately return to this cave," Ucatl orders, and immediately the warriors separate in different paths.

The first chaneque patrol finally finds the almond tree where Itzcuauhtzin killed the first chaneque. Ants have started to eat the body, but other than that there is no sign that any other animal has touched it.

"He died instantly. The ax went through the chest and split his heart. The warrior is very good."

"With this one and the one at the camp are twofold. Where are the other three?" the patrol leader Kuenú asks. The chaneques have been looking all night. The first patrol led by Kumara has been looking down by the river, and they still don't know if they have found anything yet.

"It's getting late and we have to get back. We'll take this body back to the cave. The two of you, go and bring the other one from the camp and meet us at the cave." The two chaneques quickly run toward the camp while the other two save the body in a fiber sack, like those used by farmers to save their coffee beans.

Before reaching the river, the two chaneques look at a shaved Indian examining the path. "It's just one Indian," A chaneque says.

"Might be the warrior Kumara told us about."

"Do you have any blue powder?"

"No. Do you?"

"Neither."

"He's big but we can take him very easily." So they ready their spears and prepare to attack Ucatl. They get a bit closer without being seen by the warrior.

Ucatl stands up and looks around. Seeing nothing around, he crosses the river, jumping on the few stones, and when he runs out, he dives into the river and begins to walk slowly in the water.

The chaneques cease the opportunity, since the water does not give room for speed, and jump out of the bushes with spears in hand ready to attack. Ucatl realizes his danger too late. A chaneque comes out ready to run him through when suddenly an arrow pierces his chest, killing him instantly.

The second chaneque turns to see where the arrow came from and sees Ocotlel readying a second arrow. The chaneque stops for a moment. Ucatl uses that moment to launch his bolas. They hit their target and entangled themselves between the chaneque's legs, and he falls to the ground. Ocotlel wastes no time and immediately runs over to the chaneque and disarms him. He turns him over and ties his hands behind his back.

"Let me go, you damned Pipil," the chaneque complains.

"How did you see him?" Ucatl asks.

"I saw them since they came up to the bush. I was watching from the bottom by the Achiote tree. When you got in the water, I got ready because I knew they were going to attack you when you were more vulnerable."

"Very good job. We have to question him and take him to the cave. He will tell us how to enter."

"I'm not going to say anything. *Shwissssssssssssssss…*" The chaneque whistles.

"What are you doing?" Ocotlel asks.

"He is calling his friends." Ucatl responds and ties a piece of rope around the chaneque's mouth to keep him from whistling again. "We have to cross the river before their reinforcements arrive." Ucatl takes his bolas and pushes the chaneque in front of him into the river.

The chaneques took a different route to the cave, and by pure luck they didn't hear their companion's whistles. But being closer to the cave, they notice a Pipil warrior looking for clues. "A Pipil," Kuenú exclaims. The chaneques put their dead kin on the ground and prepare their weapons. "There must be more of them in the area."

The two chaneques jump up to the branches and begin to scan the area. Kuenú takes his spear and starts heading over to the cave. A chaneque jumps down to his side. "I don't see anyone else, boss. I think he is alone."

"Very good. We will try to capture him alive. My Beloved will want to question him."

"Yes, boss. But remember, he is very dangerous. This was the one that killed the others."

"He doesn't look as big as Kumara said he was."

"Maybe not, but he's an elite Cuachicqueh Yaotecatl."

"Are you afraid?" Kuenú asks.

"Of course not. There are three of us and only one of him. We also have the advantage of having seen him first."

The second chaneque jumps down next to them. "There is no one else, boss. He is alone."

"Very good. I want him alive. Do you have a net?"

"Yes, sir," the second chaneque answers.

"I have some yellow powder Chief. We can put him to sleep," the second chaneque reports.

"Let's go get him then." The chaneques begin to move slowly hiding among the trees and rocks.

Acatlel is still sitting on a small rock, quietly drawing with his knife on the floor. It's only been a little bit over an hour ago that the others left and he quickly got tired of hitting the wall with a rock. Suddenly he hears a noise and gets up, takes his shotgun in hand and straps on his knife. He quickly exits the cave without letting down his guard. He looks around but sees nothing, so he decides to climb a rock to see better but still can't see anything.

The chaneques observe him from the bushes but they are still too far for an attack. Acatlel gets off the rock and walks to his right among the trees to investigate.

The chaneques take advantage of that moment to get closer. Kuenú jumps on some branches, scaring several birds, which draws Acatlel's attention. One of them manages to get to the rock and hides behind it while the first chaneque hides behind a thick tree.

Acatlel scans the trees and starts to get a bad feeling. Still being unable to see anything, he knows that there is something evil nearby. He takes a few steps back and readies his shotgun, ready to shoot whatever comes against him.

Kuenú knows he has lost the element of surprise and signals to the other two chaneques to get ready. "You are surrounded, Pipil. Put the gun down and we won't harm you," Kuenú lies. The first chaneque jumps toward a tree so fast that Acatlel only sees a shadow and hides behind a branch.

"What do you want from me?" Acatlel asks.

"I just want you to put that gun down. That's all." Kuenú promises, lying again. The first chaneque jumps again onto another tree. This time Acatlel sees him, but it is too fast for him to shoot.

Acatlel know he only has one shot. Then he will have to resort to his bow or his club. But he left his bow and his spear at the entrance of the cave and will not help him. His club will only help if he comes face to face with his attackers.

He has never met a chaneque and has no idea of how strong they might be, but after seeing one of them jump from branch to branch, he realizes that they're faster and stronger than him, so he decides not to shoot and save his shot till he has a better target. *How did Itzcua killed these things? They are fast.*

"Show me your face first and then I'll decide whether or not to put my gun down," Acatlel answers, trying to buy some time and improve his chances.

"You only have one shot. We are many more. It's best for you to put the gun down, Pipil."

"You're lying," Acatlel shouts in hope that the other warriors would hear him, then takes several steps back trying to seek refuge among the trees, but decides to head back into the cave instead. He'll have a better chance to defend himself there with the wall behind him.

Kuenú reads his intentions and jumps away to corner him and force him to enter the cave. The second chaneque readies his magic dust and waits for the warrior to get a little closer, while the first chaneque readies his spear.

Acatlel keeps on moving very slowly toward the cave without knowing he is walking into a trap. Kuenú hurls his spear from behind a branch toward Acatlel. He knows that his shot will not hit because he can't see very well but is not intended to kill him, just to press him. Acatlel sees the spear land very close to him so he speeds up his pace.

The second chaneque is able to see him now. Acatlel takes two more steps and stops after he sees the first chaneque jump from branch to branch getting closer.

Acatlel sees an opportunity and shoots at the chaneque when this one lands on a loose branch. The shot hits the target but only manages to hit him in the left leg, and the chaneque hangs on to the branch, wounded but able to move. Acatlel runs to the cave. The first chaneque throws blue dust on his face and Acatlel falls to the ground instantly.

"Acatlel!" Ucatl shouts when he hears the gun shot. Ocotlel immediately runs toward the cave to see if his brother is fine. Ucatl takes the chaneque by the arm and urges him to run after Ocotlel.

Up on the hill, Ocoyatl and Aquetzalli have also heard the shot and immediately run back to the cave.

"Get the rifle, we'll take it with us," Kuenú orders.

The chaneques pick up the weapons but remain very interested in the shotgun. "Boss, this is a fire arm. Do you know how to use it?" The first chaneque asks.

"No. I've never seen one so close," the leader responds. They are very dangerous. But the problem is that it takes too long to prepare a shot. They are good for hunting, but in a battle, if you don't hit your target, you are lost. They could shoot twenty arrows at you in the time you take to reload it."

"So we leave it then?"

"No, of course not. We must take it so we can find out how they work. Chilco loves new weapons." The chaneques drag Acatlel back inside the cave. Then they come back for the sack with their dead partner.

Ocotlel arrives there with his ax ready and looks at Kuenú at the entrance of the cave, huddled in front of his brother. He runs directly toward him without noticing the other two chaneques who also have not realized that a new warrior has arrived.

Kuenú rises immediately when he hears someone running. "Pipil!" He cries out at seeing the warrior. The two chaneques turn to see toward Ocotlel who is already very close.

Kuenú launches himself at the warrior with his spear in front. Ocotlel measures him and throws his bolas at him, but Kuenú is too quick and leaps up to the rock, surprising the warrior who has never seen anything like it.

Ocotlel stops a few feet from the rock. "Who are you?" the warrior asks.

"Who are you?" Chilco asks back.

The two chaneques run in Kuenú's aid. Ocotlel hears their footsteps and becomes aware. One of them throws his spear against him, but Ocotlel simply moves, and it passes by harmless.

Kuenú jumps down from his rock and attacks with his spear. Ocotlel starts backing up trying to find a better place to defend. It's only three attackers, but only two of them carry spears. *Bang!* A chaneque gets shot through the head. It's Ucatl who has thrown his prisoner to the ground and shot against the chaneque closest to him.

Kuenú and the second Chaneque jump immediately on some branches. Seeing that it is only one warrior, the second chaneque jumps down in front of Ucatl and attacks immediately with his machete. Ucatl defends himself with his rifle, stopping the first machete attack. At the same time, he uses the momentum to spin. On the same spin, he crouches and extends his rifle, hitting the chaneque in the back of his legs. This one falls to the ground, and Ucatl kicks the machete away from the chaneque. He reaches for his ax, ready to strike his enemy, but the chaneque is very agile and quickly rolls away.

Ocotlel is still busy with Kuenú, who has jumped down and continues to attack with his spear. He has thrown a couple of stings but wasn't able to run his opponent through. With his ax in hand, Ocotlel does his best to dodge the attacks and tries to attack the chaneque without losing his weapon. Kuenú is very skilled and leaps into the air while attacking with his spear. Ocotlel has never seen anything like it and doesn't know how to defend against this massive attack, so he keeps going back and using the trees to shield.

Ucatl's prisoner has gotten up, but his hands are still tied and he can't do anything to help his friends. So he runs toward a spear that has landed nearby to try to get loose.

Ucatl pulls his knife out with his left hand and prepares to fight with ax and knife in hand. The chaneque jumps up to a branch and doesn't appear to have any more weapons with him, only his satchel and yellow powder. This provides an opportunity for Ucatl to take his bow and prepares it quickly. Seeing the Pipil's intent, the chaneque jumps to another branch to cover himself from the warrior's reach. Ucatl squints over to Ocotlel and sees that he is in serious trouble, so Ucatl turns over to Kuenú and quickly loses his arrow and turns back, not waiting to see if it has hit its target. He knows he can't turn his back on his opponent.

The arrow pierces Kuenú through the back and comes out through the middle of his stomach. Kuenú falls to the ground holding the arrow with both hands. Ocotlel takes this opportunity and throws his ax against him. It hits Kuenú on the forehead, taking the chaneque leader's life. Without wasting any time, Ocotlel picks up his ax and runs toward the prisoner, who is still trying to get loose. In his run, he turns to see Ucatl. It seems like Ucatl has its situation controlled, so he keeps running. He can't see the chaneque yet, but Ucatl sees him and keeps pointing at the branches.

"Don't even try," Ocotlel shouts to the prisoner. The chaneque turns to look up and sees Ocotlel aiming at him with one of his own spears.

"Okay, okay," the chaneque responds. Ocotlel checks the bonds and sees that they are tearing. He pushes the chaneque down on his belly and ties his legs to keep him from moving. The second chaneque sees that his companions are dead and decides to flee the scene. He starts jumping from branch to branch in the river's direction.

Ocotlel runs to the cave to see if his brother is still alive. Very worried about his brother, he begins to check him and only calms down when he sees that he is still breathing.

"We must hurry, Ocotlel. That chaneque is not going to take long to comeback with more reinforcements." Ucatl pushes his prisoner inside the cave. He has been dragging him for several meters. "How is your brother?"

"He's alive, still breathing." Ocotlel keeps rocking Acatlel to wake him up, but he doesn't react.

"What did you do to him?" Ucatl asks his prisoner, but the chaneque only laughs.

The sound of footsteps calls their attention and they quickly go outside to investigate. It's only Aquetzalli and Ocoyatl who are coming to their aid.

"What happened? We heard a couple of shots," Aquetzalli asks.

"We were attacked by some chaneques," Ocotlel answers.

"Acatlel is paralyzed. We don't know what's wrong with him."

"Chaneques! How many?"

"Five. We killed three of them and we have one hostage. There was another one that got away. He won't take long in bringing back reinforcements," Ucatl responds.

Aquetzalli gets closer to see Acatlel. He opens his eyes and they are completely white. "He seems to be in some form of enchantment."

"This chaneque won't tell us," Ocotlel exclaims.

"He must be under a spell. Tenoch warned us about this. If it is a spell, we can break it with tobacco and rue." Aquetzalli takes out his pipe and fills it up with tobacco and turns it on since he doesn't have any rue. Then he releases the smoke on Acatlel's face. Acatlel still doesn't respond, so Aquetzalli tries again. After three attempts, Acatlel starts coughing from the smoke and wakes up.

"What happened?" He asks at seeing all the warriors around him.

"It seems you were attacked by chaneques," Ocotlel responds. "Do you remember anything about what happened?"

"Yes, I remember that there were three chaneques. They were surrounding me, so I tried to run to the cave. I don't remember getting there though. I remember I shot at one of them but I don't think I hit him."

"Yes, we heard the shot and ran here to help. Luckily we arrived on time. I don't know what they were trying to do, but we have a prisoner. He is going to tell us," Ocotlel promises.

Ucatl gets up and takes the chaneque by the arm and sits him up. "Okay, Chaneque. You are in big trouble. Your friends tried to kill us and left you behind. Now, we want to know what you are doing here, and what you are doing to the people you have been stealing."

The chaneque laughs and spits a little blood on the floor. "It doesn't matter what we are doing here. What matters is that you are dead. My friends are returning with a larger troop. Your miserable guns are not going to help you."

"Maybe," Ucatl answers. "But before we die, you'll die. Now tell me where the people you have stolen are."

"You'll never find them. They are underground, many kilometers away from here."

"And how do we get to this place?"

"No one can get in there and get out alive."

"Excellent, then you will have no problem in helping us enter."

"On one condition," the chaneque responds.

"Which one?"

"That you let me go after I tell you how to enter."

"No. We won't let you go until you show us the way to where my family is," Aquetzalli responds.

"No deal then. You need to get in, and I prefer to keep my head on my shoulders," the chaneque explains. "If you don't let me go, then I won't tell you anything."

"Okay," Ucatl agrees. "If you tell us how to enter, I'll let you go."

"Untie me then." Ucatl unties him and gets him up to his feet.

"Okay. Start talking," Ucatl orders.

"Down by the river, behind two large rocks, there is a hidden cave. All you have to do is move the rock and you'll find the way," the chaneque lies.

"Then you'll come with us to show us the rock, and then I'll set you free," Ucatl explains.

"Okay. Let's go," the chaneque states without any opposition.

"No. Wait. This chaneque is lying," Acatlel explains. "These chaneques were coming here to enter through this cave. All footprints end here. For sure he wants to takes us into a trap."

"Is that true, chaneque?" Ucatl angrily asks. The chaneque doesn't answer; he just angrily stares directly into Acatlel's eyes.

"This is the entrance," Acatlel declares. "You have to tell us how to get through here, or deal is off."

"Okay, chaneque, what do you say? I see you're not honest. Now you have to tell us the truth or things will go very wrong for you." Ucatl readies his ax and shows it to him.

The chaneque realizes that these Pipils are not stupid as he thought, so he decides to tell the truth. "Okay. This is the entrance."

"How do we open the door?"

"To open the door, we need some blue powder."

"Blue powder?" Ucatl asks.

"Yes. Blue powder."

"Open it then."

"I *have* no blue powder."

"Who has the blue powder?" Aquetzalli asks.

"Marak. He brought the powder," the chaneque explains.

"Go over, check those chaneques; one of them should have the magic dust," Ucatl orders.

"Ha ha ha ha," the chaneque laughs.

"What are you laughing at?" Ucatl asks.

"Marak was the chaneque that got away. Ha ha ha ha."

"Then we don't need you," Ocoyatl says and lifts his spear, ready to run him through.

"Here it is," Ocotlel announces.

"This one has two bags of powder." Ocotlel opens them. "One of them has a yellowish powder substance, and the other one has blue powder."

"Ah, it seems we have a liar among us," Ucatl sarcastically exclaims. "What do we do to liars?"

"We burn their mouth with a blight," Ocoyatl answers.

"Very good. So let's gather some firewood and if this chaneque lies to us again, I'll burn his mouth." Ucatl explains.

"I think that's an excellent idea." Aquetzalli agrees.

A PRISONER WITH AN ATTITUDE

Capturing the chaneque was easy. The tracker was looking for Pipil tracks. He had found the kids' tracks, but Itzcuauhtzin saw him first. The kids had just left the main road after leaving the tomb when they saw him checking the floor. Xóchitl wanted to shoot him with a few of her new arrows. She wanted to try her new bow, but Itzcuauhtzin convinced her that it was better to capture him and to use him as a guide.

Xóchitl hid up on the dark ceiling among the stalactites, on a very narrow passage, while Itzcuauhtzin remained hidden among the stalagmites waiting for the chaneque. When the chaneque was passing by, Xóchitl dropped a net over his head and the chaneque got tangled on it. Itzcuauhtzin pinned him to the ground and tied his hands behind his back.

"What are you doing here?" asks Itzcuauhtzin.

"You're wasting your time, Pipil. I won't tell you anything."

"Why do you have all these people captive?"

"La la la la la," the chaneque starts singing, ignoring the question.

"If you don't tell me, I'll cut off your tongue."

"If you cut off my tongue, I'll never tell you anything."

"Let's tie him up and leave him here. Maybe one of those rams will find him and eat him," Xóchitl suggests.

"No. You wouldn't do that, would you?" The chaneque asks, very concerned.

"Try me and find out," Itzcuauhtzin answers.

"Ah. This is useless." Xóchitl takes a piece of candy out from her bag and starts eating it.

"What's that?" the chaneque asks.

"This candy? It's a caramel," Xóchitl answers.

"See how easy it is to answer a question." She says sarcastically.

The chaneque starts savoring his lips. His mouth begins to water. "Can I lick it?" the chaneque anxiously asks. Xóchitl looks toward Itzcuauhtzin. Itzcuauhtzin nods in approval.

"Do you like candy?" Xóchitl asks.

"Yes, candies, sweets, and all those sweet and delicious things the market women make."

"Mmm... If I give you one, would you tell us where they took our mom?"

"No, never."

"Okay, I'll eat this candy, and then I'll give the last one to Itzcua, and you're not going to get any."

"No, gimme, gimme. Only one. Please," the eager chaneque begs.

"No. If you don't tell me where my mom is, I won't give you anything."

"But I don't know where she is. I don't even know her."

"Then tell me where the new prisoners are."

"Aaaaah, no. I can't."

"You can't, or won't?"

"Both. I think."

"Mmm... This caramel is good. Itzcua, do you want one?" The chaneque doesn't remove his gaze from the candy and is still savoring his lips.

"Yes, give me one. Do you have any suckers?" Itzcuauhtzin asks.

"I think I have one," Xóchitl says.

"Those suckers, with lots of spiral colors?" The chaneque asks.

"Yes, with lots of colors. Why?"

"Those are my favorite. Sometimes when we go to the city, we go to the market and take the larger ones."

"Don't tell me that you are the little thieves of the night?"

"Thieves! Never. We never steal anything. We just take what is ours."

"If you take the suckers without paying for them that is called stealing. Stealing makes you a thief," Xóchitl accuses.

"I'm not a thief. I told you. I just take what is mine."

"Well, this candy is not yours. They belong to some lady from market. And you are stealing."

"No. The candy was on our land. Therefore all that is in it belongs to us."

"These lands are not yours. They belong to the Pipils."

"Before they belonged to the Pipils, they were ours."

"No. Before they belonged to the Pipils they belonged to the Mayans and Lencas."

"No. Before they belonged to the Mayans and Lencas, they belonged to the chaneques. The Mayans stole them from us. But My Beloved will help us recover them. That's why all that is in them is ours, including the candy."

"Then you do admit that you took them without permission. Like all those people," Xóchitl explains, but the chaneque doesn't answer. He just keeps his eyes on the candy.

"This makes you a kidnapper and a thief," Itzcuauhtzin explains.

"I'm a warrior. All is fair in war." The chaneque tries to excuse himself.

"Your beloved? Who is your beloved?" Itzcuauhtzin asks.

"Sihuehuet."

"Sihuehuet?" Xóchitl asks. "And who is she?"

"She is the most beautiful and most powerful woman on earth."

"Powerful? In what way?" Itzcuauhtzin asks.

"In every way. In magic, wealth, and beauty. There is no one like her."

"And what are you doing with all these people?"

"I won't tell you anything else, Pipil. Save your questions." The chaneque turns around and gives them his back.

Xóchitl takes a sucker from her bag and hands it to Itzcuauhtzin. "Look, Itzcua. Grandma gave me this one before we left."

"It's really big," Itzcuauhtzin says. "Thank you. I will enjoy this one for hours."

The chaneque turns around. "No, no. That one is for me," the chaneque exclaims.

"Too bad. It is the last one. You know, I'd like to help you, but I can't. You're not helping me. Tough luck," Xóchitl responds.

Itzcuauhtzin rips a piece of cloth from a blanket that the chaneque had with him and begins to roll it up. "I'm going tie your mouth so you can't scream. Then I'll leave you in the pathway so that one of those ugly rams can find you and eat you."

"No, no. Please don't," the chaneque begs. "I'll tell you where they are, but you have to give me the candy."

"If I give you the candy, you have to take us to them. If not, we are going to leave you here in the middle of the road and without candy," Itzcuauhtzin demands.

"Okay, in that case, I also want the caramel." Itzcuauhtzin and Xóchitl look at each other.

"Okay, but no tricks. I'll give you a caramel now, and once you have taken us to the prisoners, then I'll give you the big candy," Itzcuauhtzin proposes.

"Deal."

The chaneques were heading toward the main gate to stand guard and make sure no one enter or exit. But along the way, they stopped to check the tracks they found. Behind the stalagmites they found three corpses hidden.

The discovery was by accident. A chaneque felt discomfort in his sandals and stopped to remove them. He was not used to them, but most scouts had to wear them to protect their feet against thorns and poisonous plants, so he had to put them on; but along the way his feet began to blisters and he stopped to remove them. It was then when he discovered the drops of blood on the wall.

"Roke. There is blood here." The patrol leader stopped and returned to investigate. They found the dead chaneques among the stalagmites.

"These must be three of the chaneques that are missing. Whoever killed them is still in the caves. We have to tell Chilco."

"What do we do with them?" a chaneque asks.

"Nothing. Let's leave them here. Our orders are to seal the entrance and not let the Pipils in. But you are going to go back and take the news so they can come for

173

them. Then come back and meet us at the main entrance. We are going to hurry to make sure no one enters. Tell Chilco to send reinforcements. This must be the entrance they are using to get in," Roke commands.

The warriors had no impediments entering the cave. The chaneque guided them by the same path taken by Xóchitl and Itzcuauhtzin when they went in pursuit of the chaneques.

"This is the entrance. At the end of this tunnel you will find a mine. There is a path that leads deeper into the main cave at the back. You will find your people there."

"All right, come on then," Ucatl orders.

"No, I stop here. You go ahead and continue."

"No, you're coming with us." Ocotlel pushes the chaneque and lets him take the lead.

"You promised to let me go," the chaneque complains loudly, trying to make noise in case there are more chaneques about. By his good luck, his peers have heard his voice.

"Ocotlel, tie his mouth. This chaneque is too loud," Ucatl commands.

"With much pleasure," Ocotlel responds.

"Did you hear that?" Roke asks deeper in the cave.

"Yes. They are human voices. They seem to be coming in this direction."

"Intruders." The chaneques prepare their spears and batons, and hide among the stalagmites. Roke observes how the first shadow enters the cave and signals to the others not to act rashly. One of them prepares a net. Three more shadows enter and Roke recognizes him as a chaneque but watches him carefully and manages to see the strapped piece of cloth on the chaneque's mouth, and he realizes that the one in front is a prisoner. *They're Pipil warriors.*

The group of warriors walks through the middle of the stalagmites without realizing their danger until it is too late. A net flies over Ucatl and three chaneques jump out from between the stalagmites with their spears ready to run them through. Roke and another chaneque jump at the back side, blocking the road to prevent an escape. Ocotlel, who is at the back of the line, turns around and fires his rifle, wounding Roke on the abdomen, but the other chaneque is faster and throws blue dust on his face, hypnotizing the warrior instantly.

Aquetzalli launches his spear against a chaneque, piercing his chest. Another chaneque comes at him and the two start fighting and rolling on the floor. To Aquetzalli's amazement, the chaneque is very strong and very agile. Aquetzalli gets quickly defeated. After a couple of rolls, the chaneque pins the warrior and punches him in the face, then puts a knife to his neck. "If you move, you die, Pipil," warns the chaneque, leaving him no choice but to surrender.

Ucatl is still lying on the ground with another chaneque who has used the net to subjugate him. The chaneque has put a machete to his neck and the warrior has not budged since falling to the ground. Everything happened too fast.

Ocotlel is still standing, staring at the ceiling. In his imagination, he sees an eagle flying over the hills, and his hunting companions beside him ready to mount and ride down the prairie.

"I'm hurt," Roke announces. The chaneques quickly tie Ucatl and Aquetzalli and seat them in the middle of the trail. They take Ocotlel and seat him alongside his peers. Ocotlel feels like he just sat on his horse.

"Thank you a thousand times," Yoclo expresses after being released by his fellow chaneques.

"What were you doing with these Pipils?" Roke asks while tying a piece of cloth to cover the wound in his stomach and preventing more blood from flowing.

"These damned Pipils killed my patrol and captured me by the river. Then they forced me to bring them here. What are you doing here?"

"My Beloved has ordered us to close and guard all entrances so that no one gets in or out."

"What about the patrols that are still out there?"

"Those may enter. I'm just talking about humans. It seems that there are too many Pipils around here."

"I have only seen these three, but there is more to come our way. Two warriors are waiting outside the gate. It looks like a whole army is coming. We need to seal the cave as soon as possible. One of those Pipils has blue dust and also knows how to use it."

"And how is it that they know how to use our runes?" Roke asks, very irritated.

"I taught them how. If not, they would have slit my neck open. They also promised to burn my tongue."

"Idiot. Now we'll have a lot more problems." Roke spits on the floor. "Kopán, run back and give the news to Chilco. Tell him what is happening, and tell him to send an army immediately." The chaneque wastes no time and quickly runs back.

"What do we do with these Pipils?" Another chaneque asks.

"We have no choice but to take them to My Beloved. For sure she'll want to question them." Roke stands up but his head is spinning and he falls over very weak. A chaneque tries to help him stand, but Roke begins to lose consciousness and faints. The bullet shattered a pair of vital organs and the internal bleeding is killing him slowly.

"If we don't take him to Narib soon, he'll die for sure," the first chaneque says.

"What do we do then? We cannot leave him here."

"No. We also have to take these prisoners to My Beloved. It is impossible for us to stop a Pipil army. I think it's best to go back to the main cave," Yoclo says.

"What's going on?" Elena asks one of the prisoners.

"I don't know. They put all humans on lockdown. It seems that they are preparing for a battle," Juan, a twenty-two-year-old man, answers. From him, Elena had learned that this is a mine and that workers come from all over. Most of them are young people and children. The elderly are taken to another part of the cave where their souls are stolen by a powerful sorcerer, or at least that's what they have heard.

When Elena returned from her audience with Sihuehuet, the guard took her to a larger cell where they kept the slaves after a long day of work. But today the work day ended much earlier. The guards brought in all the slaves and put them in the cells, sealing them with chains.

Elena was not allowed to see the twins. The younger children were taken further down the volcano to a special cave made just for them. No one knows what they do there, but they do know they are alive because the chefs always cook a lot more food to send to that part. Elena begged for a while to let her be with her children, but all of the guards ignored her. Eventually she fell asleep and only the noise of the troops and the roar of the panthers woke her up.

"Against whom do they fight?"

"I don't know. I've never seen this. The only ones I've seen that go out well armed are the patrols when they go to the surface for more slaves, and hunters," the young man answers.

"It must be the Pipils," a man with brown skin exclaims. He is one of the newest prisoners.

"The Pipils?" The young man asks.

"Yes, the Pipils. They are the indigenous people that live in this region. My people."

"You are Pipil?" Elena asks.

"Yes. I'm Pipil of birth. I come from Lamatepec. And you?"

"I'm half Mayan, half Spanish, but my family is Pipil. How did you come to this place?"

"I don't know. I just remember going on a trip back to my village and then showed up at this place. Almost everyone here has the same story. We dreamed an immensity of times with a rescue. And you?"

"Precisely last night, we were on our way back to Coatepeque. We were coming from Tazumal. But since then I have not seen my family, I know nothing about them. I've only seen my two young children."

"I hope your family is well."

"Thank you. I'm sure it is the Pipils. My husband was a Pipil warrior before marrying me. Everyone in his family are Pipil warriors. I'm sure it must be them who are coming for me," Elena explains, a little worried.

"I hope they brought reinforcements. There are about five hundred chaneques here."

"And how many people are captives here?"

"Nearly two hundred, including children, without counting the small kids that are taken deeper into the volcano," Juan answers.

"My name is Atlahua. Pleased to meet you." The older man offers a hand in a gesture of friendship.

"Nice to meet you, Atlahua. Mine is Elena. How long have you been here?"

"I'm not sure, maybe one or two years. Most people have grown up here. Most of them don't know at what age they got here. There are many who don't even remember the surface, or the sun. To be honest, there have been times when I've lost all hope. But to see you here and see how worried the chaneques are gives me hope. This means they have a very strong threat to have to assemble the whole army. Your husband must have very good and powerful influences in the tribe."

"Yes, he was part of the elite warriors before marrying me. His brothers are still part of them."

"Excellent. That explains why everyone here is getting very nervous."

A chaneque wearing red robes approaches the cell and starts spraying a bright blue powder on the bars. The humans go back to the rear. The sorcerer draws a couple of runes in the air, and the bars begin to shine with a dim and yellowish light.

"Who is he?" Elena asks.

"That's the chaneques' main wizard. They call him Notchím," Juan answers. "He seals the cells with a spell so that no one escapes. That's why there are no guards here. The guards only guard the entrances. That wizard makes experiments with humans. Many say that he steals their souls to make magical potions. One day while working at the bottom of the cave removing earth, I saw some chaneques pull a man from his room. The man's eyes were white as lime, and he could hardly walk."

"Maybe he was a blind man. Many blind people are born with white eyes," Atlahua says.

"No. This man had been here in the cell with us. He was old. Maybe about forty and some years old, but he could see very well."

"Why do they only do it with older people?" Elena asks.

"If you don't have any work talents, such as carpentry, crafts, or jewelry, you're expendable to these chaneques. Notchím takes those people and steals their soul. That's why most people here are young. Occasionally, My Beloved comes to the cells and chooses a good-looking boy and takes him with her," Juan explains.

"And why does she take the young boys?"

"Nobody knows. We never see them again though."

"It's true," Atlahua adds. "This is one of the few occasions where being ugly is a good thing."

"How many warriors are there?" Chilco asks. At the same time, another chaneque slaps Ucatl, breaking his lip.

181

"A thousand warriors, all armed to the teeth," Ucatl responds while spitting out blood.

"What kind of weapons do they bring?"

"Every kind. We bring firearms, spears, bows, batons. You have no escape. Once my warriors get here, they'll annihilate you. You better surrender."

"You lie," Yoclo, the chaneque that had been captured by the Pipils, exclaims. "The Pipils don't have as many warriors. The whites took it upon themselves to destroy your army. There's no way you have as many warriors."

"Yes, I'm sure he's lying," Chilco adds. "It doesn't matter how many they are. Today is the day that the Pipils die, and their army will be reduced to nothing. I'm going to finish the job that the whites couldn't do. Hang these three Pipils amid the main cave, so that all can see." Chilco orders.

"Immediately, boss." The chaneques grab the three warriors and take them to the main cave and hang them by the arms on the posts in the center of the cavern in front of the cells.

"Good God, it's Aquetzalli," Elena exclaims.

"Is it your husband?" Atlahua asks.

"No, my brother-in-law. He is the one on the left. The one in the middle is one of the commanders. Ucatl, I think he's called. But I don't see my husband anywhere."

"You were right, Atlahua. They are the Pipils. But these ones must have been captured. This means that there are more Pipils within the volcano. They must have come to our rescue," Juan says, very excited.

"No. They are not coming for us. They come for Elena. Nobody knows we're here," Atlahua answers.

"Maybe so, but they'll free us all," Elena exclaims. "My husband must be coming with them."

"That is if they make it. This is a large army, and since the whites conquered this land, we haven't seen any Pipil warriors. I'm not sure if they even exist. Perhaps these were it."

"They do exist, and there are many. There is a large group of great warriors at Tazumal that still preserve the ancient traditions," Elena answers.

"How many?" Juan asks.

"I don't know. About three hundred, I guess."

"Three hundred will not be sufficient to defeat a big army of chaneques. There are about five hundred chaneques just in this cave alone, and there are many mines and hidden places we don't even know about. Three hundred is not going to be enough," Atlahua adds.

UNDERGROUND AMBUSH

"The warriors are coming," Ocoyatl announces from the top of a tree. "Let's go down to the camp and meet them." Both warriors had remained behind after Aquetzalli and the other two warriors entered the cave. Their orders were simple— just wait until the others arrive and show them the way. Luckily the warriors did not take long, and they only waited a little over half an hour.

The chaneque had confessed that there was another chaneque patrol in the area. So rather than risk it, Ucatl decided to leave two warriors behind to watch each other's backs, but the patrol of chaneques never returned.

"Niltze." Acatlel salutes the warriors when they got back to the camp.

"Niltze," the group answers.

"Where are the others?" Atlanezi asks.

"We found a cave. It is an entrance to the caves of the mountain. Apparently that's where your family was taken to. Ucatl took Aquetzalli and Ocotlel. We captured one chaneque, and he is leading them to the place," Acatlel explains. "But I don't trust that chaneque. He might be leading them into a trap."

"Then it is true. These creatures do exist," Teutli exclaims. "And they can speak Spanish?"

"No. But they do speak Nahuatl. That's how we communicated with him."

"Come on. There's no time to waste," Ocoyatl says. "Leave the horses here. We won't need them."

"All right, let's go. Yanixté and Tenoch, you stay here and take care of the horses."

"But why?" Tenoch protests. "It's my family that's in there. I have to go get them."

"No. It is very dangerous and we can't risk it."

"That's not fair," Yanixté protests as well. "I'm already a Telpochcalli cadet and I have the right to go with you. Tenoch already had his first fight and also has the right to go."

"You are not a seasoned warrior yet. You still need a lot more training, and Tenoch is still too young. He's not even a Tameme yet. You stay here until it's over," Atlanezi orders.

"There is one chaneque patrol around here, and they could return at any moment. They might even be watching us right now. I think it'd best that we take them with us," Acatlel explains.

"Okay. Teutli, the decision is yours," Atlanezi finally says.

"Let them take their weapons and supplies. Surely they're going to need them," Teutli commands. "And let's go already; I don't intend to waste any more time here."

The warriors take their weapons and supplies. They tie the horses and let Ocoyatl show them the way. Acatlel updates them on the current events while they walk.

Ocoyatl opens the door of the cave with some blue powder, and all the warriors get astounded. Once inside, hey follow the trail and the footprints their peers have left behind.

"Halt," Teutli orders all of a sudden. Everyone stops and keep silent.

"It sounds like an army," Acatlel exclaims.

"Let's go back to the main road. There must be some place we can hide down the trail," Atlanezi suggests. Everyone quickly runs back to the main road. Yanixté and Tenoch do their best to keep up with the others.

The chaneques reach the main trail, and Chilco immediately begins to give orders. "Shut that entry. If the Pipils enter, I want them stopped here."

Chilco chooses twenty of his warriors. "You take your blowguns and nets. I want you up there in the dark. When the Pipils come in, let at least a couple dozen pass. Then shoot them with poisoned darts. The first unit will be waiting down the road to finish them off. We don't know how many warriors are coming, but we'll have to stop them here. The more Indians we kill, the easier it will be to defend this entrance. Is that understood?"

"Yes sir." Most of them answer and begin to climb the walls like spiders.

In the larger space of the cavern, Chilco prepares a unit of chaneques, all of them ready with shields and spears. Chilco also places his troops around the walls, along the walkway, hiding many among the stalagmites.

"Lord Chilco, I found some Pipil tracks. They are heading downward," Xilo, one of the most effective trackers, reports.

"How many?" Chilco asks.

"A dozen Indians at most. A couple of tracks belong to children. Maybe Tamemes."

"Kolektlak, take thirty warriors with panthers and go after them. Xilo, go with them and take a couple of coyotes to help you track them. Bring me their heads." Chilco turns around but then retracts. "Oh! I also need one or two of them alive for questioning. Try not to kill them all."

"Yes, sir." Kolektlak takes his warriors and wastes no time in starting the persecution.

After running for about a mile, the road becomes narrower. It makes a small turn to the right, with the cliff on the left and a small furrow of stalagmites on the right. Further up the wall, Teutli observes a slightly wider gap. "Over here." Teutli guides his warriors among the stalagmites and starts climbing the wall. "Come up quickly. This is a good place to make a stand. If the chaneques come, we will have a better advantage from up there."

Tenoch and Yanixté climb up after Teutli. There is little light in this place, and that gives them hiding advantage. The wall is solid and has many stones for support. Yanixté and Tenoch have no problems climbing it. The top is about twelve meters high, and it takes the boys about one minute to climb.

"Listen up, Yanixté. You and Tenoch will serve as Tamemes to reload shotguns. Do you know how to do it?" Teutli asks the boys.

"Yes," Yanixté responds.

"I don't," Tenoch answers, a bit ashamed about it. "My dad never lets me touch his rifle."

"Very well, then you're in charge of the arrows and spears, in case we need them. You're also in charge of bringing the empty rifles back to Yanixté for reloading and then back to us."

"There are no rocks or anything else, other than the bare ground for cover," Ocoyatl points out.

"Let's hope these chaneques don't have fire arms then," Teutli responds. "That will give us an advantage. The narrow trail is also in our favor."

"I just hope they don't come after us," Acatlel adds.

"You think they caught the others?" Ocoyatl asks Acatlel.

"I hope not. But it looks like a big army. I have a bad feeling about this. We should have sent someone back to Tazumal for reinforcements."

"Too late for that." Atlanezi points out.

"We will wait here about an hour, and if there's no movement, then we will continue our way down and look for another entrance. There must be more trails around here," Teutli exclaims.

"The council was wrong. They should have let us bring more people," Atlanezi complains.

"Well, in their defense, our orders were only to investigate and report our findings," Teutli says.

"Well, we are still investigating, but it appears that it has turned into a war," Atlanezi adds.

"The fact that there is an army on its way tells me that Ucatl and the others have been captured. And these chaneques are coming to meet us," Teutli exclaims.

"No! My dad is there," Yanixté exclaims.

"So is mine, and my mom and my brothers," Tenoch adds.

"They also have my brother," Acatlel responds. "The best thing is to stay calm. Don't let despair overcome us. If we face the chaneques with a dense mind, we're not going to survive this encounter. It's best to let things take their course. Tlaloc is with us, that's for sure."

Atlanezi pulls his paint out and begins to paint his face with black and red stripes. Other warriors begin to do the same. They also put on their armor and prepare their shields. Tenoch pulls out an armor made of cotton and rope that his grandfather gave him before embarking on this expedition. The armor had been used by Itzcuauhtzin when he was in training and it was a little too big for Tenoch, but it is still better than nothing. "Yanixté, give me some paint. I don't have any."

"The Tamemes don't use paint," Yanixté responds.

"And why does that matter? Just give me some. I was already in a battle," Tenoch responds.

"Okay. Here."

Tenoch takes some red paint and a draws a few diagonal stripes on his face, then takes white paint and draws more stripes between the red ones. "I'm ready," Tenoch announces.

"If you say so. In this darkness I can only see your white stripes," Yanixté responds.

"Silence," Atlanezi orders. "I hear something."

"Whatever it is, is coming very fast. Might be a horse," Ocoyatl adds.

The chaneques did not take long to arrive. The coyotes appear first with Xilo riding a big wolf the size of a panther. Xilo passes through the narrow gap with his wolves, and the rest of the crew follows closely on their panthers.

"Ahhh!" A couple of warriors exhale, including the boys, at seeing the panthers. Luckily, the chaneques pass without noticing them.

"Stop," Xilo shouts and halts the whole troop.

"What is it?" Kolektlak asks.

"The coyotes have lost the trace. Wait a minute." Xilo gets off his wolf and begins to examine the path. "There's no sign of them. They must be back up the trail. We have to go back. They must be hiding among the stalagmites." Xilo gets on his wolf and breaks through the line, taking the lead again. The chaneques are forced to go a little further down to thin up the line, since there is only one wall on one side and an immense fall to the other.

"Ready boys? Here they come," Teutli whispers.

"They're about thirty chaneques," Tenoch whispers. "I counted them as they passed."

"We won't use our rifles. They will only attract more chaneques. Let's use the arrows and spears. Try not to shoot at the same target. The tracker is mine. And be careful with those panthers. Yanixté, Tenoch, ready your bows; I want you to kill the beasts. That will take some of their edge away," Teutli orders.

Tenoch's heart begins to beat faster. "Relax," Yanixté whispers. "These are Cuachicqueh warriors. They are the best. Everything will be just fine."

"The tracks end here," Xilo declares. The army stops and prepares to dismount. An arrow hits Xilo on the chest, then eight more chaneques fall to the ground. A couple of them fall over the cliff, dragging their panthers behind them. Tenoch shoots the wolf through the throat and Yanixté hits one of the coyotes through the ribs.

"Pipils!" One chaneque shouts. He still hasn't finished saying the word when an arrow runs him through. Six more chaneques fall down. The panthers get in between the stalagmites and try to climb the wall, but the top is too high. The boys continue to fire their arrows at the beats. Yanixté kills the second coyote, while Tenoch skewers another panther. The panthers are harder to kill, and despite being wounded, they are still trying to climb. But Tenoch and Yanixté don't stop shooting. In less than a minute, they have shot nearly thirty arrows between the two.

The chaneques take refuge behind the stalagmites. "Up there on the roof!" Another chaneque shouts. The rest of the chaneques turn back, trying to flee the area and seek shelter further down the trail. One more chaneque gets pushed over the cliff by another beast that Yanixté wounded when it was trying to flee.

"One wolf and four panthers," Tenoch reports to Yanixté.

"Two coyotes, five panther and one chaneque," Yanixté answers.

"Cowards!" Kolektlak cries out. "It's an ambush." In less than a minute he has lost more than half his troops. A couple of chaneques throw their spears against the Pipils, but it's too dark up there and they can't see very well. The spears pass by harmlessly, since most of the Pipils are on their bellies.

The chaneques raise their shields to take cover from the arrows. Not having a better angle, the Pipil cease firing, except Tenoch and Yanixté who are still shooting at the beasts that have taken cover among the stalagmites.

"What are they doing?" Acatlel asks.

"I think they are planning an attack. Get ready for hand-to-hand combat," Teutli commands.

Suddenly half a dozen chaneques jump up covering nearly four meters in the air. They grab on to the rocks. The Pipils shoot but the chaneques are too fast and skilled. One single arrow hits its target, and one chaneque falls to the ground injured by the shoulder and bruises his head. Yanixté and Tenoch shoot him right away. The two arrows hit the chaneque simultaneously—— one on his chest and the other on his stomach.

While the Pipils are distracted watching the chaneques climb up, the rest of the chaneques also jump. Three chaneques make it to the top where they are received by two Pipils. One of them gets pushed into the abyss, but his agility allows him to spin in the air like a cat, and he pushes himself with his legs away from the wall and lands on his feet. Yanixté loses an arrow on him and hits him through the chest.

The other two chaneques cover themselves with their shields and start attacking the Pipils with their spears. One more chaneque reaches the top, but Ocoyatl throws a spear at him, running him through. The chaneque falls to the abyss with the spear buried in his chest.

The Pipils defend themselves with their shields and use their batons to attack back. A Pipil gets pierced through his shoulder by a spear. Atlanezi seizes the moment and throws himself to the ground in a somersault and cuts the chaneque's hand with his macuahuitl. When the chaneque turns, Atlanezi rips the head off in one lunge.

The rest of the chaneques reach the top and Kolektlak realizes that there are too many Pipil warriors. "Retreat," he immediately commands. But two more chaneques have fallen at the hands of the Pipil warriors. Kolektlak and three chaneques jump back into the abyss. Tenoch and Yanixté shoot them, wounding one on the leg and another on the shoulder. Acatlel launches one of the chaneques' spears and hits the third chaneque on its back, but Kolektlak escapes unharmed.

The remaining chaneques left alive are quickly overcome by the Pipils. Kolektlak climbs on top of a panther and tries to escape, but Yanixté shoots the panther on the leg and it falls forward, throwing Kolektlak over the cliff. Tenoch loses one more arrow, hitting the panther through the head.

"Look for prisoners," Teutli commands. "Yanixté, what happened to the panthers?"

"Several of them ran up, but most are dead. A few fell over the cliff and a couple of them are injured," Yanixté reports.

"Good work, boys. Collect the arrows that are still good and let's get out of here."

"There's a couple of chaneques still alive down there," Tenoch announces.

"Excellent." Teutli takes a rope and ties it to a stone.

"How are you boys doing?" Atlanezi asks.

"We're okay uncle. A bit nervous but fine," Tenoch answers.

"Is it always this fast?" Yanixté asks.

"Yes, melee fighting always ends quickly. The persecutions and hunting are the ones that take long." Atlanezi takes his weapons and start climbing down the rope that the other warriors put in place. The Tamemes are the last to climb down.

"Throw all dead chaneques over the cliff. Also throw the beasts if you can," Teutli orders. Two warriors drag a pair of chaneques that have survived and sit them between two stalagmites, while Ocoyatl bandages Ziquetl's shoulder.

"You think you can go on like this?" Ocoyatl asks.

"If you're asking if I can keep up, the answer is yes. But I don't know how useful I could be in a battle," Ziquetl answers.

"At the moment that's all we need, as long as you don't faint. You weigh too much to have to carry you out of here."

"Ha ha. Ouch."

"What happened?"

"It hurts when I laugh. Ha ha, ouch."

Yanixté and Tenoch finish off the surviving beasts and collect the arrows. Then they start collecting ears as trophies. "Nine beast ears and two chaneques," Yanixté proudly exclaims.

"Nine panther ears, a wolf, and a chaneque," Tenoch responds. "Excellent job. If you continue like this, soon you two will graduate from the Telpochcalli." Acatlel exclaims while pushing another chaneque over the cliff.

Teutli approaches the chaneques. One of them has an arrow through his left side. The other one has two arrows buried, one in the right shoulder and one on the right foot. "Where were you going in such a hurry?" Teutli asks them in Nahuatl. The chaneques do not answer; they don't even turn around to look at him.

"I asked you a question." Teutli squats down and grabs one of the arrows buried in the foot of a chaneque and applies pressure. The chaneque screams in pain. "Let's try this again. Where were you going?" He asks again.

"To look for you. We were only looking for Indians," the chaneque responds in pain.

"And the army up there, where are they going?"

"We just came to seal the entrance so no one enters."

"And why so many people for just one door?"

"They are waiting for the Pipil army. Our orders are to keep them out. It's all I know."

"What about the other Pipils? Where are they?"

"I don't know. We are still looking for them. We've only seen three of them," the chaneque answers.

"And where are they?"

"They were taken to the main cave for questioning."

"In that case, you will take us to the main cave. And no tricks. At your first attempt, I'll slit your throat." Teutli doesn't wait for a response and stands up. "Do not draw the arrows. He could bleed too much and die. Just break them so he can walk with us. He will be our guide."

"What about the other chaneque?" A warrior asks.

"I don't think he'll live more than half an hour. Leave him here; let Tezcatlipoca have mercy of his soul." The unfortunate chaneque stares at Teutli with a sorrowed look as if pleading for his life. But there is nothing that the warrior can do for him.

"Elena, I think you have not been honest with me," Sihuehuet exclaims. She takes a small blue ball made of crystal in her hand and looks at it for a moment, then saves it in a hidden pocket on her dress. "Your friends are out there. You saw them?"

"Yes, My Beloved."

"You know them?"

"Yes, My Beloved." Elena wanted to say no, but she had seen the warriors hanging by the prison corridor, and this witch is too wise and cunning. So she decided to tell the truth to prevent further violence.

"Who are they?"

"They are Cuachicqueh Pipils from Tazumal."

"Very good. There is a large Pipil army marching this way. Tell me something. Why are you so important? What family are you from?"

"I'm from the Pipil family, from the house of Ohtocani," Elena answers.

"Ohtocani? I don't know him. Who is your father?"

"My father was Don Manuel Rodriguez, but he died three years ago."

"I don't know him either. But you told me that you are part Maya."

"Yes, My Beloved. On my mother's side."

"And who is she?"

"Her name is Yaretzi from the Copan region."

"So why are you so important then? Nobody raises the Pipil army for just one person. You're lying to me. Why are you so important? Are you Spanish royalty?"

"No, My Beloved. I'm just a housewife and a mother."

"Then it's your husband who has influences. Who is he?"

"He is Pipil. But he doesn't have strong-enough influences to raise a big army."

Sihuehuet turns around and takes two more crystal spheres, and saves them on her dress pockets. "This battle will end soon. I hope your husband survives the battle. It will give me much pleasure to meet him." Elena tries her best to contain her tears.

"You will stay here with me until my chaneques return."

"May I see my children?"

"No."

"Please. They must be very scared. I beg of you."

"Don't worry about them. They are fine."

"Please. Don't you have any children?" Elena asks and pleads.

"I had a son a long time ago, but I lost him. He was a very lovely and playful child."

"What happened?"

"That's none of your business," the beautiful woman answers, very irritated.

"I'm sorry. But as a mother, you can understand my pain."

"I understand it very well. But trust me, your children are fine. Nothing bad will happen to them."

"Where are they?"

"They are in a wonderful place, in an enchanted place that I built for orphans—— lost and abandoned children."

"But my children are not lost or abandoned, and they are not orphans."

"Not yet but soon will be."

"Why are you doing all this? If you love children as much as you say, then why do you cause them this pain?"

"They don't feel pain. Soon they won't even remember their parents. They are happy with me, and I with them."

"How is that possible? What kind of creature are you?"

"Sometimes it's better not to know things, dear. Let it be enough for you to know that your children are well." With those words, the beautiful lady leaves her room, leaving Elena crying in a chair.

THE EMPTY CAVE

The kids found the mine empty. There are stones, precious and unknown metals separated in wooden barrels and metal pots, among them precious gems— emeralds, diamonds, obsidian, and jade stones.

"You can see that the whites have never been here. If they had, all this would already be in Spain," Xóchitl exclaims.

"Why isn't anyone guarding all this or working the mine?" Itzcuauhtzin asks.

"I don't know," the chaneque responds. "There are always people working here. This is one of the richest mines in the volcano."

"Something very serious must be happening for them to leave everything behind," Xóchitl says.

"Come on. We have to find mom and the twins. How much longer to the main cavern?" Itzcuauhtzin asks.

"About five minutes. The main cave is at the end of this trail," the chaneque answers.

"Excellent. Here is your prize." Xóchitl hands the candy over to the chaneque, and he happily starts licking it like a five-year-old.

"Xóchitl, we need a plan. We can't go in there with so many people. Surely there is a great army in there. Also there must be guards along the way."

"So what do you propose?" Xóchitl asks.

"Well, first of all, we can't take the chaneque with us."

"We can't release him either. He would warn his people about us for sure," Xóchitl adds.

"Then we have to lock him up in one of those caves or tie him up somewhere until we get out."

"Sounds good." Xóchitl looks around trying to find a place to lock the chaneque in but can't find any suitable place.

"There. That place is perfect." Itzcuauhtzin points at the privy.

"There?" The chaneque and Xóchitl ask at the same time.

"Yes. There is no other place. I'm sorry. I was starting to like you, but I can't let you go. Your friends will rescue you later." He takes the chaneque by one arm and pushes him into the privy booth. Then he closes the door and seals it with a wooden bar.

"What are you doing? We don't have time." Itzcuauhtzin exclaims at seeing Xóchitl pointing an arrow toward the ceiling.

"Let me try the bow first. I still don't know how good it is," Xóchitl responds. The girl points to a wooden column nearly a yard wide and releases the projectile. The bolt goes through the trunk with great power. Itzcuauhtzin looks at the trunk with great astonishment.

"Ah! What a wonderful shot. It crossed the trunk completely. Try to shoot a little further, like that rock up there."

Xóchitl takes another arrow and points up, fixing her eyes on the center of the rock. She loses her projectile, impacting the rock right in the center. The bolt buries itself easily into the rock without breaking.

"This is wonderful," Xóchitl exclaims. "I hit the very center as I wanted, and the arrow pierced the rock like a melon." Xóchitl quickly pulls another arrow and points to the rock. She fixes her eyes on the same spot where she buried her first projectile. She let go of the string. The arrow whistles, breaking the air in its path, then hits the rock in the same place as the previous arrow, without breaking.

"That was a great shot," Itzcuauhtzin exclaims. "I've never seen anyone do that."

"I think it's the bow. I'm hitting all my shots in the exact spot I'm looking at."

"This is great. Nobody is ever going to believe us. I'm glad you decided to bring it with you."

"Yeah. I love it."

"Let me try." Itzcuauhtzin takes an arrow and places it on the bow. He looks straight into another rock and releases the string. The arrow hits the rock without breaking, right on target.

"Extraordinary!" Itzcuauhtzin exclaims.

"I told you."

"Well, don't waste any more arrows. Let's go." Itzcuauhtzin collects his weapons and the two get on their way. The tunnel is empty and quiet. Itzcuauhtzin expected at least to hear some noise from the main cavern when they were approaching, but the ambience seems to be dead.

The kids approach the cave entrance. They don't see anyone anywhere. Gingerly, Itzcuauhtzin takes the lead and gets closer to the end of the tunnel. Upon entering the cave, he discovers that it is a very large cavern, with steps to the side and two trails that trace along the outside of the walls and follow their route around, leading to more tunnels and lots of doors. There are four sets of steps going down to the bottom of the cave, all built at the four cardinal points.

Down at the center of the cave, Itzcuauhtzin observes three figures with their hands tied, hanging from wooden studs. Several chaneques are sitting at a table playing with bones. All armed and wearing their armor. Itzcuauhtzin signal to Xóchitl to come closer. "Look, guards. This is the main cavern," Itzcuauhtzin whispers. "I think they are guarding those prisoners."

"Shouldn't they be guarding the entrance?" Xóchitl asks.

"I don't know. This is very strange. I thought there would be more people here."

"Maybe that chaneque lied to us."

"I don't think so. This cavern is the largest I've seen. And those doors look like they are for dwelling rooms. Or maybe they are prisons."

"I think those prisoners are indigenous."

"Yeah. You're right. Cuachicqueh Pipils!" Itzcuauhtzin quietly exclaims.

"What do we do?"

"We have to rescue them."

"What about the guards?" Xóchitl asks.

"We have to beat them. They're not going to let us leave here without a fight. Get ready."

"They're too many."

"Yes, but it's only a dozen or less. With your bow we can beat them," Itzcuauhtzin explains.

"What if there's more?"

"Then we'll flee back to the mine. We have no other choice. We're already here."

"Okay. If you say so."

"They are too far away. I don't think my bow can shoot at that range. Maybe yours can. But we have to get closer. There's no place for cover. If we go down, they'll see us for sure and we'll lose the advantage of surprise," Itzcuauhtzin explains. "I have an idea. Get ready to shoot and shoot fast. I will draw their attention. Stay crouched to avoid getting caught." Itzcuauhtzin checks the hallways along the walls and not seeing anyone, walks down the stairs with his spear in his right hand and his shield on the left. He walks down the steps and stops midway. "Hello, friends. How are you?" the brave young Pipil shouts, attracting the attention of everyone in the cave, including the prisoners in the cells.

"Another Pipil warrior," Atlahua exclaims.

"But it's just a boy," Juan points out. The crowd of prisoners piles up against the bars to see the brave Pipil.

The chaneques turn to look toward the stairs. "Pipil," a guard announces when he sees the warrior's painted face with thin armor, spear, and Chimalli.

"I want you to free those Pipils." Itzcuauhtzin points to the prisoners. The prisoners are facing backward and can't see what's happening.

The chaneques run toward the center of the cave and begin to check the area, expecting to find more Pipils. Seeing no one else, the group leader gets closer to the stairs where the young warrior waits. "How did you get in here, Pipil?" the chaneque leader asks. The rest of chaneques spread around, trying to surround the young warrior, but Itzcuauhtzin is on the steps, and their move doesn't help because they can't surround him.

"I told you to free those Pipils. I'm only going to say this once. If you don't, you will regret it," Itzcuauhtzin threatens.

"But you're just a little brat. We outnumber you. You think you're so strong? Why don't you come down? We'll talk about it." The chaneques continue to advance and reach the foot of the stairs with their spears ready to attack. An arrow flies through the chaneque leader's forehead, then three more chaneques drop, one after another. The rest of chaneques jump in the air, dodging a couple of bolts. Xóchitl wounds two more of them while they are still in midflight.

Itzcuauhtzin takes his spear and throws it into the air. The lance soars through the air so fast, as if it had been thrown by an atlatl, and it impacts a chaneque on the chest. Itzcuauhtzin cannot believe how strong and effective his shot has been. Wasting no time, he takes his ax in hand and starts running down the stairs, dodging a couple of spears that have been thrown at him.

Xóchitl shoots two more arrows with much more confidence. One hits its target, but the other one passes over one side of a chaneque who managed to dodge the arrow by pure chance. Xóchitl loses one more against another chaneque. The chaneque raises his shield in front to stop the projectile, but the arrow passes through the shield like paper and buries itself on the left side of the chaneque.

Itzcuauhtzin gets to the bottom with no problems, but two chaneques are waiting for him with clubs in hand. One gets pierced by an arrow from Xóchitl, but the other one runs toward Itzcuauhtzin and attacks. Itzcuauhtzin runs to meet him and slides on his knees across the floor, dodging the attack and buries his ax in the chaneque's stomach. The chaneque falls to the ground holding his stomach. Itzcuauhtzin stands up ready to face his next enemy, but Xóchitl has already taken care of them. Itzcuauhtzin looks at her, giving her a look of approval on her excellent work.

"Free the Pipil, Itzcua," Xóchitl cries out and starts her way down the stairs in a hurry. Itzcuauhtzin takes his knife and runs toward the warriors.

"Ucatl, Uncle Aquetzalli, Ocotlel. How did you get here?" Itzcuauhtzin asks them while cutting the Ucatl's ropes. The warrior falls to the ground like a sack of potatoes.

"Tenoch told us, and we came to your aid," Ucatl answers. Itzcuauhtzin finishes liberating the others.

"Uncle," exclaims Xóchitl who has come down rapidly.

"I'm so happy to see you," Aquetzalli exclaims.

"Are you okay?" Itzcuauhtzin asks.

"Yeah, just a little bruised and tired, but okay." Ocotlel responds.

"What about my dad? How are his wounds?" Xóchitl asks.

"Your father was very badly injured. By the time he came to Tazumal, he had already fainted. My mom is watching over him. She says that everything will be just fine," Aquetzalli responds.

"Are you all the warriors the elders sent?" Itzcuauhtzin asks.

"No. We couldn't wait for their decision, but we trust that there are more reinforcements coming to help. Ocoyatl and Acatlel are waiting for them at the cave's entrance," Aquetzalli responds.

"We haven't found Mom or the twins yet. Have you?" Itzcuauhtzin asks.

"No. Not yet. We haven't seen any humans since we came to this place, but we did find a witch. She is the boss here. I think she must be the queen of the chaneques."

"Witch?" Both kids ask.

"Yes, a very pretty woman whom everyone calls 'My Beloved.'"

"Oh yeah, we heard about her. That explains why the chaneques use magic powder," Itzcuauhtzin says.

"She must know where the twins and my mom are," Xóchitl adds. "Where is she? Show us the way."

"Her throne is up there. It's a very large room, but it's not easy to get in there. She has several chaneques guarding her, and she also has black magic powers. She's very dangerous," Ucatl answers.

"So am I." Xóchitl gets up and readies her bow. "Let's go get her."

"Come on," Itzcuauhtzin agrees.

"No. Wait." Ucatl stops them. "Even if we make it to her room, nothing guarantees that she will tell us anything. Going after that woman is a suicide mission."

"Maybe you're right, Ucatl. But she has my family and I will not leave without them," Itzcuauhtzin states with a very firm and decisive voice.

"So be it then," Ucatl adds. "Warriors, collect as many weapons as you can. We're going after that witch."

"What a beautiful bow, Xóchitl." Aquetzalli can't stop staring at the marvelous bow.

Xóchitl just smiles in response. She prefers to avoid having to explain that she has found a magic bow for fear that someone might want to take it from her for not being male and having no right to bear Pipil arms as Itzcuauhtzin and the warriors.

The warriors armed themselves with the chaneque weapons. Ocotlel picks up Itzcuauhtzin's spear and thinks it a little weird, but very nice.

"That spear is mine," Itzcuauhtzin states.

"It's beautiful. How'd you get it?"

"I'll tell you later," Itzcuauhtzin responds and takes his magic weapon.

"Very well. Let's go," Ucatl orders.

From the cell, the prisoners watch the warriors. They have witnessed the fight and all have been amazed to see how two young kids have so easily defeated a group of combat-trained chaneques. The group continues shouting very loudly to release them, but the warriors can't hear them.

"Why are they ignoring us?" Juan asks.

"I don't know. Perhaps the spell that Notchím put in this cell prevents them from hearing or seeing us."

After collecting their arrows, Xóchitl passes very close to the cell without realizing that the wall on her right is only an illusion that covers the slave's prison. Juan extends his arm trying to touch her but Xóchitl walks too fast and too far out of reach.

210

The five warriors, led by Ucatl, reach the throne room door. "This is strange. There are no guards," Ocotlel exclaims.

Ucatl tries to open the door but is unable to. "It is sealed. The witch must have locked it."

Aquetzalli tries to push it but it doesn't open. "We'll have to tear it down."

"And how will you do that? This door must weigh a thousand pounds or more," Ocotlel asks.

"With this." Aquetzalli pulls out a small blue dust bag and shows them.

"Where'd you get that?" Ocotlel asks.

"From one of the guards. I thought it would be useful for occasions like this." Aquetzalli spreads a little dust on his finger and draws the rune he learned from his first prisoner. The rest of the warriors get ready for their next battle. The door opens inward very slowly. The warriors wait for a moment, but nothing happens. Aquetzalli looks at Ucatl, waiting for his orders. Ucatl goes in first with his spear at the ready. The rest follow his example and go in after him.

"There's no one here." Ucatl exclaims.

"Where has that witch gone to?" Aquetzalli asks.

"Aquetzalli!" A female voice calls from behind a cabinet full of cups and clay pots. The warriors direct all their attention to the furniture, and Elena comes out of her hiding place.

"Mom." The kids run after their mother. Elena receives them with a hug.

"My children. I'm so happy to see you. I thought these chaneques had kidnapped you too."

"Yes, but Itzcua rescued us," Xóchitl responds.

"Where are Tenoch and your dad?"

"They are fine. We'll tell you everything later. Right now we must leave this place. Where are the twins?" Itzcuauhtzin asks.

"I don't know. My Beloved took them to a place below the cave, but I don't know where that place is."

"So where is the witch?" Aquetzalli asks.

"I don't know. She brought me over here half an hour ago, then she left with a couple of guards. But I don't know where she was going."

"Why would she leave you alone and unguarded?" Aquetzalli asks.

"Maybe she didn't expect us to come so early," Itzcuauhtzin responds. "Maybe that's why the door was sealed."

"Elena, we have to go before that witch comes back with reinforcements," Aquetzalli exclaims.

"The prisoners. We must free them. Maybe they know where the kids are," Elena responds.

"Okay. Where are the prisoners at?" Ucatl asks.

"Down in the cells," Elena responds.

"Very good. Take us with them then." Everyone leaves the room and run down the stairs.

"The prisons!" Elena looks around and touches the walls. "The cells were here, but I don't see them."

"Elena. Elena, help us." The prisoners shout from behind the cells, but the Pipils still can't hear them.

"There's nothing here," Aquetzalli says. "We were hanging over here for about two hours, and we never saw any prisoners."

"They were here. I was here," Elena responds. "Witchcraft. This must be a spell from that witch." Elena approaches a wall and knocks on it. The wall is solid and there are no signs of the prison cells. The prisoners keep shouting from inside without any success.

"If it is a spell, maybe a little magic dust can open it," Aquetzalli suggests while pulling out his blue powder bag. He draws the rune but nothing happens. "Mmm...It did not work. Are you sure that the cells were here?"

"Yes. There were several prison cells here. I was here most of the night and saw when they brought you over and hang you in the middle of the room."

Xóchitl and Itzcuauhtzin look at each other. "Let me try," Xóchitl exclaims. The girl approaches the wall and touches it with her left hand. *Open up.* The ring emits a yellow light and the wall deforms into a liquid wave, and the cell gets exposed. The clamor and the cries of joy of the prisoners almost deafen the ambient, but the face of the Pipil's amazement to see the magic of the ring is indescribable.

"Juan, Atlahua!" Elena calls.

"Elena, you came back for us," Juan calls from behind the bars.

"How'd you do that, Xóchitl?" Aquetzalli asks.

"It's a long story. I promise to tell it to you when this is over. Right now we must break this chain."

"It's a lock," Ocotlel exclaims. "We need the key to open it."

"The guards have the keys." Juan points to the dead chaneques.

Ucatl and Ocotlel run to find the keys. The leader of the group had a ring with several keys and different sizes. "Here they are," announces Ocotlel and immediately begins to try his luck. The third key he tries finally opens the lock. The warriors quickly open the cell and the prisoners start to come out slowly.

"We need to open the other prisons," Atlahua demands.

"More prisons?" Ocotlel asks.

"Yes, the entire cave is full of prisons." Xóchitl and Ocotlel follow Atlahua. Xóchitl breaks the spell and Ocotlel opens the locks.

"Come on, get out of here. This is our chance to be free." Juan explains to more than a quarter of prisoners who refuse to leave their cells.

"There's nothing for us out there. Besides, if the chaneques catch us, it's going to get worse for us. We shouldn't leave. Five Pipils can't stop Sihuehuet's troops," a young man responds from behind the cell.

"They are only five, but we are much more. Chilco doesn't have enough chaneques available to stop us. Also these kids have Pipil magic. Didn't you see what they've just done? Don't be afraid."

214

"What's going on?" Xóchitl asks when she returns with the others.

"These people refuse to go with us. They are afraid of the chaneques," Juan responds.

"Leave them here then. We don't have time to help people who don't want to be helped," Ucatl explains.

"I think Ucatl is right." Itzcuauhtzin adds. "Leave them here. Maybe they want to work twice as hard to make up for all the work that the others are going to leave behind. Let's go."

"There is a large army up there, so we can't go back through there. We must find another way to get out of here," Ocotlel exclaims.

"Who knows how to get out of here?" Ucatl asks aloud. Nobody answers.

"We only know the mines, but we don't know of a way out." Juan explains. "Many of us have never even seen the light of day."

"I know someone who knows this place very well," Xóchitl responds. "Follow me."

"Wait, what about the twins? We can't leave them behind," Elena exclaims.

"Does anyone here know where they are?" Itzcuauhtzin asks.

"The cooks," Juan answers. "The cooks bring them food every day. They must know the way."

"Then find a cook immediately," Itzcuauhtzin orders. "Ucatl, listen well. We have to get all these people out of here. Do you see that tunnel up there?" Itzcuauhtzin points to the tunnel where they came in from.

"Yes."

"The tunnel will lead you to a very wide mine. We locked a chaneque who served as our guide. He is locked in one of the outhouses. He can help you get out of here. Just offer him some candy; he loves them."

"But I have no candy."

"Don't tell him that. Just tell him you will give it to him when you get out of here."

"Xóchitl and I will go get the twins."

"I'm coming with you," Aquetzalli exclaims.

"Me too," Ocotlel offers. "I have a score to settle with that witch."

"Okay. I'll come back for you once we get this people out," Ucatl responds.

Elena and Juan return with an older man. "This is Mario. He is going to show you the way."

"Excellent," Itzcuauhtzin exclaims.

Ucatl climbs up a few steps and turns to face the people. "Listen up. We'll get out of here by a different route. But that doesn't mean that it will not be dangerous. Those who can arm yourselves, do it. Look for anything. Clubs, spears, knives, whatever you can find. I'm going to lead, and I need everyone to stay together," Ucatl explains, and without waiting for an answer, he begins to pace toward the tunnel.

"Come with me," Mario suggests. Elena, Juan, and the warriors begin to walk after the cook.

"Mom, wait." Itzcuauhtzin stops Elena. "It will be better if you go with Ucatl. He's going to need you more."

"But... the twins?"

"Don't worry, we are going to get them. It will be very dangerous. I'll feel better if you go with Ucatl. He will need help with all these people. It's better that you go with him."

"Sounds like a good idea," Juan says.

"Be very careful."

"Yes, Mom. My uncle is coming with us."

"Xóchitl, you shouldn't go. You're still a child."

"Don't worry, Mom. Tlaloc will take care of me, and Quetzalcoatl has given me some very good gifts. I'll be fine. Go with them," Xóchitl responds. Elena gives her a big hug and then lets her go.

"This way," Mario points out.

The cave gets empty in less than ten minutes. The prisoners who have been left behind start coming out one by one. "They are all gone," one of them announces. "I'm going with them too. If Sihuehuet returns and finds us here, for sure she'll make us pay for their transgression. If you don't want to come, good luck to you all. I'm going with the Pipils." The man begins to run after the Pipils. Once at the top of the stairs, he turns to look back and sees a large crowd running up the stairs behind him.

WARRIOR HEART

Teutli stops his warriors near the mine. "Halt. Do you hear that? It sounds like a crowd of people. They are coming this way."

"Chaneques or humans?" Acatlel asks.

"I don't know, but it sounds like a very big crowd."

"If you want, I can go investigate," Acatlel suggests.

"Okay. Atlanezi and I will go with you. We can't run with Ziquetl hurt." Teutli turns to face his warriors. "Ocoyatl, go back and hide between the stalagmites of the previous cave. We'll go investigate and return as soon as possible." The three warriors draw their weapons and rush to investigate the crowd. Ocoyatl takes his prisoner and leads the group back to the previous cave.

"It's people," Acatlel says, seeing a couple of figures approaching. A chaneque comes behind them with his hands tied, and a Pipil warrior holding the rope.

"Ucatl!" Teutli calls, very happy. "You did it. Ha ha." The three warriors come out of hiding.

"Ucatl," Acatlel calls. The people stop at seeing the three shadows approaching.

"Acatlel?"

"Yes. It's us."

"I'm so happy to see you," Ucatl exclaims. "Are you all the reinforcements the elders sent?"

"No, of course not. There are six more in the back," Teutli answers.

"Only six! I thought they were going to send at least fifty."

"No. Pacotli is very stubborn. Who are they?" Teutli asks, changing the conversation.

"They were prisoners. This chaneque is leading us to the exit. There is a large army of chaneques that went to guard the entrance."

"Yes, we saw them. We had a little altercation with one of their squads. Ziquetl is hurt. Did you find Elena and the twins?"

"We didn't find the twins, but we found Elena. A band of chaneques band captured us, but Itzcuauhtzin and Xóchitl came and rescued us. You should have seen them fight. They are an indestructible pair."

"Itzcua and Xóchitl?" Atlanezi asks.

"Yes."

"But Xóchitl is just a girl. I didn't know she could fight."

"Not at face-to-face combat, but she is lethal with the bow."

"And where are they now?" Teutli asks.

"Elena is back there. She is helping me keep order. Itzcua and Xóchitl went to look for the twins. Ocotlel and Aquetzalli went with them," Ucatl responds.

"They are only children. How could you let them go?" Atlanezi complains.

"I couldn't stop them. Itzcua is just as stubborn as Atecaltzin and Ohtocani's entire house. There is also a very powerful witch who has black magic. Xóchitl has a powerful magic ring. She believes that with that ring, she may be able to counteract the witch's magic. And on top of all that, we need to get these people out of here, now that the chaneques are distracted waiting for the Pipil army. They have been in captivity for years. When they are outside, then we'll come back for the kids."

"It may be too late by then," Atlanezi exclaims. "I'm going to go get them. Just tell me where they went."

"Wait. I'm going with you," Acatlel offers. "My brother is with them."

"Wait a minute," Teutli orders. "I'm coming with you. Just let me give my orders to the others." Teutli runs back to his companions.

"Listen up, everything is okay. It's Ucatl and a big crowd of people who have been in captivity for years."

"Is my family with them?" Tenoch asks.

"Only your mom. The others went to rescue the twins," Teutli responds. Tenoch starts running immediately. Yanixté follows right behind him.

"All right, listen up. We have some problems. The main goal just changed. I need you to help Ucatl get these people out of here as soon as possible. Acatlel, Atlanezi, and I are going to go after the kids. Is that understood?"

"Yes, My General," everyone answers.

"Here they come," Teutli announces. Ucatl and his people don't take long to arrive. "Ucatl, all these warriors are yours. Good luck."

"What happened here?" Ucatl asks.

"Ziquetl is hurt," Yanté responds.

"What about this chaneque?"

"He is our guide."

"And why are you carrying him?"

"Because his foot is injured, and he can't walk."

"Tie him up and leave him here. We're not going to need him. We have our own guide," Ucatl orders. "Ocoyatl, I need you to come with me and this chaneque. We'll go ahead and inspect the road. The rest of you, keep walking with these people, and I need two of you to go to the back and protect the people."

"Immediately," Tlacoyotl responds.

"Yanté, hasten the pace. We need to get out of here before the chaneques return."

"As you command," Yanté responds.

Tenoch makes his way among the crowd as good as he can, looking for his mother, but Elena comes all the way in the back with Juan and Atlahua. Atlanezi seems to be talking with one of the men.

"Mom, Mom." Elena hugs Tenoch as she has never done before.

"Tenoch, son, it's so good to see you. What are you doing here? Ucatl said you were with Atecaltzin at Tazumal."

"I came to show them the way, but a lot has happened since, and now I'm here. Yanixté came with me."

"Niltze," Yanixté salutes.

"Niltze, Yanixté."

"Where's my dad?" Asks the young boy.

"He went with Itzcua and Xóchitl to look for the twins," Elena answers.

Yanixté turns to face Atlanezi. "Uncle, I'll go with you to rescue the twins. My dad is in there with them."

"No, you're not. This is very dangerous, and your dad would never forgive me. Besides, you have orders to take care of Tenoch. You stay with him and aid Ucatl to get these people out of here. I'll get your father; we'll see you outside."

"But uncle."

"No. I already said no."

Teutli finally reaches the end of line. "Ready?" The General asks.

"Yes, ready. Further down this road is a mine with other tunnels that will take us to the main cavern. We have no time to lose," Acatlel answers, and the warriors start running immediately in rescue of their family and kin.

The sound of the door silenced everyone in the cave. The chaneques on the ceiling prepare their blowguns and get ready to start shooting, but only a small group of warriors enter the cave. The chaneques on the ceiling wait for them to pass. They can only see their hats. The stone door closes and darkness returns to the cavern.

"Give me a mango."

"Here, and leave me alone. You should have picked up some for yourself instead of pestering me."

"Shut up, you two, and pick up the pace," Kumara orders from behind the group. After taking the last bend and reaching the large cave, a shower of spears falls down on them. Kumara and one other chaneque take cover between the stalagmites. "What's going on?" Kumara shouts. "Why are you attacking us?"

"Stop!" One chaneque shouts when he recognizes Kumara's voice. "They are chaneques. Do not shoot." Luckily the chaneques on the ceiling have followed the instructions not to shoot until a couple of dozen have passed through the door.

"What is going on here?" Chilco angrily demands. "We are killing our own people."

"But you were the one who gave the order sir," one chaneque responds.

Kumara comes out of his hiding place. "Why are you attacking us?"

"We thought you were Pipils."

"No, it's us. What a tragedy! You killed my entire squad." Kumara spits on the floor.

"Where are the Pipils?" Chilco asks.

"I don't know. But there are several dead chaneques out there. We hid them in the undergrowth of the forest. I'm sure they came through here," Kumara responds.

"Where's Kuenú?"

"He's dead. Pierced by an arrow."

"So there are no Pipils out there?" Chilco asks.

"No, we haven't seen any."

"They must have come in already. Xilo went after the trail of several Pipils, but they weren't many, maybe a dozen or less. Are you sure there is no one else?"

"I'm sure."

"Then stay here with a group of forty. I want you to make sure this entrance is secure from the outer side. We will return to the main cavern. If there are problems, let me know."

"Yes sir."

"Kompa."

"Yes, My General."

"Take a group of twenty warriors and panthers and go after Xilo. If the Pipils came through, they must be on the path to mine number seven. Narib, go with them. I'll send another squad from the other side to trap them." Kompa makes a sign with his fist in the chest and leaves with his group.

Chilco and the rest of the army were quick to return to the main cave. When they arrive, they find the guards dead and the cells empty. "My Beloved!" Chilco exclaims. "You come with me." Chilco runs into the throne room with a group of chaneques. The door is open but there's no one inside. "Damn. There's no one here. Those Pipils tricked us." Chilco exclaims.

"My General, everything indicates that the slaves escaped through the mine seven's path."

"Go after them," Chilco orders. "Where is Notchím?"

"I don't know My General. Maybe he is with My Beloved."

"Find them. I want you all looking for My Beloved and Notchím. You come with me. We are going to the children's garden to look for them." Chilco takes about fifty warriors with him, and sends the rest after the prisoners.

"There was a great battle here. There's blood everywhere. I think the ambush came from above. The Pipils must have shot Xilo from above," the tracker reports.

"So, where are the dead?"

"They must have thrown them into the ravine. There are signs of a couple of panthers being dragged."

"Let's go, they can't be too far ahead," Kompa orders.

"Which way?" Ucatl asked the chaneque when they reach the main trail.

"It's this way," the chaneque points up.

"No. The chaneques are up there. There must be another way."

"There is, but it is across the Boiling River."

"Boiling River?"

"Yes. Further down, about five kilometers, there is a bridge. The bridge was put there to cross to the other side without falling into the river."

"Why is it called the Boiling River?" Ocoyatl asks.

"Because the water always boils."

"And why does the water boil?" Ucatl asks.

"Because of the volcano's magma. That's why we don't come here a lot, because it is always too hot on this side of the cavern."

"Excellent," Ucatl exclaims.

"Ucatl. I'm sure the chaneques already realized that there aren't any more warriors coming to our rescue. They could be coming in this direction. I will go up to investigate. You guys keep going down. I'll catch up," Ocoyatl offers.

"Okay, be careful."

Yanté and the rest of the people arrive shortly after. "Is everything all right?"

"Yes. It's down that way. Take this chaneque and lead these people down the path. He will show you the way." Ucatl addresses the people and loudly calls for their attention. "Listen up, everyone. I need strong and armed people who are willing to defend themselves and their freedom. We have an army of chaneques up there that could be coming after us. We need to protect these people. Women and children please keep walking. Yanté will direct you to the exit." Over a dozen young men with spears and machetes volunteer. While people are still passing by, Ucatl continues to recruit people till he gathers a little over thirty men.

Atlahua and Tlacoyotl are the last to pass. They also stay with Ucatl, along with Yanixté and Tenoch.

"All right boys. Ocoyatl is investigating the road up ahead. We'll wait here. Tenoch, you can't stay here. You have to go with others."

"But I want..." Suddenly a shadow appears at the turn of the road.

"Chaneques!" Ocoyatl announces with a cry. Behind him, another shadow appears, bigger and faster. The rumblings of war animals and people can be heard quite loud. The shadow attacks Ocoyatl with a club trying to raze him. Ocoyatl jumps to the side, dodging the attack, and rolls on the floor. Immediately more shadows come to light. Ucatl and his warriors run in Ocoyatl's aid. They take their bows and start firing against all chaneques. Most of young men get paralyzed by fear at seeing the action. Only a dozen of them join Ucatl, while the panthers roar and close in at great speed.

Yanixté and Tenoch quickly climb up onto a couple of stalagmites and start firing against the beasts. A couple of panthers fall to the ground, wounded by the youngsters' missiles.

"Come on," Ucatl cries out. "Form a defensive line." A couple of spears pass close to Ucatl's head. One of them runs through a young man. At seeing that, the men who had stayed back run away from the place, abandoning the Pipils to their fate.

"Where are you going? Cowards, come back," cries Atlahua at seeing their cowardice.

Ocoyatl defends himself with his shield, blocking a few attacks. Tlacoyotl shoots the chaneque's panther that is attacking Ocoyatl with a spear. Ocoyatl stands up and uses his baton to get rid of his attacker, but a panther without his rider jumps on him. Ocoyatl dodges a claw and uses his shield to block the panther's bites. He pulls his knife out however possible, but the panther's weight is too much, and it has started to attack him with its claws. The great weight starts to crack his ribs. In his desperation, Ocoyatl launches a stab against the panther, wounding it on the neck. The panther's blood begins to paint him in red, but that doesn't stop the panther from scratching him in the stomach. Ocoyatl screams in pain and brings his hand to the wound to prevent from bleeding. The panther stands up on two legs ready to deliver the final blow when one of Tenoch's arrows hits it. The panther falls backward. Ocoyatl touches his stomach and sees the blood. He quickly tears off his shirt and covers the wound with it.

Ucatl and the Pipils keep busy fighting the few remaining chaneques. A couple of teens have gone into action and have managed to get rid of a chaneque. Tenoch and Yanixté keep shooting against the panthers. One of Yanixté's arrows hits Kopán on the left side. This one drops his weapon and turns his panther around with intent to flee. Narib realizes that the Pipils are too many and this battle is lost. He decides to follow Kopán. Half a dozen panthers do the same. A couple of them still have arrows embedded in their bodies.

The chaneques are eventually defeated by the Pipils and the young men. "Ucatl!" Ocoyatl shouts.

Ucatl approaches the warrior. "What's wrong?"

"I think I have a couple of broken ribs and a severe wound in my stomach."

"Let me see." Ucatl lifts the piece of cloth. The wound is long with four deep scratches, but only one is heavily bleeding. "It's not too deep. I think you'll live, my friend."

"That's good news. I like living."

"Do you think you can walk?" Ucatl asks.

"I hope so. Help me up."

Ucatl carefully lifts his friend up. "How is it?"

"I think I can."

"You're a beast with that knife," Tlacoyotl happily says, the adrenaline still running strong within him.

"I don't know who shot the panther, but thanks. I thought I was done for."

"Ha, you? No. Never. Bad weed never dies," Ucatl teases.

"A young man has died and two more are injured," Atlahua reports.

"How serious are the injuries?" Ucatl asks.

"They are minor. They'll be fine."

"What do we do with the young man who died?"

"I'm sorry. There's nothing else we can do. We'll have to leave him behind. We can't take him with us."

"In that case, let's get out of here before they return," a young man with tears in his eyes suggests. The boy who died was his friend, and he died defending everyone's freedom. It was a high price to pay.

Tlacoyotl doesn't need to ask; he already knows and places a hand on the boy's shoulders. "Don't let his sacrifice be in vain."

The boy just looks at him and wipes his tears off.

"Collect all weapons. We have to take them with us so we can arm more people," Ucatl orders.

"What people? Didn't you see how they all fled like cowards?" Atlahua says.

"They were just scared. They've been locked up so long; I don't think any of them have ever seen a confrontation. They will do better next time," Tlacoyotl exclaims.

"I hope there isn't a next time," Ocoyatl says.

Two young men help Ocoyatl walk, while others collect spears and weapons for their peers.

"Tenoch, Yanixté, excellent work," Ucatl congratulates. "It looks like you were born with a heart of a warrior."

"Thank you," the boys respond while they finish cutting ears and collecting arrows.

Further up the trail, Narib and Kopán stop. Narib pulls the arrow from Kopán's side. He puts some yellow powder on the wound and draws a rune, then recites a spell. The yellow powder starts to bubble, and Kopán's wound closes.

"Thanks, Narib. These Pipils are very dangerous. I thought there would be less of them."

"Yes. It would be better to go back to the main cavern and give notice to Chilco. They were not all Pipils. Many of them were slaves. Something is very wrong," Narib exclaims.

THE BURIED PARADISE

Sarnik and three companions escort Sihuehuet to the entrance of the children's paradise. Sihuehuet does not allow any chaneques inside the garden, preferring to maintain the children's innocence intact until they reach the appropriate age. So Notchím, Sarnik, and the guards wait outside.

"What do you know about the Pipils?" Sarnik asks Notchím.

"The Pipils have always been a peaceful society—— farmers, fishermen, and hunters—— but their warriors are very dangerous, although after the conquest of the whites their numbers have declined. Their warriors are not as wild as they used to be. The absence of war has made them soft. I don't think Chilco will have much trouble with them."

"But they have firearms."

"Yes, that could give them an advantage, but firearms take too long to prepare. Even the fastest gunman can't fire more than one shot per minute. One minute is a long time. How many men could you kill in one minute?"

"With the right weapons, about ten; hand-to-hand, at least five," Sarnik proudly responds.

"You see? The Pipils will try to use their firearms. After that, it will be a melee battle. With our numbers and in our caves, they won't have a chance. For sure, Chilco will hide blow-gunners among the darkness of stalactites. By the time the Pipils realize what's happening, it will be too late."

"I wouldn't be so sure."

"You don't need to worry about the Pipil army. What you have to worry about is a couple of heavenly warriors sent by Quetzalcoatl to destroy us."

"Heavenly?"

"Yes. Quetzalcoatl has sent two warriors to fight his war. I've seen them in my visions, within the divination bones. They are two warriors who wear the symbol of the feathered serpent and the jaguar. I've seen them fight terrestrial monsters and beings of the Transcendental World."

"Is that why you're here?" Sarnik asks.

"Yes. My Beloved suffers much danger."

"But her magic is very powerful."

"It could be, but these Pipils have very good medicine, and I've seen that they carry the power of Quetzalcoatl just like it was carried by Ce Ácatl Quetzalcoatl, Quetzalcoatl Acxitl Topiltzin II, the very same Atlacatl and many other chiefs before them."

"How do we fight against such power?"

"I don't think it's possible."

"Then we should better retreat."

"And where would we retreat to? If Quetzalcoatl has sent his warriors, they'll find us wherever we go. It's best to be prepared for anything."

"Notchím. And how do we prepare for that?" Sarnik asks, losing patience with the sorcerer.

"My Beloved has a plan. That's why I came with her. We'll seal this cave and the treasure room till this war against Pipils is over. Then we will seal all entrances to the caverns but one. That way we'll make sure the Pipils can't re-enter. And about the Quetzalcoatl's warriors, well, we better find Chalchiuhtlicue's bracelet. My Beloved believes that the bracelet will give her the power to beat the celestial warriors. But first we'll need to capture them."

"Capture them?"

"Yes. We only need one. Don't underestimate My Beloved's power."

"You said we need the bracelet to beat them. And now you want us to capture at least one? This is absurd. We've spent years looking for that *blessed bracelet* and we have never found it. I don't even think it's here."

"Of that I'm sure. The bracelet is here. But it's protected by Mayan magic that prevents me from locating it. I know it is hidden among the skirts of the Lamatepec volcano."

"We have looked all over this place, and we searched every cave. There's nothing here," Sarnik complains.

"I'm sure it was buried by an earthquake, and these warriors have found the place. That's why My Beloved is anxiously waiting for these warriors. One of them could be wearing the bracelet. And if not, at least we could get information about the Mayan cave, if we can catch them."

"You mean Topiltzin Acxitl had the magic of the bracelet?"

"Yes, but he never used it. What he did was save it among his treasures. The shamans and priests of that time buried their chief along with his belongings."

"So how is it, that he was protected by Mayan magic, if he was not Mayan?"

"The Mayans had a better understanding of magical things. They advised Topiltzin not to wear the bracelet and to keep it in a safe place. Mayan magic and medicine were far superior to that one of the Pipils. So they helped the priests seal the tomb."

"How do you know so much?"

"I like reading the history of my ancestors, and I also like knowing my enemies. The stories and the events change a bit. So you can never be sure of the actual facts. But every story always keeps its essence, and the essence is that the bracelet is buried around here. My Beloved knows more about this subject and how that bracelet came to be in the hands of the Pipils, but she has never told me that story, and I've never found anything that explains that enigma."

After an hour, Sihuehuet finally comes out of the garden, very satisfied. "Notchím, seal this cave. I don't want anyone going in or out. Leave some guards nearby. I do not want them by the door. That would only mark the entrance."

"Yes, My Beloved." Notchím closes the front door and puts an illusion spell on it to cover the identity of the cave.

"Pipils!" a guard cries out when he sees Teutli and a group of Pipils.

"My Beloved!" Ocotlel exclaims and immediately fires his rifle, hitting a chaneque in the chest. The chaneques scatter, taking defensive positions with shields at the front.

"This way, My Beloved." Sarnik takes his protégée by the left trail, escaping the reach of arrows and bullets.

Xóchitl fires a couple of bolts that pass through the shields of the chaneques, running through their wielders. A couple of spears are thrown at the Pipils, but the warriors are too few and dodge them very easily. Itzcuauhtzin also throws his spear running through another chaneque. The last two remaining chaneques decide to flee the scene and go after Sihuehuet.

"This must be the place," Aquetzalli exclaims. "Surely the kids are here."

"Let's go after the witch," Ocotlel suggests. "This is our chance."

"Let's go," Itzcuauhtzin agrees.

Ocotlel approaches the turn, pressing his back against the wall and poking his head slowly to see if the way is clear. "Come on," the warrior announces, seeing no one. Itzcuauhtzin takes his spear and is the first to run after the chaneques.

Sarnik and company reach a larger hallway, with just one outlet on their right. "This is a good place for an ambush," the warrior says.

The other two chaneques that escaped from the Pipils enter the hallway. "It's only three Pipils and a girl, but they are very dangerous," one of them reports. A bright and very straight arrow runs him through the skull, and the chaneque falls face first to the ground. Sarnik and the other chaneque run to meet their foes, covering themselves among the wall and out of reach of any arrow.

Sihuehuet waits patiently at the end of the hallway. Notchím casts a spell, turning the walls into steaming mirrors. One of Aquetzalli's arrows hits Sihuehuet on the chest, but she doesn't move. She only pulls the arrow out without paying any attention to it. Her wound closes immediately without bleeding.

"By Tlaloc! What kind of demon is she?" Aquetzalli exclaims when his attack doesn't make the slightest damage. The Pipils enter the hall aware of the chaneques. Sarnik is the first to attack Ocotlel with his macana. Ocotlel blocks the attack with his Chimalli and the two begin to circle each other. Ocotlel attacks Sarnik with his macana, but Sarnik is very fast and dodges his attack, and counterattacks.

Aquetzalli and the second chaneque have already engaged into action, but Aquetzalli is faster; and after only two attacks, the chaneque lies dead on the ground with a spear running through his body.

Sarnik and Ocotlel engage into a fervent battle. Sarnik has hit Ocotlel very hard and Ocotlel has lost his shield, but his agility gives a small advantage and spins his body to the left, releasing a very strong blow on Sarnik's right side. Sarnik tries to block the blow, but his shield is in his left arm and he has no choice but to block the attack with his macana. The impact is so strong that Sarnik drops his macana. The chaneque immediately drops to the floor, taking Ocotlel by his legs and knocking him over. The two warriors start rolling on the floor. Ocotlel gets the advantage and pins Sarnik to the floor, but Sarnik uses his legs and sends Ocotlel flying through the air. Ocotlel lands five meters away on his back. The impact leaves Ocotlel holding on to his back. Sarnik stands up, ready to finish his opponent off, but a bullet runs him through and then a spear finishes him. Aquetzalli, who was already on his way to help Ocotlel, turns around to see who did the shooting, and to his joy, it's Acatlel, Teutli, and his brother Atlanezi who have come to their aid.

Itzcuauhtzin and Xóchitl get confused by the mirrors. Everything looks dark, and Sihuehuet and Notchím are everywhere. Notchím seems to be working on another spell, and Sihuehuet only watches the teens in amazement, especially Itzcuauhtzin, who's dressed in ancient armor. *Topiltzin's armor.*

"Who are you?" Sihuehuet demands.

"It's a spell," Itzcuauhtzin warns.

"I noticed." Xóchitl approaches a wall. *Show me what's real.* The ring shines and the mirrors explode in a thousand pieces, revealing the dark walls.

Sihuehuet opens her eyes wider in wonder at what Xóchitl has done and realizes that she won't be able to counteract Xóchitl's magic. At that moment, two arrows and a bullet pierce her chest, but she doesn't even flinch. She puts her hand into her dress' pocket and pulls out two blue crystal spheres. Sihuehuet drops them on the floor, while the Pipil warriors quickly reload their guns.

"What kind of sorcery is this?" Teutli asks, very amazed. Ocotlel finally stands up and looks around.

Two small cyclones get formed on the ground where the spheres fell, and two gray and very large creatures rise from the ground. The warriors fire their rifles at the beasts, but they don't seem to pay attention, and they keep coming at them quickly. Teutli attacks one of them with a spear. The spear gets stuck in the body made of rock and sand, but the creature doesn't feel any pain and keeps gaining ground.

Notchím runs up to Sihuehuet "My Beloved, we need to go."

"No, these warriors know the whereabouts of Chalchiuhtlicue's bracelet."

Xóchitl shoots an arrow from her bow. The projectile hits the monster on the chest, and the creature explodes. Sand and stone pieces fly everywhere. Sihuehuet opens her eyes and mouth with disbelief at seeing the success of Xóchitl's arrow. Itzcuauhtzin throws his spear at the second monster, causing the same effect done by Xóchitl's arrow.

"Quetzalcoatl's weapons." Sihuehuet angrily shouts. "How is it that a couple of brats like you have these weapons?"

"Where are my brothers?" Xóchitl raises her bow. The Pipil warriors have also been shocked in disbelief at the power of the weapons and they are just standing there looking at the powerful duo.

"Where did you find those weapons?" Sihuehuet looks furious.

"That's none of your business. Tell me where you are keeping my brothers. If you don't, I'll put the next arrow through your heart. If you know these weapons, then you should know that I can't miss," Xóchitl threatens.

Sihuehuet raises her hands. "Ahrrr!" She cries out in anger, raising a cloud of dust that covers the entire area, blinding the warriors. Sihuehuet takes the opportunity and runs through the tunnel. Notchím follows after her.

"Over here." Itzcuauhtzin, who was closer to Sihuehuet, shouts. The Pipils follow his voice. Itzcuauhtzin is much faster than the others and runs in pursue of the beautiful lady. When he takes the first bend, Sihuehuet grabs him by the neck and puts her right hand on his head. The images of the cave are immediately projected onto her mind. Including the path they used to get to it. Itzcuauhtzin screams in pain. He wants to move but the beautiful lady's siege is too strong.

"Itzcua!" Xóchitl shouts while running to his aid. Sihuehuet pushes Itzcuauhtzin against the warriors. Teutli and Acatlel shoot at the witch. The arrows bury themselves into her flesh but nothing happens.

"Ha ha ha. Useless Pipils," Sihuehuet exclaims. Xóchitl loses one of her arrows against her, hitting her in the left shoulder. "Ah!" The fair lady screams and falls wounded to the ground. See pulls the arrows off of her, but only Xóchitl's bolt was able to seriously hurt her. The wounds of the common arrows close immediately, but the wound of Xóchitl's arrow doesn't close and she starts bleeding. A black circle begins to form around the opening. Sihuehuet rolls over, evading Xóchitl's second shot and quickly flees the scene, leaving a layer of dust behind her covering her retreat.

"Itzcua. Are you okay?" Xóchitl calls from afar, but the teen doesn't respond.

Aquetzalli takes Itzcuauhtzin and checks him. "He's still breathing. He is only unconscious."

"Where's the witch?" Ocotlel asks when he finally catches up with everyone else.

"She escaped, but she is bleeding. I don't think she'll get very far," Acatlel answers. The air begins to clear and the warriors can now see clearer.

"Our weapons can't hurt her. Only Xóchitl's magical bolt managed to hurt her. We must find the children first. Leave that witch be, she is very tricky," Teutli exclaims.

"I think he's under a spell," Atlanezi says.

"Tobacco. Does anyone have any tobacco?" Aquetzalli asks.

"What for?" Teutli asks.

"To break the spell," Aquetzalli responds.

"Yes. That's what my dad did when Tenoch and I were under the spell," Xóchitl adds.

"Here," Acatlel pulls his pipe and a bit of tobacco from his satchel and hands them over. Aquetzalli doesn't waste any time and quickly turn the pipe on and begins to exhale smoke onto Itzcuauhtzin's face. Soon the youngster reacts and starts coughing.

"Are you all right, son?" Aquetzalli asks.

"Yes, thank you. That witch took me by surprise."

"What did she do to you?" Aquetzalli asks.

"I think she was reading my mind. I felt how she invaded my mind and began to see how we found Topiltzin's tomb."

"Topiltzin Acxitl's tomb! You guys found the tomb of the chief?" Teutli asks.

"Yes, I think so. We're not sure. But that's where we found these magical weapons. I think that's what that woman was looking for. She tried to kill me with her magic after she read my mind, but she couldn't. I think the ring protected me. I felt the hotness of the ring covering me with its magic. If you had not arrived in time, for sure she would have killed me some other way."

"Well, seems like you two have had a formidable adventure," Ocotlel says.

"The children!" Xóchitl warns. "We should go get the kids."

"Come on. Our mission is not that witch but to rescue the children," Teutli orders.

"How did you find us?" Ocotlel asks Acatlel.

"We found a cook and he gave us directions," his brother responds.

The seven warriors return to the small cave. "Can you open this door?" Aquetzalli asks Xóchitl.

Xóchitl gets closer to the wall and breaks the spell, and opens the door easily. Inside they find a large room with long banquet tables, made of fine wood, but there are no children in the room. There are several doors along the far walls, so the warriors go through the nearest one. The door opens easily without the use of magic.

Outside, they find a hidden paradise, with trees, and exotic plants. The ceiling is very high and without stalactites. It's been decorated with rhinestones emanating light to illuminate the place. In the middle lies a gigantic pond of water that's fed by a cascade that falls from the ceiling along the wall. It also has a small stream that flows freely through the green terrain. There are many domestic animals such as dogs, pigs, goats, sheep, and even horses can be seen running freely everywhere.

"Unbelievable!" Atlanezi exclaims. "How can anything grow in here without the sun?"

"Magic. The chaneques are supposed to be nature's guardians. I'm pretty sure it's their magic that makes everything grow so strong and vivid," Teutli answers.

"Those are only legends," Atlanezi says.

"Well. Just this morning, we thought they were a myth. And here we are fighting them. Their magic must be real," Teutli adds.

The children continue to play without realizing that the Pipils have entered their dwelling place. There is not a single child over eleven years old in this place. All of them play and have fun without any worries. Some of them are playing in the pond, while others play on swings made out of ropes and boards.

"How are we going to get all these kids out of here?" Teutli asks. "They look so happy."

"Felipe!" Xóchitl shouts and runs after her little brother and takes him by the shoulder. "Felipe. It's me, Xóchitl."

"Xóchitl," the boy happily responds.

"Are you okay?" she asks with watery eyes.

"Yes. Where are we?" the child asks.

"In a very large cavern. We came to get you out of here. Where's your brother?"

"I don't know. He was by the pond a while ago. Where's My Beloved?" Felipe asks.

"She ran off. I don't know where to."

"Oh, what a pity. She said she would bring us new clothes and new toys. What about my mother?"

"Our mom is waiting for you. We have to get out of here as soon as possible."

"What are we going to do with all these children when we get them out?" Acatlel asks Teutli.

"I have no idea. We'll let the council worry about that."

"We have to gather all these children and get out of here as soon as possible. Surely, My Beloved will be coming after us," Ocotlel warns.

"I don't think so," Itzcuauhtzin interrupts. "That witch is on her way to the chieftain's tomb. There is something in that room that catches her attention."

"Even more than Quetzalcoatl's weapons?" Aquetzalli asks.

"Yes. There's a great treasure there. Maybe there's something else that we didn't see. Or maybe she thinks that there are more weapons. I think its best that you take the children out of here, and Xóchitl and I go after her."

"No. It's too dangerous. Plus we also need your help getting these kids out of here. There are too many chaneques everywhere. We can come back later," Aquetzalli exclaims.

"Yes. This will not be so easy. There is a large chaneque army waiting for us up there," Ocotlel explains.

"There must be another way out. We should follow My Beloved's tracks and then find another route. We can't go back by the way we came from," Teutli exclaims.

"Xóchitl, gather up the children. We have to go," Atlanezi orders.

Xóchitl climbs on a wooden bench. "Listen up. We have to get out of this place, so everyone gather up and follow me." The children turn to look at one another in puzzlement.

"And who are you?" one of the bigger kids asks.

"I am Xóchitl, and these are the Pipils. We're going to get you out of here and take you to the surface."

"But we like it here."

"Yes, I know, but it is time to return to your families. Your parents miss you a lot. There are lakes and animals up there."

"My mom. Do you know my mother?" a small child asks.

"No, I don't know her, but once we get out of here, we are going to help you find your parents."

"I want my mommy," one of the newest kids cries.

"I don't know my mom," another one says.

"Listen up. We are going to help you find your parents. But first, we have to get out of here," Xóchitl exclaims.

"What about My Beloved?" an eight-year-old girl asks.

"She's not coming back. She went to find another treasure. Come on everyone, gather up. We'll go through the kitchen," Xóchitl explains.

"Xóchitl! Xóchitl!" Sebastian screams from the back.

"Sebastian!" Xóchitl's screams with great joy.

Gradually all the kids get together and start walking toward the kitchen. Some of them walk with their pets following behind them. Some have dogs, others pigs, some mules and a pair of horses.

"Well, this is going to be harder than I thought," Teutli says. "Atlanezi, you and Acatlel take the rear. The rest of us will go to the front in case that witch reappears. Be very careful."

"Tezcatlipoca!" a ten-year-old indigenous girl exclaims at seeing Itzcuauhtzin with his armor, Chimalli, and weapons.

"Tezcatlipoca?" Itzcuauhtzin asks. The other warriors stare at him up and down.

"Yes. I see it too," Ocotlel answers. "Dressed like that, you look like the god of discord."

The girl kneels before Itzcuauhtzin. "What are you doing? Don't kneel. I'm not Tezcatlipoca. I'm just a Pipil Indian."

"No. You are Tezcatlipoca. I saw you in my dreams. You and Xochiquetzal freed us." The girl stands up. "Only that your face was painted in orange with black stripes across the middle. And you said you would take us back to our homes."

"What's your name?" he asks as the two walk beside each other.

"I am Calixta of the Maya tribe, from the land of Lake Güija."

"How long have you been here?"

Bang!

"Chaneques! Everyone fall back," Teutli cries out from outside the cave after shooting a chaneque. Chilco and his fifty warriors have arrived at the cave at the same time that Teutli and Aquetzalli were directing the children out. Everyone runs back inside the cave except for Xóchitl and a few children who had already exited. They had taken the path to the left, following Sihuehuet's path.

Xóchitl runs with seven girls and nine boys toward the large cave where she had her first encounter with the beautiful lady. "Hide yourself among the stalagmites and make no noise. I'll be right back."

Itzcuauhtzin runs to the door along with his uncles and Acatlel. Teutli has dropped two tables in front of them by the door to use for cover. Aquetzalli and Ocotel have already fired their rifles and have managed to contain the group of chaneques between the stalagmites and around the bend. Acatlel aims at the chaneques, waiting for an opportunity to shoot, while the others reload their rifles and arrows. "How many?" Itzcuauhtzin asks while he readies his bow.

"We don't know. It could be the whole army. There are many more hidden back there, around the bend."

"You better give up, Pipils," Chilco demands in Nahuatl.

"Teutli, what is your plan?" Itzcuauhtzin asks.

"I'm still working on it. I think if we stop them here, we could take the children by that direction." Teutli signals with his head to point to the left side. "Xóchitl managed to escape with several children through there."

"We still have more than thirty here though, and many of them are scared." In the back you can hear several small children crying of fear.

"Where is My Beloved?" Chilco demands.

"They are too many. I don't think we can contain them," Aquetzalli exclaims.

"Anyone else have any ideas?" Teutli asks.

"I got it," Itzcuauhtzin exclaims. "Uncle, do you have any orange paint?"

"Yes. What for? I don't think you have time to paint yourself," Atlanezi explains.

Itzcuauhtzin just smiles at him. "I want to talk to your boss." Itzcuauhtzin responds out loud to the chaneques.

"I'm the boss," Chilco answers.

Xóchitl shows up with her bow at the ready. Teutli signals to her to stay put.

"What's your name?" Itzcuauhtzin asks, trying to buy some time.

"I am Chilco, general of My Beloved's army."

"Okay, Chilco. We have My Beloved's children, and many more surprises, all of them very unpleasant for you."

"Who are you?" Chilco asks.

"I'll come out so you can see me and we can talk face to face. Do not shoot or all this will end badly. Okay?" Itzcuauhtzin paints the finishing touches. He has painted his face orange with a black stripe across his face. *Quetzalcoatl, Tezcatlipoca. Protect me.* The young man takes his macana and locks his spear over his shoulder.

"All right," Chilco responds after thinking about the proposal for a while.

"Are you crazy? They're going to tear you apart," Aquetzalli says.

"I don't think they will. These chaneques love their Beloved. They would not put at risk her most precious treasure." Itzcuauhtzin comes out of the cave with his Chimalli ready to block any attack. "Here I am," the young warrior announces. Xóchitl gets a little closer, giving him a look of confusion and disapproval, but even she can't deny that with his armor and painting, Itzcuauhtzin looks like a formidable warrior. He would even look like a chief, if he only had a crown.

Chilco comes out of hiding. Three more chaneques come out beside him. When he sees the young man, Chilco stops and stares at him up and down. One chaneque immediately kneels down when he sees Itzcuauhtzin's ring. Chilco gets a little closer for a better look. Itzcuauhtzin's ring begins to shine brighter. Chilco looks at him more intensely, trying to see his eyes. More chaneques kneel down before the young warrior. One by one the chaneques begin to come out of hiding after seeing their companions kneeling down.

"Tezcatlipoca!" Chilco exclaims in awe.

Itzcuauhtzin doesn't answer. The Pipils look at each other in disbelief of what they are seeing.

"These children are captives." Itzcuauhtzin exclaims out loud and authoritative. "I will not allow this to continue. No one deserves to be a captive. You are miners and nature conservationists. Why are these children captive?"

Chilco kneels immediately upon seeing Itzcuauhtzin's ring begin to glow stronger, completely covering the young man's body with a radiant light. Jaguar patches form up on his body as if they were tattooed and even the weapons start to glow, including the ordinary macana.

"Forgive me, my Lord. It was not our idea. It was Sihuehuet's idea. She convinced us to help her find Chalchiuhtlicue's bracelet. She was the one who brought these children captive."

"You lie," Itzcuauhtzin interrupts him before Chilco can say anything else. Chilco crouches even lower.

"Forgive me, my Lord. Just command us, my Lord, and we will obey."

Acatlel kneels inside the cave. "What are you doing?" Ocotlel asks him.

"It's Tezcatlipoca," Acatlel answers.

"Are you crazy? It's only Itzcuauhtzin."

"I can't believe it," Teutli says. "This boy is not the same Itzcua we know." With that, he also kneels.

Xóchitl can't believe it either. She looks at the jaguar ring and then at hers, but hers is not shining like Itzcuauhtzin's. Finally all of the chaneques kneel.

Calixta exits the cave and takes Itzcuauhtzin's hand. "Ah!" the girl gasps. "My Beloved is about to do something very bad."

Itzcuauhtzin looks at the little girl and sees that her eyes have gone completely white. "All rise," he commands. "I need you to take these children out of here as soon as possible. I want you to escort my warriors to the surface."

"Yes, my Lord." Chilco rises and bows his head. The rest of the chaneques follow his example.

"Chilco, you're coming with me; I have another task for you."

"Yes, my Lord, as you command." Chilco answers. "Solak, guide these people to the surface," Chilco commands.

"There are many people on their way to the surface. Your army is blocking the exit. Send someone to tell them to let them pass."

"Immediately, my Lord." Chilco answers. "Chales, take five chaneques and your panthers and bring the news to Kompa. This is my ring. Show it as evidence of my direct orders."

"Acatlel, you better go with them in case they reach Ucatl first," Itzcuauhtzin commands.

"But I don't ride on panthers," Acatlel responds.

"Don't worry. Go with Chales, he'll take you on his," Chilco says.

"Excellent," Itzcuauhtzin exclaims. "Teutli, get the children out of here. Xóchitl and I will go after My Beloved."

"No. There's no way I will allow you two to go alone," Teutli responds. "Ocotlel, you and Aquetzalli take care of the children. Atlanezi and I will accompany Tezcatlipoca," Teutli orders.

BRIDGE ON FIRE

The heat becomes unbearable. The lava can be seen a kilometer down the ravine. The air is scarce and the people are tired of jogging. Since they left the main road, they have been walking in a fast pace for over three kilometers. Finally Ucatl stops the crowd and orders everyone to sit along the wall as they investigate the way on the other side. Ocoyatl lies on the floor. Beside him sit two young men who have been carrying him.

"That looks dangerous," a girl says.

"Don't worry, we will all cross together, but we have to make sure the path is clear first," Ucatl explains.

The bridge is nothing more than a Ceiba tree trunk placed over the ridge, and barely a meter wide. The good news is that the gap only measures six meters long. Ucatl, Yanixté, and Yanté cross without any problem and quickly follow the trail to their right. The road becomes narrower with barely enough space for two people. After running for a couple of minutes, the road becomes steep, uphill, and leads into a dark and wider cave. Ucatl draws his green crystal he received from the chaneque and they begin to walk more cautiously.

They have barely walked half of a kilometer when they hear voices. "Throw it, throw it. It's taking you too long. Just throw it."

"Don't rush me, I'm still thinking about the play," answers the second voice.

Yanté gets a little closer to the corner and can now see five chaneques at the end of the trail playing with bones on a rock. "Only five," Yanté whispers. "I think we can take them by surprise."

"The ones above are the most dangerous," Ucatl points at the two chaneques with weapons in their hands. Ucatl puts his bow on the ground and readies his rifle, so does Yanté while Yanixté readies his bow. "I'll take the one on the left," Ucatl whispers.

Bang, bang! The shots hit their target and two chaneques fall to the ground. Yanixté loses his arrow and hits a chaneque on the chest. The rest of the chaneques react and rise quickly. "Don't even think about it." Ucatl points at them with his bow. The chaneques look at the three Pipils and decide to stay still with their hands in the air, showing that they are not armed.

"Yanté, tie them up," Ucatl commands. Yanté immediately takes out a rope and ties the chaneques' feet and hands. "Are there any more chaneques in these parts?" Ucatl asks. A chaneque only nods.

"Okay. Where's the exit?" Ucatl asks.

"Is that brown rock over there," the chaneque beckons toward the door.

"What are you doing here?" Ucatl asks.

"We just came to guard the entrance so that no one goes in or out." Ucatl takes a magic dust bag from the chaneque and draws a rune. The rock opens and daylight enters into the cave.

"It is still daytime," Yanixté exclaims.

"Yanixté, go get the others. Tell them the way is clear and bring everyone here immediately, the injured first." Yanixté takes the crystal from Ucatl and runs through the cave at top speed.

"I'm going to go make sure all is clear out there. I want to be sure that there are no more chaneques," Ucatl exclaims. "Stay with these chaneques here and wait for the rest. It looks like the sun is already setting. That is good. It will help us escape."

"Okay. See if you can figure out which side of the volcano we are at," Yanté responds.

"Help me pass to the other side," Ocoyatl tries to get up. The young men immediately help him stand up.

"We will have to cross sideways," one of them explains. So the two helpers take Ocoyatl supporting his arms on their shoulders and cross the bridge sideways, taking very slow steps. Below they can see the lava flowing slowly and a few bubbles occasionally bursting.

"The chaneques will not take long to come," Juan says. "They should have realized that the prison cells are empty by now."

"Yes. We should start crossing now," Atlahua answers.

"No. We can't cross until we know for sure that the way is clear," Tlacoyotl explains.

"So why are they taking that Pipil to the other side?" a young man asks.

"That is a very stubborn Pipil. He just wants to be on the other side to avoid delaying the others if there is a rush," Tlacoyotl responds.

"Someone is coming," a young man across the bridge exclaims. Everyone stands up, ready to run in any direction. Tlacoyotl runs to the other side of the bridge with rifle in hand. In an instant, Yanixté appears and the people relax.

"Everything is fine. We found the exit. We can cross now," Yanixté announces.

"Great," Tlacoyotl says. "Listen up, everyone. Yanixté will guide you to the exit. I want everyone to carefully cross. We have not come all this way just for someone to fall over. We will cross one by one until all have passed. Wait until the person in front of you has crossed completely. Is that understood?"

"Yes," the crowd answers. Tlacoyotl crosses the bridge to the other side to bring order and starts sending people one by one. Ziquetl and the chaneque are the first to cross.

"Atlahua, please go to the end of the line, bring the news to the others," Atlahua immediately obeys.

"Ocoyatl, the gap becomes very narrow further on. Two people can barely fit. You will have to be very careful to pass. It would be better for them to carry you by the arms and legs so you can pass."

"Okay," Ocoyatl responds. "I think I can take it," the young men take him as Yanixté suggested and follow the young man by the narrow way.

Behind the crowd, Tenoch, Elena, four warriors, and the young volunteers impatiently wait for the crowd to move or the chaneque army to come for them. "They are moving," Elena exclaims.

"It was about time," Tlanextic responds.

"Tenoch, get down from there. They are moving now," Elena calls.

"I'll come down in a moment. I think I see movement up there," the child responds from the top of a stalagmite.

"Let me see," Tlanextic exclaims and climbs up next to Tenoch.

"I don't see anything."

"Let's go. They are moving," Elena exclaims.

"You go; we'll stay here to make sure no one follows. Tenoch, you go with them," Tlanextic orders.

"I'm staying with you," Atlahua offers when he reaches the end of the line.

The line starts moving faster. Most people keep crossing smoothly. There are a couple of them who walk very slowly and sometimes have to hold someone's hands to get across, but nothing major.

"Chaneques!" Tenoch warns. Two panthers appear at the top of the road, but they stop.

"Only two," Tlanextic says. "Stay here. I'm going down."

The news of chaneques runs very fast through the crowd, and the people become impatient. "Hurry up," a very distressed girl shouts. Several of them start to push their peers to hurry them. "What is it? Stop pushing. We're all going to cross," Tlacoyotl demands.

"The chaneques," a young man answers. On hearing the news, those who have already crossed start running, giving the news to the rest of them.

"Why don't they attack?" Elena asks.

"Maybe they are only scouts," Atlahua answers.

"Form a line here," Tlanextic commands. "We're going to protect these people. If these chaneques decide to attack, they won't have it easy. The road is very narrow and they cannot attack all at once. It will be easier to defend this pass. Tenoch, what do you see?"

"I see only two. They are not moving. They are just watching us."

"The line is moving faster. Elena, please go with them," Tlanextic tells her.

"Tenoch, get down from there. Let's go."

"No, wait. There's more chaneques. Like a dozen more panthers just arrived," Tenoch reports.

"Okay. Get down and go with your mom," Tlanextic orders him.

"But I can help."

"Yes, but you better give your bow to someone else. This battle will be much stronger than the previous."

"This is not fair. I am a Pipil warrior too," the boy complains.

"Don't argue with me. Obey," very upset, the child gets off his stalagmite and gives his bow and arrows to a young man.

"They are moving very slowly. Why?" Atlahua asks.

"I don't know. Maybe they think we are a lot more. Guys, those of you with shirts, take them off and paint stripes on your chests, and your faces as well. I want them to think that we are a large army. I will try to negotiate with them to gain time," the young men quickly obey and start painting themselves with paint that the other warriors brought. With the paint and weapons they took from the previous battle, the twenty young men look like true warriors.

The chaneques get a little closer; a pair of panthers are still roaring. Tlanextic decides to take two steps forward. "I want to talk to your leader," the warrior demands. "I'll leave my weapons here as a sign of good faith."

A chaneque climbs down from his panther. "I am the leader. My name is Kompa," he shouts and walks down to meet the Pipil.

"I am Tlanextic from the Pipil tribe. What do you want from us?" he asks as he walks over to meet the chaneque.

"I think you know what we want. You have something that belongs to us," Kompa answers.

"No. These people don't belong to you. These people are free and are no one's property."

"You have to return them. If you don't, this floor will be painted with color red," Kompa threatens.

"It will also be painted in purple."

"I have a large army behind me. You have no way out."

"You're wrong. Just like your colleagues did a while ago. Or didn't you find their bodies? I also I have an army behind me," Tlanextic responds.

Kompa looks at the Pipil army and at the group of warriors with firearms. All young people are standing with their chest up; spears, shields, bows, and painted faces. "Yaoquizqueh?" Kompa asks.

"Cuachicqueh," Tlanextic responds. "All experts in the art of war."

"You are trapped. You can't leave. What's your plan? To live here in the back of the volcano? You'll never survive. It would be better to come back with us. We could come to an agreement."

Tlanextic doesn't answer; he just stares at the bulky chaneque. "Wait a minute," the warrior finally exclaims and walks back over to his warriors. Tlanextic huddles. "Have they all crossed yet?" he asks in low voice.

"Not yet. But almost," a young man answers.

"Very good. This chaneque thinks there's no other exit, or he is trying to deceive me."

"What are you thinking of doing? Are we going to fight them or are they going to let us go?" a warrior asks.

"They're not going to let us go, that's for sure, but they want to negotiate our surrender. I will continue to talk with him for a while. Let me know when they all have crossed," Tlanextic walks back. "What do you propose?" he asks Kompa.

"If you let the people go back with us, we will let the Pipils leave without harm."

"That's all you offer? I think it's better if we paint these walls in purple."

"I have no authority to offer something better. But if you come with us, I promise you will be treated well."

"Who has that authority?" the Pipil asks, ignoring the chaneque's offer.

"My Beloved and My General."

"Bring your General so we can talk then."

"My General is not available. And My Beloved is very busy at the moment."

"Well, I need to talk to someone who can offer me something better. If not, many chaneques will die today, and you will not recover your slaves. These people prefer to jump into the ravine, onto that lava before giving up and continue to be slaves."

"Don't threaten me Pipil. You're not in that position," Kompa angrily demands.

"I don't think the negotiations are going well," Atlahua says. The warriors prepare their rifles.

Tlanextic takes a step back. "Think well on what you're going to do. I have a lot of people, and you know well how dangerous we are," Tlanextic turns to look back, and a boy beckons at him signaling that everything is ready. Tlanextic starts walking backward slowly.

"Where are you going?" Kompa asks.

"To wait, while someone goes out and calls your superior to negotiate a truce. Don't worry, I have no hurry," Tlanextic answers.

Kompa looks around but sees nothing unusual. It's a very small area with a ravine to the left full of lava. To his right, there is a large and smooth wall. The few stalagmites around are too small. He looks at the Pipils and realizes that most of them carry chaneques' weapons, not Pipils'. "Okay. Wait a while. I'll send someone with a message," Kompa offers and retreats.

"What happened?" Olontetl, one of the Pipil warriors, asks.

"I don't think he bought it. Get ready to run. But first, we have to shoot the panthers first. They are the fastest. Wait until they make the first move."

"They're lying," Kompa tells his subjects. "I don't think they have that many warriors. Most of them carry our weapons. I think those are the slaves."

"Even so, they are still a lot," one of them comments.

"I don't think so. Maybe around the bend they have more people, but I haven't seen any movement back there. Who has a map? I need to see where this trail leads to."

"There's no need. This trail leads to the bottom of the volcano, all the way down to the lava lake and the boiling river," one chaneque answers.

"Yes, but there is a bridge that leads up to the east side exit of the volcano and is just half a kilometer from that bend," another soldier adds.

"We should go after them then," another chaneque exclaims.

"Cheaters, they were just trying to buy time. After them!" Kompa commands. The riders climb on their panthers with their weapons ready.

"They are moving," Atlahua exclaims.

"Now!" Tlanextic shouts. Five shots hit directly into five panthers and they fall to the ground. The young people immediately start running at full speed toward the bridge.

"After them!" Kompa, who is now without a panther, commands again and runs after the Pipils. The road is so narrow that two chaneques are pushed over the canyon by the ferocious panthers.

The Pipil warriors shoot their arrows against the panthers, momentarily halting the chaneques advance, but the rest of them are still coming and in half a minute they will be on them. The youngsters finally finish crossing. "Hurry up," one of them shouts, and between all of them, they form a defensive line, using their shields to cover themselves from the attacks.

"We have to drop the bridge," Tlanextic orders. Two youngsters bury their spears between under the trunk, ready to push the bridge into the void.

The Pipil warriors run to the bridge. A couple of spears pass very close to the warriors as they cross but cause no damage. Only Tlanextic has stayed behind shooting arrows. The warriors turn around and start firing from the other side of the bridge. "Tlanextic, now!" a young man shouts. Tlanextic runs over the bridge. A lance passed so close to him that it manages to rub his left leg. Tlanextic's body falters and heads straight into the void. Using his right leg for support, he jumps to the edge of the ravine. A young man grabs him by the arms safely, avoiding the warrior's death.

Three young men take over the defense and cover his teammates with their shields so that they can push the bridge. The warriors continue to heavily shoot against the chaneques, who have been hampered by three dead panthers and against a couple of chaneques that have been hiding behind them.

The bridge is finally thrown down to the ravine between all four youngsters. The trunk falls on the lava, sets itself on fire, and then sinks. "Let's go," Tlanextic orders and starts running toward the exit. The youngsters run after him, leaving Atlahua and three warriors behind covering their retreat.

Upon reaching the first bend, Tlanextic and Tlacoyotl stop to cover the rest, while the rest run. One chaneque tries jumping with his panther to the other side, but by the weight of the chaneque and his weapons, the panther barely puts its front paws on the ground but is unable to sustain itself and falls to the ravine with the chaneque on his back. Other chaneques climb down from their panthers and jump to the other side without any effort.

"Tlanextic, let's go. There must be a better place where we can defend ourselves up there," Olontetl exclaims. Tlanextic shoots one more arrow and runs after the others.

The chaneques keep jumping the gap without difficulty. While further up ahead, the people have started to exit the volcano, and several have started pushing again.

"What's going on?" Ucatl asks.

"The chaneques are coming right behind us," a girl answers.

"To the river." Ucatl points out and enters the cave whichever way he can.

"Yanixté, guide these people to the other side of the river."

"Immediately, sir. Follow me," he yells to the people and runs in front of them. The river is about two kilometer downhill which helps the tired people put some distance between their pursuers. The woods are thick and still damp from last night's rain. It's getting darker by the minute, making it harder to see. But at that moment, that's the least of Yanixté's problems, as he has just inherited a great responsibility.

"Yanté, come with me," both warriors run back to the ravine. They encounter the youngsters first.

"How many?" Ucatl asks.

"The entire chaneque army," Atlahua responds without stopping. Tlanextic is the last to arrive. Behind him, the chaneques have already begun to enter the darkness of the cave. Ucatl and Yanté fire against them, wounding two chaneques. That makes the rest of them stop. The Pipils recede slowly, walking backward while reloading their rifles, and fires them one at a time, not letting the chaneques enter freely.

The youngsters come to the exit but the exit is already closed, and they don't know how to open it. "Yanté, open the door," Ucatl orders. Yanté runs up with a magic dust bag and opens the door for the young people to exit, and finally the warriors also exit, leaving Ucatl last. The chaneques run up to the door, but Yanté shoots again, critically injuring a chaneque that was at the front just before the door closes.

The chaneques stop at the door. No one dares to go out for fear of being shot by the Pipils. "Come on," one of them shouts from behind.

"If you want to be the first, then go ahead and pass," one of them answers.

"What's going on here?" Kompa asks when he finally reaches the exit.

"The Pipils are outside and they have guns. This gate is too narrow. We would be killed one by one without any problems," a warrior answers.

"Worse things will Chilco do to you if you don't go through that door. Also, do you think that these Pipils will stay to wait for us? They don't have enough ammo for that. Exit immediately," Kompa orders.

The chaneques open the door with great fear, covering themselves with their shields. Not seeing anyone, everyone starts exiting one by one, like ants out of an anthill, just in time to see the sun setting on the other side of the mountain.

The crack is very narrow and dark. Sihuehuet has to duck to get through several places. "This is it," Sihuehuet announces at reaching the top of the gap. "The cave is up there. Those kids were here. We have to climb."

"I'm going to go investigate, My Beloved," Chilco exclaims. The old chaneque jumps over the wall without using the rope that the Quetzalcoatl's warriors left behind. He supports his legs on the wall on the left and pushed to the right, jumping from wall to wall, all the way up to the top. Sihuehuet takes the rope and climbs up more slowly.

"This is the cave, My Beloved. Look how many runes. There are so many I have never even seen. This is wonderful."

"Let's find the Mayan calendar; that's what the girl used to enter."

"No wonder we couldn't locate it. Look how many Mayan symbols—— Olmec, Aztec, and Toltec's. This is incredible. It is designed to keep intruders out. It will take a very powerful shaman to open it," Chilco says.

"No. We just need some Mayan blood. Look, here's the key," Sihuehuet points to the image of a sacrifice.

"Then we just need to sacrifice a Mayan to use their blood. That's good. That means that those brats are Mayan not Pipil," Chilco exclaims.

"No. Those kids are mixed. Their mother is Mayan and their father is Pipil," Sihuehuet explains, while pulling a small knife from her bag.

"I would give anything to know what's inside," Chilco exclaims.

Sihuehuet cuts her finger and let a few blood drops fall on the calendar. The center of the calendar moves inward and a weak and tiny light flows from the calendar. Then Sihuehuet approaches the graph of Quetzalcoatl and tries to move the bow just like Xóchitl did. The whole image of Quetzalcoatl releases an immense light of fire. The rest of the hieroglyphics lit up with a big and bright light, illuminating the entire cave.

"By Tezcatlipoca! What kind of blood do you have in your veins?" Chilco asks. Sihuehuet just smiles at him without answering the obvious.

THE CALENDAR'S SECRET

The singing of crickets, owls, and the howling of coyotes kill the silence of the night. The wind is the only one who has decided to rest while the full moon hides amidst a couple of clouds. The chaneques relax among the trees, and a group of them have fallen asleep, while a couple of them try to woo the moon with a soft and melancholic melody—— product of their flutes.

Kumara gave orders to remain silent, but the sun has set more than an hour ago and there are no signs of Pipils anywhere. Even the road is empty. If not for the cry of the coyotes, the chaneques would feel desolate. At least there is a pair of rabbits that still lies roasting on the slow fire.

"This is going to be a long night," Kumara says.

"Do you think Chilco found the Pipils that slipped through?" Tokis asks.

"Yes, I think so. But they are going to leave us here until morning for sure. Did you erase the Pipil's tracks, like I ordered?"

"Yes, sir. We destroyed the camp and filled it with dry leaves. That place looks virgin."

"Excellent work."

"Do you want some coffee?" Tokis asks.

"Coffee? What is that?"

"It's a drink that humans make out of beans. It's really good, but humans sweeten it with sugar. But I like it better without it.

Besides, we don't have any sugar."

"And how did you get it?"

"In Tecupán Ishatcu. We visited a farm that is starting to grow coffee trees. They have a few barns and mills, that's where they prepare it. We brought a full sack. My squad and I have been drinking it for a few days. Drink up, you'll feel much better after you've taken it."

Kumara takes the cup and tries the coffee. "It's hot," he complains. "But it's very good."

"Ha ha. You will like it more than firewater. And this one won't daze you. It'll energize you. I think it's the drink of the gods."

"That's what you said about the firewater."

"Yes, but that was before trying the coffee," Tokis responds. Suddenly the cave starts to open and the chaneques stand up with weapons ready.

"Kumara, Tokis. Niltze," Solak salutes.

"Niltze," the patrollers greet back. "What news?"

"Great news," Solak answers. "Tezcatlipoca has visited us tonight."

"Tezcatlipoca?" both warriors answer at the same time.

"Yes. He appeared to us in the children's garden and ordered us to free the slaves. Chilco is with him at this very moment."

"And why would Tezcatlipoca come to visit us?"

"Well, it seems that he doesn't approve of My Beloved's plans. And at this very moment, he is looking for her. For now, he has ordered us to free the slaves and the children."

"And how do you know he is not an impostor?" Kumara asks suspiciously.

"Because I saw him with my own eyes. His body transformed into a leopard man in front of the whole army. At first, he seemed as a very young boy. But then he turned into a strong warrior with leopard patches all over his body. He has magical weapons and a powerful ring. Also, My Beloved fled from him."

"This is unbelievable," Kumara answers. "Are you sure you didn't dream it?"

"Of course not."

"Then it's true. Tezcatlipoca is among us," Tokis exclaims.

"Yes. And he is very angry. His eyes were like fire. I thought he was going to incinerate us."

"And where are the children and slaves now?" Tokis asks.

"The children are with us, but they are walking slowly. I don't know about the slaves though. The last time we heard of them, they were being chased by Kompa and the rest of the army. Chale went looking for them to let them know," Solak responds.

"What do we do with the children then? Do we leave them here alone or what?" Kumara asks.

"No. A couple of Pipils are coming with us. They'll take care of them. But we have orders to guard them until morning or until Chilco returns."

Kumara leaves the cave with a face full of concern. "Listen up, everyone. Our orders have changed."

"Everyone, to the river. Don't let anyone get to the road. Ready your blowguns," Kompa orders. The chaneques immediately use their speed and quickly spread themselves over the sides.

Across the river, the Pipils relax for a moment not seeing chaneques behind them. Most people take the opportunity to drink some water and recover from the hot volcano.

Four young people are still trying to cross with Ocoyatl on their shoulders. "Leave me here. Save yourselves." He had told the young warriors, but they insisted in carrying him. "No one is left behind. All or none," the boys had responded. That did not soothe the warrior's heart. He was conscious and convinced that he would die anyways. He couldn't feel his ribs anymore. Maybe it was that the pain was gone, or that his nerves had given up. The only thing Ocoyatl was sure of was that he would soon see a white horse coming for him.

"Ucatl, what is the plan?" Tlacoyotl asks.

"I don't know. I never thought we'd make it this far. I thought maybe once we were out, these chaneques wouldn't follow us anymore, but it is already nighttime. If it were daytime, they might not pursue us, but with it being dark, I'm sure they will try. What do you think?"

"We cannot fight them. They're too many, and we don't have any advantage. I think it'd be best to head for the main road and we head toward Tecupan Ishatcu. It is the nearest town."

"Sounds good."

"Ucatl, you have to get these people out of here," Elena cries out when approaching the warriors. "The chaneques won't take long to come. There are many people who are thinking about running away, and I think a few already fled down the river."

"No. We have to keep the people together. Make sure no one gets separated. If the chaneques don't get them, the coyotes for sure will."

"And what about Teutli and the others?" Tlacoyotl asks.

"They are no longer within reach. They depend on Itzcuauhtzin and Xóchitl now."

"Itzcuauhtzin and Xóchitl? They are just kids," Tlacoyotl exclaims.

"Do not underestimate them. If you had seen what they can do, you'd have a lot more faith in them," Teutli responds.

"Faith? I only have faith in God."

"Yes, let's trust that God will protect them," Elena says, extremely worried about her family.

The boys finally cross the river with Ocoyatl. "How do you feel?" Tenoch asks at seeing the warrior in a very bad shape.

"Very good. Couldn't be better," the warrior lies. "What about Ziquetl?"

"Ziquetl is talking with the chaneque. They both love sweets," Tenoch answers. "Don't worry, my grandmother will cure you.

I've seen her heal worse wounds."

"Thanks, Tenoch. I think I owe you my life."

"Why do you say that?"

"Yanixté told me that it was one of your arrows that killed that panther. If it wasn't for you, I would be with Quetzalcoatl right now."

"Don't mention it. Did you see Xóchitl and Itzcua?"

"Yes. They saved me the first time. I think I owe my life to you all."

"Don't worry. How did they look? Is it true they have magical weapons?"

"I think so. Xóchitl's bow is wonderful. Itzcua has an impenetrable Ichcahuipilli that makes him look almost like a chief."

"What's an Ichcahuipilli?"

"It's an ancient armor worn by ancient warriors."

"I saw them just two days ago, and it seems that it's been an eternity."

"Ahhhhhh!" the crowd shouts.

"What's the matter?" Ucatl asks, but when he stands up, he realizes that they are surrounded by chaneques. Several of them are still on their panthers. A young couple who had fled lie on the ground at the chaneques' feet. Ucatl looks around and there are chaneques everywhere, even up on the tree branches.

"It's over," Kompa announces. "You are surrounded. You better give up."

Ucatl looks at the people. Most of them are still gathering in the middle of the woods.

"I'm not going back to that miserable place," Atlahua cries out and raises his rifle to shoot at Kumara, but a dart hits him on the back. Atlahua feels his whole body turn on fire, his blood boils and loses his legs' strength. His body hits the ground, but not before his eyes turn off.

"No!" Elena shouts and runs to his aid, but before she can get there, a dart hits her in the chest.

The hollow and accusive eyes of Topiltzin Acxitl observe her, as Sihuehuet inspected his suit. "This is not his armor. This one is only a replica. The crown is original, but it's almost disintegrated."

"Unbelievable. I never thought we'd find it," Notchím exclaims.

"The best thing that could have happened to us was for those Pipils to discover us. Help me find the coffer," Sihuehuet orders.

"There are many coffers here. How do you know which one it is?"

"It's silver, with Mayan runes." Sihuehuet keeps looking behind the throne, while Notchím is still admiring the calendar.

"This calendar is huge. It must have taken a long time to see it completed," Notchím says, then keeps looking at the walls and studying the runes. "This is Mayan magic. The Pipils must have gotten along with them very well to allow them to do all this."

"Want to help me find the coffer?" Sihuehuet complains from a corner.

"Maybe it's not here. Those kids could have moved it or hidden it," Notchím answers while reviewing the other skeletons. "These were the foremost warriors—Tlacateccatl and Tlamani, all of them. It seems as if they are giving tribute to the king. But at the same time..." The old wizard does not finish his sentence. The direction in which they are looking at is not toward the chief but toward the calendar.

"At same time what?" Sihuehuet asks as she turns over another coffer full of jewels and obsidian stones over.

"They are not offering tribute. They are looking at the calendar, like waiting for something."

"Waiting?"

"Yes. Waiting for something. Maybe they are pointing at the time of a prophecy or something else." The sorcerer runs to the throne and begins to inspect the calendar. Knocking and listening closely, reading runes and hieroglyphs, while Sihuehuet keeps looking for the coffer. Finally, she moves to the other side of the cave and starts searching.

"My Beloved, I think this is another door. The bracelet may be in here."

"Let me see." Sihuehuet abandons her search and runs alongside Notchím. "No, I don't think so. If the brats had opened this door, there would be dust everywhere." Sihuehuet reopens her wound and drops a couple of drops of blood on one of the runes. This one shines a bit and then goes off.

"It didn't work."

"If it were a door it wouldn't be so easy to open. Besides, what could be behind it? More obsidian and gold? The kids found those weapons here. That, and the bracelet. What else could be in there? I don't think it's a door."

"You're right. Maybe it's nothing." Notchím responds, resigning to his task. He turns to see the warriors and their weapons. "Why would these guards be here?" he asks himself. "I've never heard of a chief who was buried with his guards. I think they are protecting something."

"Protecting? They are dead. For sure they were dead before they were put in here. They were put here for their importance and for the honor they earned when they were alive. Surely they were heroes, and the Pipils and Mayans decided to grant them the honor of being buried here."

"What do you know about this cave?" Notchím asks.

"Nothing. Only that the bracelet is here." Sihuehuet responds, trying to sound as innocent as possible. But Notchím's suspicions are too well advanced by now, and he knows that Sihuehuet is hiding something from him.

"Here it is," Sihuehuet joyfully exclaims, removing a couple of old blankets and discovering the silver coffer.

Notchím moves quickly to see the famous coffer. "We have to open it. Let me see. Here I have blue powder."

"That doesn't work. This is not a chaneque spell, it's a Mayan spell," Sihuehuet explains.

"Then open it." Sihuehuet touches the coffer with her hands and tries to open it, but it doesn't budge."

"With blood," Notchím suggests.

Sihuehuet ignores him and recites a spell in Nahuatl and the coffer opens up slowly, emanating bluish light between its bars. "Ah!" Sihuehuet exclaims with great joy and ecstasy. Sihuehuet takes the clothes out of the silver coffer, and there in the middle of it all lies Chalchiuhtlicue's bracelet. Without wasting time,

Sihuehuet takes it and puts it on her left arm. The bracelet's jade stones sparkle and Sihuehuet stands up.

"How do you feel?" Notchím excitedly asks.

"Excellent," Sihuehuet exclaims. She raises her hands and looks at the walls, as if studying the hieroglyphics. Then her gaze fixes on the calendar and walks toward it.

Notchím looks inside the coffer but can't find anything more than clothing and a jade mask. Sihuehuet taps the calendar and through the bracelet's magic she can see what's inside. "This is not a simple calendar." Sihuehuet touches the stone and the bracelet shines with great force. The more the bracelet shines, the brighter the calendar gets. The light becomes as bright as the sun. The light completely covers the entire tomb and envelops Sihuehuet. Notchím can't see anything else. Everything is too bright.

A strong earthquake takes over the hill. The tremor can be felt throughout the Cuzcatleco territory all the way to Escuintla. The calendars in the crypts of every Mayan pyramid lit up simultaneously.

In the tomb, the stones that form the calendar fall one by one, discovering another huge and dark cave. This cave is at least ten times larger than Topiltzin Acxitl's tomb. The calendar's light ceases to exist and finally Notchím can see Sihuehuet in her shining robes. Sihuehuet walks up into the cave. Notchím gets up and runs after her. The darkness is overwhelming, but that's no problem for Notchím. The chaneques can see very well in the dark. They also have a kind of bat-like radar touch.

"Do you know what this place is?" Notchím asks when he finally catches up to the beautiful lady, but Sihuehuet doesn't answer. She just keeps walking among the rubble, searching for something. Deeper in the center of the cave, they finally find a stone sarcophagus full of runes and Mayan hieroglyphs. Notchím studies them but what stops his heart is a word written in large Letters: ITZALKU. "Itzalku! No. By god! My Beloved, we have to leave this place. Itzalku is buried here—— the ancient demon that almost destroyed the palace of the gods!"

"Silence," Sihuehuet commands, and begins to recite an ancient spell. The sarcophagus starts to open with great rumble.

"My Beloved, please don't. This monster could destroy everything. There is nothing that can stop him," Notchím begs, but Sihuehuet is not listening and keeps reciting her spell. Gradually the sarcophagus runes begin to light up and continuously shine. The sarcophagus lid rises up, emanating light from within, illuminating the cave completely. Notchím decides to take a couple of steps back. As the sarcophagus keeps on opening, Notchím continues to take small steps backward. Finally, the lid opens up completely and falls over to the left. Notchím fixed his eyes on the sarcophagus. The light ceases to exist and Sihuehuet elevates herself into mid air and enters the sarcophagus.

Notchím waits a couple of minutes and nothing happens. He finally decides to approach the sarcophagus, very slowly regaining his courage, and takes a few steps forward. Little by little he leans from afar to see inside as if he was standing on the edge of a cliff. It's dark inside the sarcophagus, but Notchím can still see the steps that descend into the depths of the volcano.

The cave is empty by the time the warriors get there, but the tacks of Sihuehuet and Notchím are everywhere. "This is the place," Itzcuauhtzin announces. "Sihuehuet must be inside."

"Inside where?" Teutli asks.

"The tomb is behind this wall," Xóchitl responds.

"I thought this was the tomb," Atlanezi says.

"No. This is only the door." *Open.* Itzcuauhtzin's ring shines and the door opens. The warriors immediately take their weapons and war positions, including Chilco.

"You did not use blood," Xóchitl comments. "That's good. You are learning to use your magic." Itzcuauhtzin just smiles and enters the crypt.

"Xóchitl, look. The calendar." Itzcuauhtzin points out.

"It was destroyed. That must have been the earthquake we felt," Xóchitl responds.

"What kind of place is this?" Acatlel asks.

"I think it's a crypt." Teutli answers.

"A crypt?"

"Yes, a crypt. Like the one the Mayans use to build within their pyramids to bury their kings," Teutli answers.

"My beloved was here for sure," Chilco exclaims.

"Chilco?" A thick and tired voice exclaims. All warriors turn in the voice's direction with their rifles ready.

"Notchím," Chilco responds and walks over to the old wizard who lies hidden behind some jars of gold. "What happened here? Where is My Beloved?" the General asks. The kids approach them while the other warriors inspect the site, making sure that there is no danger.

"My Beloved found Itzalku's prison."

"Itzalku!" All respond at once in great amazement and disbelief.

"Yes. I think this crypt is the beast's prison. That's why there are celestial weapons and magical items—— to keep that monster imprisoned. My Beloved found Chalchiuhtlicue's bracelet and she managed to break the spell on the calendar that was there." Notchím points to the hole behind the chief's throne. "And I think she is on her way to Itzalku's prison to free him."

"Why would My Beloved unleash that monster?" Chilco asks.

"I do not know, but I think that's what she wanted all along. She deceived us, Chilco. She just used us for her own selfish purpose. The gods must be angry with us." Notchím turns to look at Itzcuauhtzin from head to toe. "You must be Tezcatlipoca's sent. You have all of his qualities. I hope you have the power to contain that beast."

"Who is Itzalku?" Itzcuauhtzin asks innocently.

"You never heard of Itzalku?" Xóchitl asks, but it's more of a reprimand than a question.

"No," the boy answers.

"Itzalku," Notchím begins, "was a powerful god. He was one of Tezcatlipoca's sons—— a very strong and handsome god. He fell in love with Yeisun's girlfriend, Sihuehuet."

"You mean My Beloved?" Chilco interrupts.

"Yes. My Beloved had a romance with Yeisun, son of Tlaloc. Sihuehuet's beauty was too much for Itzalku to resist. Sihuehuet had many lovers though. The legend says that Yeisun found out about her betrayal and he confronted Itzalku. Yeisun was a much more powerful god though. He had control of the wind and water. Itzalku was no match for him and barely escaped alive, but Yeisun wanted to kill him and persecuted him without rest. Itzalku was afraid and sought Sihuehuet's help. Sihuehuet made him a potion that would transform him into a big and powerful beast. She combined Tezcatlipoca's and Quetzalcoatl's powers, and promised him that he would be as powerful as the creators, but the potion did not work as they thought it would. Instead, it transformed him into a two headed beast. Itzalku felt all powerful, but he couldn't control the power and it took control of his mind. All of Itzalku's wits were lost to him and he became more beast than god. With his new and increased powers, he went to the palace to look for Yeisun. He defeated Yeisun easily. The guards tried to contain him, but even with all of their mighty weapons they weren't able to stop him. It wasn't till Tezcatlipoca and Quetzalcoatl got involved, that the beast was defeated. By then he had destroyed most of the palace."

"What happened to Yeisun?" Chilco asks.

"Yeisun survived, but he was so angry at Sihuehuet that he decided to banish her from the kingdom. But before she left, Sihuehuet poisoned his drink and when he drank it, he also turned into a big beast, just like Itzalku did, except that he was much more powerful and gigantic. He also lost his wits and tried to destroy everything. The gods and the guards fought fervently one of the hardest battles in history to try to contain him. Tlaloc did not want the beast destroyed, since it was his son. So they locked him up in a prison."

"Why didn't they destroy Itzalku?" Itzcuauhtzin asks.

"Same reason. Tezcatlipoca intervened. So they both were imprisoned. What I didn't know was that Itzalku was imprisoned here on earth, and that's why My Beloved wanted the bracelet—— to set him free."

"But why?" Xóchitl asks.

"Because she loves him, because she wants vengeance; I'm not sure, my dear."

"We must not allow her to free him," Itzcuauhtzin demands.

"My Beloved's powers have increased tremendously," Notchím points out. "She is much faster and stronger. I saw her rise into the air and move very fast without touching the ground. Only heavenly warriors can fight her."

"In that case, Itzcua and I are going to go after her," Xóchitl responds.

"My dear child," Notchím exclaims. "You are the living reincarnation of Xochiquetzal."

"Xochiquetzal? The goddess of beauty?" Aquetzalli asks.

"Among other things, but she's also a great warrior. Take this, my child. You must wear this." Notchím takes one of the garments from the silver coffer that My Beloved had set aside and gives it to Xóchitl. "It's an old garment that will protect you, just like your brother's armor. They are impenetrable by human weapons, but their runes have powers that will protect you against supernatural attacks from the Transcendental World." Notchím explains.

"I don't think it fits me," Xóchitl responds.

"Do it, Xóchitl. Quickly, we don't have time to waste." Itzcuauhtzin orders. Xóchitl takes the dress and runs to a private dark place behind some jars full of jewels.

"Come on," Teutli commands from behind Topiltzin's throne. The other warriors run after him, including Chilco. Itzcuauhtzin is the only one who does not attend to his call.

"If you know anything that can help me defeat My Beloved or beat that monster, you better tell me now," Itzcuauhtzin demands.

"No. I really don't know much about Itzalku's powers. I don't know how powerful your weapons would be against him. But they should work fine against Sihuehuet. She is mortal, not a goddess anymore. If you can catch up to her, do not hesitate to shoot her in the heart. It's the only thing that can kill her. Although with the bracelet, her powers have increased so much that the wound caused by your sister has already healed."

"Ready," Xóchitl announces. "How do I look?" They both turn to look at her and their eyes open up wider than normal.

"Extraordinary!" Itzcuauhtzin says. "You look like a Pipil princess."

"Goddess," Notchím corrects. "Your beauty is beyond comparison, my child." Notchím takes an old bandana with a jade stone in the middle, adorned with Mayan runes and color patterns. Notchím approaches her and places it on her head. "This is the bandana of wisdom. It will help you see and understand hidden secrets."

"If these clothes have powers, why didn't Sihuehuet take them when she was here?" Xóchitl Asks.

"Because she doesn't need them. She just needs Chalchiuhtlicue's bracelet. The bracelet has enough power to let her get into the very same god's realm, if she desires."

"By Tlaloc! Let's go," Itzcuauhtzin implores. "We must catch up to that witch as soon as possible."

"I'm coming with you," Notchím exclaims. "If this will be my last day on this world, it better be with honor and not as a coward," Notchím exclaims.

The warriors are still waiting by the sarcophagus. "It's dark in there," Teutli says when the kids finally arrive.

"All right, gentlemen. This is the end of the road for you. From here on, only Xóchitl and I will continue forward," Itzcuauhtzin exclaims.

"There's no way. I am the General of the chaneques, and My Beloved is my responsibility," Chilco responds.

"And I'm Tlacateccatl Pipil. I'm going with you," Teutli adds.

"And you're crazy if you think I'm going to let my nephews go alone after a witch and an old monster. I would never forgive myself," Aquetzalli exclaims.

"Okay then, let's not waste any time," Acatlel smiles.

LAKE OF FIRE

The air is scarce and the suffocating air fills every corner of the cavern with steam. The rivers of lava running in branches are responsible for illuminating the place. Thousands of stalactites on the ceiling of the cave drip water, which vaporizes instantly as they fall on the lava lake.

Sihuehuet looks around, but there's no sign of any prisons in this side of the river, so she decides to rise and float to the other side, on an island formed from a gigantic rock surrounded by the lake of lava. The beautiful woman descends bare feet on the seething rock and her feet instantly start to smoke, but for Sihuehuet that kind of pain doesn't exist. She rises to the top of the rock discovering a small plateau with thousands of ancient runes completely covering the surface. In the middle, she can see the face of Tlaloc and a feathered serpent. "My love," the beautiful lady whispers. "It's time to come out of your prison." Sihuehuet studies the runes and starts reciting a spell.

"My Beloved, noooooooooo!" Notchím shouts from the other side of the river, the Pipils behind him, but Sihuehuet has entered a meditative trance and can't hear him. Sihuehuet raises her arms and a soft blue light covers her entire body and begins to cover the area where Sihuehuet is standing. The light continues to advance, covering the entire island. The top surface starts to crack, releasing a red light from inside. Sihuehuet rises into the air to prevent from falling.

Xóchitl shoots an arrow against Sihuehuet, but it bounces off Sihuehuet's light and falls into the lava lake. Xóchitl tries again but without success. "By Tlaloc! It's not working," Xóchitl groans. The ground begins to shake again, but this time the quake is stronger. The chaneques on the surface can feel it as well and stagger. Part of the Lamatepeque hill crumbles inward into its crater. Many stalactites fall from the ceiling on the Pipil warriors. Luckily, none of them get hurt.

The surface of the island finally crumbles and two giant manlike guards rise from the depths of the island, their bodies made of solid stone and lava. Their heads are Olmec stone heads, with thick lips and gigantic helmets. Burning fire veins run through their bodies, like burning brands just like their eyes.

The guardians attack Sihuehuet with their spears, trying to prevent her from entering the island. But Sihuehuet floats away from them rising to the top of the cave, without losing her concentration. The bracelet continues to glow stronger.

The guards jump but can't reach her, making the ground shake as they fall back down. One of them looks at the Pipil warriors and immediately runs to them, jumping over the lava on top of stones. The last river has no stones but the guard gets into the river, warming his body without burning.

"By Tlaloc! Let's go." Atlanezi shouts while firing his shotgun against the guardian without causing any harm. "They are made out of stone."

Xóchitl shoots the guard, burying her bolt in his chest and momentarily stopping its progress. Teutli and the rest fire on the guard without success.

Tezcatlipoca! Itzcuauhtzin's ring begins to glow, covering him with jaguar patches. The young man takes his spear in his hand and runs toward the giant. "We're friends," the young warrior explains in Nahuatl. "We've come to stop Sihuehuet," The guard looks at the teen and kneels on one leg.

Sihuehuet's body gets completely covered in light. The guard closest to her hurls his spear at her, but it crashes against Sihuehuet's light and falls down to the lava lake without causing any damage. Sihuehuet's arms point toward the crater of the island and a beam of light shoots out of her body, illuminating the entire island once again. The light beam enters the crater, and an even stronger earthquake gets activated, knocking stalactites from the ceiling and the island starts erupting lava and rocks.

The children are crying of fear. The whole camp has turned to chaos. The chaneques try to calm them down, but most kids are more scared of them that the earthquake itself.

"By Tlaloc! What's going on in there?" Aquetzalli wonders out loud. It had been about half an hour since they came out of the caverns and the children were still afraid. With the earthquake, fear had taken over them and they were insatiable.

"It Tezcatlipoca," Solak answers.

"Yes. It's Tezcatlipoca and Xochiquetzal," Calixta confirms.

"Let's get these kids out of here. We must take them to a safer place," Aquetzalli exclaims.

"This place is safe," Tokis responds.

"It's not safe. We are too close to the hill. If it collapses, it would bury us for sure," Aquetzalli explains. "We have to get them out of danger."

"We have to hit the road. The Coatepeque Lake and Tecupan Ishatcu are the nearest cities, but there are also several farms near to the south and several hamlets," Kumara explains.

"Then we'll go down the road. We will take the road to Lake Coatepeque," Aquetzalli orders.

"We cannot be seen by the humans," Kumara explains. "It would cause many problems for us."

"I don't think there are people on these streets this late at night," Ocotlel answers. "But if you want, you can stay here. We'll take care of children."

"No. Chilco gave us specific orders to care for them until their return, or until dawn," Solak explains. "We'll take you to the edge of the forest where it is safer and wait till morning."

"Sounds good," Kumara answers. Ocotlel and Solak take the lead with a group of chaneques while Aquetzalli takes responsibility for maintaining order among the children.

The exit on the east side crumbles with the tremor completely sealing the Cuntetepeque caverns. Luckily, Chale, Narib, Kopán, and company emerged from the cave, just before the earthquake.

"By Tezcatlipoca! The second earthquake was stronger," Narib says.

"It must be Tezcatlipoca. Surely he found My Beloved," Chale adds.

"With all that power, they could destroy the whole Lamatepeque volcano," Narib exclaims. The poor healer had found the main cave empty. Kopán had decided to follow the route of the mine number thirteen. Everything pointed out that the army had gone in that direction. Luckily, Chale caught up to them and took them with him as well as an injured chaneque they found tied up. He was sure that the chaneques had caught up to the Pipils and there would be many people hurt.

"There they are," the chaneque announces, seeing the crowd gathered across the river. Chale breaks through the chaneques. "Kompa. What's happening here?" the warrior asks.

"We caught them," Kompa answers, very satisfied with his work.

"Excellent work. But we have to let them go."

"What? Are you crazy? It cost me a lot of men to catch them. I lost a lot of people. In addition, My Beloved will have our necks if we let them go."

"No. My Beloved no longer has dominion over us. These are Chilco's orders, and by order of the very same Tezcatlipoca," Chale explains.

"Tezcatlipoca?"

"Yes. Tezcatlipoca commanded us to free the slaves. At this very moment, he's battling My Beloved."

"You mean that these earthquakes were caused by Tezcatlipoca?"

"That's right. Chilco went with him to find her. I think they found her. By orders of the General and Tezcatlipoca, we must release these hostages," Chale explains.

Narib finally enters the camp and starts looking around. Pipil warriors lie sitting with their hands tied behind their backs. Several young people also lie tied up. A child with a painted face like a Pipil warrior sits beside a wounded Pipil.

Narib approaches the wounded warrior. "Leave him alone," Tenoch tells the chaneque at seeing him approaching his friend.

"Do not worry, everything is fine. I'm a healer," the old Chaneque explains. "How do you feel? Where does it hurt?" he asks the warrior.

"I have a broken rib," Ocoyatl explains with a very weak voice.

"And what happened to them?" the healer asks when he sees Elena and Atlahua lying on the ground.

"They were hurt by your chaneques with poisoned darts," Ucatl answers in reproach.

"Oh, I see. Don't worry, they were just tranquilizer darts. I'll wake them up in a moment," Narib explains and quickly starts looking for medicines, potions, and herbs in his handbag.

"Untie the Pipils," the resigned Kompa orders. The grumbling among chaneques and slaves instantly fills the air, many in disagreement and others in confusion. However, the main guards obey without further questions.

"Listen up," Chale calls out. "Everyone is free by orders from Black Tezcatlipoca. But no one can go until him and My General return. The earthquakes you felt a while ago were caused by a battle between My Beloved and Tezcatlipoca. General Chilco is with them at this moment. By his orders, we'll release the slaves until morning."

"So we are not free," Tlacoyotl exclaims. "You will when My General gets back."

"What if he doesn't come back?" Yanixté asks.

"If Chilco does not return, Tezcatlipoca will. Then he will tell us what to do."

"And what about the children?" Ucatl asks.

"The children are safe on the other side of the mountain. I will send several chaneques to go get them so we can all be together when my lord returns."

"My Beloved," Sihuehuet exclaims.

"Noooooooooooooooo!" Chilco shouts. "We must stop her."

"How do we cross the lake?" Teutli asks.

"There's no need. Look." Acatlel points to the top of the island where the lava has stopped flowing. A figure like a man of normal size and two heads rises from the crater. One of its heads is like a dragon with golden feathers—— a green gem on his forehead and three horns behind his head, with red eyes, large and sharp fangs like a cobra. The second head is like a yellow leopard with black patches and brown eyes.

The first guard reacts and tries to stop the prisoner, but the prisoner is very strong and stops him in his attack with one hand and immediately strikes back, ripping the guard's head off with a single blow. The giant's head falls into the lake of fire and sinks, while his body is thrown into the crater by the prisoner.

"Itzalku, my love. I am Sihuehuet." The beautiful lady descends next to her beloved. Immediately Itzalku joins his heads together to form a single one as one of a very handsome man.

"Sihuehuet." Itzalku exclaims holding her tight with his right arm and launches her hard against the ceiling stalactites. The stalactites break and Sihuehuet starts falling, very badly hurt from the impact, but Itzalku jumps and catches her amid flight, avoiding the lava lake and landing on firm ground.

"Why?" Sihuehuet asks in a weak and agonizing voice.

"For having fooled me and turned me into this. Because of you I have spent centuries imprisoned, just waiting for this moment." Itzalku answers and with one single blow rips her heart off. The astonished eyes of Sihuehuet open wide and the beautiful lady loses her charm, becoming a sparse white-haired old woman. The horrible woman takes her last breath, losing all of her strength and magic. Itzalku sheds the old, lifeless body into one of the rivers of fire. The body instantly catches on fire and flows with the current. Chalchiuhtlicue's bracelet dims and turns off without burning.

"My Beloved! Nooooooooooooooo." Notchím cries out and runs up to her, jumping the first river with no problems. His eyes full of tears.

Chilco stands still trying to absorb what has just happened, with the Pipil warriors at his side. His Beloved, the most precious of creatures of the earth, lies dead in the middle of a lake of fire. "By Tezcatlipoca," Chilco finally exclaims. "My Beloved is dead."

"Let's get out of here," Atlanezi suggests. "We don't have a chance against that beast."

"No. We can't allow this monster to leave this place," Itzcuauhtzin responds and quickly runs up next to the guard who waits patiently for Itzalku at the riverbank, with smoky eyes and a huge spear ready.

Itzalku turns to look at the warriors and jumps over the rivers at high speed. The guard waits for the beast to get closer and throws his spear at him, but Itzalku dodges it easily, spinning in midair and descending on firm ground. The guard throws himself at him and takes him to the ground, but Itzalku is stronger and easily rotates under the guard and pushes him toward the lava river. The giant stands up and quickly advances against Itzalku. Xóchitl uses the distraction and shoots an arrow against Itzalku, impacting him on the back. Itzalku screams in agony and angrily turns against the Pipils. The guard attacks him once more, but Itzalku jumps backward, turning around in the air to avoid the fury of the guard, and grabs the giant by its head. He supports his feet on the giant's back and pulls with all his might, ripping the guard's head off. The giant's body falls forward while his head falls at the edge of the lava river.

Itzalku yanks the arrow from his back and starts to bleed. Xóchitl fires a pair of arrows, but Itzalku dodges them easily. "Quetzalcoatl!" he shouts with great fury. His head splits again in two, losing his human form and taking the form of a dragon and leopard. The beast turns to the warriors and looks at Itzcuauhtzin, who is waiting in front of the group, his body fully lit and leopard patched. Xóchitl stands beside him with another arrow ready. "So you are the envoys of Tezcatlipoca and Quetzalcoatl. Those cowards, always sending someone else to do their job."

Xóchitl shoots again, but this time Itzalku simply catches the bolt in the air. Teutli fires his shotgun against the beast, but the bullet doesn't cause any damage. Acatlel and Atlanezi also shoot without any luck. Itzalku takes the arrow and launches it at high speed at Teutli, impaling him in the chest. Teutli falls back to the hot ground painted in red.

"Tezcatlipoca, help me," Itzcuauhtzin cries out and runs to confront Itzalku before he gets closer. The young man puts his shield in front for defense and takes his spear in attack position.

"Quetzalcoatl, help me." Xóchitl whispers. Her ring begins to glow and covers her completely. The runes on her garments also begin to shine. The jade stone in her forehead activates and Xóchitl can see more clearly. Her mind starts to work quickly. "Chilco, the Bracelet," she exclaims.

Notchím has already pulled Sihuehuet's incinerated body from the river. Chilco runs up to them and takes the bracelet but quickly drops it.

"Quickly," Xóchitl shouts. The General makes another attempt and drops it again.

"It's too hot," the old warrior responds.

"Notchím, Teutli is hurt," Acatlel cries out. The old sorcerer gives one last kiss to his Beloved and lets her float in the river of fire. He never really knew how much he loved her, until this day. The only regret for Notchím is that his Beloved never knew it despite having lived together for over a century.

Itzalku launches himself and clashes against Itzcuauhtzin. The young warrior manages to block the attack with his shield. The leopard roars as the dragon blows fire from his mouth. Itzcuauhtzin's ring shines even stronger, protecting the warrior. Itzcuauhtzin attacks with his spear but his attack is too slow for Itzalku who grabs the spear and easily pulls it away. In the same pull of the spear, Itzalku turns around to his right and hits Itzcuauhtzin behind his legs, knocking him backward. Itzalku intends to run him through with the spear, but Itzcuauhtzin rolls to his left, missing the attacks and gets up as fast as possible. Itzalku is faster and Itzcuauhtzin has not yet finished standing up when a kick puts him down again.

Xóchitl fires just before Itzalku can attack his brother again. Itzalku reacts at the last moment and the arrow barely roses his leopard's face. The leopard roars as the dragon blows fire on Itzcuauhtzin. Xóchitl keeps shooting, forcing Itzalku to withdraw.

Itzcuauhtzin stands up and takes his ax. The ax shines with the power of the ring and the teen launches himself back against his attacker. Itzalku dodges a few attacks and jumps over Itzcuauhtzin like a Jaguar with his claws in front. Itzcuauhtzin arches his body backward, dodging Itzalku's claws, but Itzalku manages to connect his knee on his chin, and the boy falls to the ground bleeding from the mouth.

By god. Xóchitl fires once again, trying to keep the monster away from her brother, without connecting a single bolt. Itzalku takes Itzcuauhtzin's spear and throws it against the girl. Xóchitl tries to move away but the spear comes at high speed and impacts her directly on the chest. There's a big spark and an explosion sound as Xóchitl gets thrown three meters back by the impact. Xóchitl's dress absorbs the impact, saving her from certain death. The girl screams from the pain which begins to disappear quickly. The runes of her dress shine while Xóchitl lies on the floor trying to understand what just happened.

Atlanezi runs up to his niece and lifts her up. "Are you okay?"

"Yes, I'm fine. I think the dress absorbed all the pain."

Chilco finally picks up the bracelet and quickly jumps over and runs up to Xóchitl. The girl quickly puts the bracelet on as Itzcuauhtzin defends himself as best as he can from Itzalku's ferocious attacks, using his ax to strike back. If not for his armor and Chimalli, the boy would be dead.

"Tezcatlipoca!" the leopard cries out with great fury. Itzcuauhtzin ignores him and attacks with his ax at seeing an opportunity, but Itzalku dodges his attack at the last moment and connects his right fist on Itzcuauhtzin's chest. The young warrior flies about five meters back, dropping his ax in midflight. Acatlel runs over to his aid while Notchím keeps reciting incantations and using yellow powder to resurrect Teutli who lies unconscious on the floor, but at least the bleeding has stopped.

"Itzalku!" Xóchitl, her body completely covered in radiant light, shouts, calling the monster's attention. Itzalku stops for a moment to look at the girl, expecting a fierce attack from her, but nothing happens. Xóchitl doesn't know how to use the bracelet, let alone any of Sihuehuet's enchantments. So without knowing what to do, Xóchitl takes her bow and starts shooting at her enemy. Itzalku dodges the bolts, but Xóchitl continues to shoot, forcing Itzalku to back up again.

"Itzcua, are you okay?" Acatlel asks.

"Yes, I think so. Give me your macana." The teenager stands up, still a little dizzy from the hit and bleeding from his mouth. The young warrior stops for a moment to admire Xóchitl's fierce attack. His sister has shot so many arrows that will soon run out. "Acatlel. Take all of your arrows and give them to Xóchitl. She's almost out."

"But they are only common arrows." Acatlel complains.

"Yes, but her quiver is magical. Do it quickly," Itzcuauhtzin orders and quickly runs to pick up his ax.

Itzalku runs on the walls, jumping high and taking cover among rocks and stalagmites. He grabs a couple of arrows from a wall and begins to move against Xóchitl.

Suddenly Xóchitl shoots her last arrow. Itzalku realizes the situation and uses Xóchitl's distraction to throw two arrows against her, but the arrows are stopped by the bracelet's light, protecting its bearer.

Itzalku angrily runs up to her. Atlanezi takes his bolas and throws them against the beast. The bola entangles between Itzalku's legs, and he falls down with great force, rolling several times before stopping on the hard and hot ground.

Acatlel uses the distraction and runs up to Xóchitl with a quiver full of arrows. "Xóchitl, I got some more. Here, take them." Xóchitl quickly crouches down to let Acatlel fill her quiver with common arrows.

Itzcuauhtzin runs at high speed against Itzalku who is now sitting up and trying to break free from the bolas. Itzcuauhtzin grabs his ax from the floor and throws it with great force. The dragon turns around too late, and the ax embeds in his forehead, breaking his green gem. The leopard roars in pain and Itzalku falls backward, his body trembling and agitated. The warriors hold their breath for a moment. Itzalku tries to bring his heads together but his magic does not work. Without his second head, the beast has lost much of its power. His body starts to squirm and roll on the floor. The leopard's roar does not stop and his body gets closer to the river of fire, standing on all fours like a leopard. Itzcuauhtzin runs up to him with his glowing macana in his hand.

Xóchitl takes one arrow and puts it on her bow. Itzalku stands up showing his dead bleeding head and his leopard eyes in flames. Xóchitl shoots her bolt and connects it directly on his chest. Itzalku staggers back and pulls the arrow out of his chest.

"Ay yay yay yay yay!" Itzcuauhtzin shouts while launching a devastating attack on his opponent. The macana furiously hits his neck, chopping the leopard head off. Both Itzalku's head and body fall on the lava, which starts boiling fervently. The bubbles begin to grow stronger, bursting off lava on its surroundings.

"I don't like this," Atlanezi exclaims.

"We have to get out of here immediately," Chilco warns.

"Let's go. There's no time to lose." Acatlel shouts while lifting Teutli and throwing him over his shoulder.

"Itzcua, let's go," Xóchitl shouts. "He's already dead."

Itzcuauhtzin still remains near Itzalku not believing that they have been able to defeat a powerful monster. The land slightly trembles again and the young warrior finally reacts and starts running behind his peers, but not before picking up his precious spear. The earthquake becomes stronger and stalactites start falling from the ceiling.

"This whole place is going to crumble," Acatlel exclaims as he runs up the stairs with Teutli on his shoulders.

"How do we seal the door?" Xóchitl asks once they reach the top.

"There's no need. This place seems to be crashing down anyway," Notchím answers. "We better get out of here as soon as possible."

"I'll take the Pipil from here; I'm stronger," Chilco offers.

"Okay," Acatlel answers and everyone runs out of the crypt and enter the Cacique's tomb. Xóchitl opens the door and all run out of the tomb, leaving the old chief and his warriors to await their sad fate.

The lava begins to climb the stairs, breaking through the crypt's door. It slowly begins to fill the place, spreading to Topiltzin Axcitl Quetzalcoatl's tomb.

The lake of fire keeps boiling and the lava continues to grow. The island erupts with great force, causing an even greater earthquake which begins to collapse the roof. The pressure of the lava breaks through roof. A small cone of dirt and lava emerges on the surface, on the southwest side of the hill of Cuntetepeque. The pressure of the lava gushes out with great force trough the crater and the cone begins to distill lava, giving life to a new volcano.

A GIFT FROM THE GODS

Ocotlel feels great satisfaction at finding the adults' camp and seeing his friends. Ocotlel and Solak were at the front mounted on a black panther. They had just reached the road when Kompa's chaneques found them. The chaneques took the children to the new camp, moving them away from the streets and taking them by the river.

The children were no longer afraid of the chaneques, and many of them talked quietly among themselves as they walked through the woods. The chaneques used their magic tricks and knowledge of ancient history to gain the children's trust.

Seeing the warriors and the children, Yanixté and Tenoch run to meet them. "Felipe, Sebastian," Tenoch cries out in happiness at seeing his brothers behind the warrior.

"Tenoch, Yanixté," the twins shout when they see their family. Elena stands up, waiting with tears in her eyes, full of joy at seeing her twins safely. The children run to meet their mother while she shakily walks toward them.

"Where are Itzcua and Xóchitl?" Tenoch asks the warrior.

"In there." Ocotlel points toward the hill. "They went looking for Sihuehuet."

"Is it true that Tezcatlipoca is with them?" Yanixté asks, very excited.

"Yes, he is," Ocotlel answers, trying not uncover that Itzcuauhtzin is the Tezcatlipoca the chaneques speak of.

"This is incredible," the boy exclaims as they walk toward the camp. "What about my dad?"

"He's back there at the back of the line." The young warrior leaves the group and quickly runs out to find his father.

"Niltze." Ucatl salutes.

"Niltze," Ocotlel answers.

"Is everyone all right?"

"Yes, everybody is. We haven't had any problems, just a couple of bruises from a fight, but nothing serious. The chaneques have treated us well since Tezcatlipoca ordered it. And you?"

"We're fine. We had several problems and several injuries, but their shaman cured them all."

"Wounded? How?" Ocotlel asks.

"It's a long story. I'll tell it to you later."

Ocotlel looks around and sees fires everywhere, with humans on one side and chaneques on another. The chaneques have gone hunting and brought a couple of deer, two coyotes, and half a dozen rabbits that the people immediately started cooking over the coals. After a long and exhausted day, hunger among the crowd had grown greatly. The hunt was Atlahua's idea. Since the chaneques wouldn't let them leave, Atlahua asked them to please bring some food. So Kompa sent a group of chaneques hunting. The expert hunters soon returned. Their speed and skill in hunting is really impressive. They knew where to find their prey and their agility gave them an advantage far greater than that of any human.

"Ucatl, I need to talk to you." Ocotlel stoops down pretending to tie his shoe laces.

Ucatl understood and squats down next to him. "What's in your mind?"

"I'm worried about Acatlel and the others."

"They're going to be fine. Tezcatlipoca is with them."

"Uh...I don't know how to tell you this. But the Tezcatlipoca they talk about, it's Itzcua," Ocotlel whispers.

"What?"

"Yes. I saw it myself. Itzcua painted his face as the god and then went to meet with the chaneques. His body began to glow and turned into the very same Tezcatlipoca. The chaneques knelt down to him, but my fear is that if it was a trick from Itzcua, he may not be able to do it again."

"But they have magic weapons. I saw them when we were rescued."

"Yes, but that witch is very powerful. I saw her do some pretty amazing things inside the cave," Ocotel responds.

"Don't worry, I'm sure they'll beat her. Xóchitl also has magical powers. But, if they don't return, the chaneques promised to let us free by dawn."

"Yes, that was Chilco's order, their General."

"Very well, then we'll have to trust in the kids. I suppose Teutli also went with them, right?" Ucatl asks.

"Yes, Teutli went with them, Acatlel and Atlanezi as well."

"Then we'll have to wait until morning and then we'll see. Come, let's go warm up a little by the fire and eat something."

Further back in the line comes a group of chaneques with Aquetzalli and several small children. Many of them are mounted on the chaneques' shoulders and even Aquetzalli is carrying a little white girl.

"Dad, Dad," Yanixté calls out, very happy to see Aquetzalli at the tail of the group.

"Yanixté, son. Are you okay?"

"I couldn't be better."

"So you came after all. Teutli told me how well you fought down by the cliff."

"Yes. I got several ears for my collection."

"Excellent work; I am very proud of you. The gods have really been good to us tonight."

"That's right. Who is this little girl?" the boy asks.

"Oh, she's someone very special, but no one knows her name. Everyone calls her Chele, because she is so white," the warrior answers.

The children enter the camp and reunite with their families and relatives. The rest are orphans or children who were taken very young that they no longer remember their family or where they came from. They just stay together with friends in the middle of the camp, Calixta in front of them all.

"Who is she?" Tenoch asks at seeing Calixta, with her long braids and tapatío eyes.

"I don't know," Tlacoyotl answers. "It must be one of the slave kids. Most of these children must be orphans."

Elena looks at the orphan children and immediately approaches them and begins to gather them so they can eat something.

"Niltze." Tenoch welcomes Calixta as he gets closer.

"Niltze," Calixta answers.

"I am Tenoch. This is Elena, my mother."

"Nice to meet you. My name is Calixta."

"Is everyone all right?" Elena asks.

"Yes, and very hungry," Calixta answers.

"Then come with me. We have a couple of rabbits that we can share." Elena leads the group to her campfire and the warriors start distributing the rabbit meat among the children.

"Where are you from?" Tenoch asks Calixta.

"I am from Lake Güija."

"Oh. That's far from here. I am from Coatepeque Lake, but we all come from Tazumal. But my mom's family comes from the north of Copan."

"She is white," Calixta points out.

"Mestiza. My grandfather was white, but my grandmother is Mayan."

"Then you are Mayan."

"I'm mixed. Mayan and Pipil. And you?"

"I'm Mayan, and I can't wait to return to Güija."

"Maybe we can help you. My mom always wanted to go visit my grandmother at Copan. Maybe we can convince her and we can take you with us."

"That would be wonderful. Thank you," the girl answers while grabbing a piece of rabbit meat to eat.

"You saw Tezcatlipoca?"

"Yes. At first he was a young warrior, but then Tezcatlipoca possessed him and gave orders to the chaneques to get us out of there. It was awesome."

"A young warrior?" Tenoch asks.

"Yes, a boy of about fifteen years old."

"Oh. I hope he comes back later. I also want to see him." Suddenly the earth begins to shake very slowly. Everyone stops, and several children get frightened and begin to cry again. The tremor becomes stronger and continues to progress slowly until a very small explosion is heard several kilometers south of the camp.

"What is that?" Atlahua asks.

"It looks like an explosion," Juan responds.

"It's Tezcatlipoca destroying our home, and sinking it," Narib answers.

"No. That is too far out. Our home is further to the north," Kopán says.

"Yes. That explosion was further down." Kumara, who has more experience on the surface, confirms. "That's very close to the valley of rams. Tezcatlipoca must have caught up to My Beloved."

The cone starts to grow and the lava begins to rise from within, sending rivers of lava and rocks several meters into the air. The lava is visible from the camp, and they can see it lighting up its surroundings and incinerating everything in its path.

"God Almighty," Elena exclaims. "What's that?"

"I don't know. It seems as if the earth is bleeding fire," Ucatl answers.

The strength of the earthquake begins to wane, and they can now only feel the vibrations of the earth as the volcano rises slowly over the plains of Cuscatlán.

The stalactites keep slowly falling, while the warriors keep running for their life. Xóchitl keeps trying to use the bracelet but without success. She tried to give it commands and tried several words in Nahuatl but without results, except for the bracelet's protective light that covers the bearer.

There was a mist that clouded the corridors throughout the cave. "The lava must have reached the boiling river." That was Notchím's explanation, when he saw the steam rising everywhere. The earthquake has sealed several corridors, and made it impossible to return by the main cavern. Chilco's biggest concern was for his chaneques to have gotten out in time. The Pipils feared the same for the slaves and the warriors.

The road that Chilco took led them to the main road that the Pipils took toward the bridge while they were fleeing. The lava had grown so much that the river had overflowed with lava and they couldn't pass to the other side. The warriors had to return toward the north exit where they initially entered through, but the canyon had collapsed and they had to climb over the rubble to get through. At the top there was only a small gap between the ceiling and the fallen rubble, with barely enough space for one person, but it was enough to escape without further complications.

"We're almost there," Chilco exclaims at seeing the end of the road and the green crystals on the top.

Notchím takes the lead, climbing over several stalagmites and stalactites that fell during the quake. Finally they reach the door, which fortunately is not blocked. Notchím takes his magic dust and draws a rune to open the door.

"Finally," Atlanezi shouts with great joy.

"Ha ha. I thought we'd never get out of there. These earthquakes had me on my last nerve," Acatlel confesses, while everyone runs down the hill into the woods, following the trail the chaneques and the children left behind.

Grrrrrrrr. A black jaguar with yellow patches roars, almost invisible at night. It looks like a combination of a leopard and a panther, but larger and more robust, its bright yellow eyes burning like fire. The warriors raise their weapons, ready to fire. Xóchitl also takes an arrow and readies it in her bow, while her bracelet begins to glow along with her ring. Itzcuauhtzin's ring activates again, covering him with light and similar patches as the jaguar's.

The jaguar starts to surround them, doing nothing but roar. Itzcuauhtzin walks to the front of the group to protect them. The black jaguar stops in front of him. His ring shines even brighter.

Tezcatlipoca!

"Put down your weapons," the young warrior commands. The Pipils obey his orders without question. Chilco slowly sets Teutli on the floor.

The jaguar walks toward the young warrior and stands up on two legs, as his body takes human form. A great warrior with a quetzal feather crown and indigenous armor stands in front of the boy. His black body like a jaguar with patches and long braids. He looks like a larger and stronger version of Itzcuauhtzin.

"Tezcatlipoca!" the others exclaim and kneel immediately. Only Itzcuauhtzin and Xóchitl remain standing, but at seeing the others, Xóchitl also kneels.

Itzcuauhtzin keeps looking at the god straight in the eyes without flinching, his blood boiling, but he doesn't know if it is for fear or anger.

"Itzcuauhtzin," the god finally says in a thick and authoritative voice.

"My Lord," the young man exclaims and finally kneels on one leg.

"Excellent work." The god applauds three times and takes him by the shoulder, forcing him to stand up.

"Ah!" Itzcuauhtzin exclaims at feeling his patches burning his body. The feeling only lasts a couple of seconds and the boy feels as if he had just taken a mint bath.

"All rise," the god commands. They all stand up, including Teutli, who has just woken up. Tezcatlipoca's power has finished the healing work that Notchím begun.

"Tezcatlipoca?" Teutli asks, very confused. The god simply nods.

"Teutli?" Atlanezi exclaims when he sees his friend standing up.

"What can we offer you, my lord?" Chilco asks.

"I just came to congratulate you. You have fulfilled the task entrusted to you by the gods."

"What task is that?" Teutli asks as he gets closer.

"The one of destroying Itzalku," Tezcatlipoca answers.

"Itzalku is dead?" Teutli asks.

"Yes. We finally did it. I'll tell you later," Acatlel responds quietly.

"Itzalku has threatened this land since its creation. Finally he and his creator are no longer part of this world. The gods are very grateful for your services. We have built a volcano in your honor. The volcano will serve as evidence of your achievement to all the natives of this region and for generations to come."

"Volcano?" Itzcuauhtzin asks.

"Yes, Itzalku is a god and cannot die. With your defeat, he has turned into a volcano. On the other side of this hill you will see your great feat. There, along the river, you will find the children and the rest of your people waiting." The jaguar god answers while walking toward the girl. "Xóchitl."

"Yes, sir?"

"The bracelet please." Tezcatlipoca extends his right hand. "That bracelet should not stay here. I will return it to its owner."

Xóchitl removes the bracelet immediately. "Who is the owner?" the girl asks.

"Chalchiuhtlicue. Tlaloc's wife," Tezcatlipoca confesses.

"So all the gods that the elders and the storytellers have told us about exist?" Xóchitl asks.

"Of course we do. As long as there are people like your grandparents and warriors like you, we will continue to exist and be part of your world, although today there are new gods in these lands."

"I'm sorry. I always thought they were just stories," the very embarrassed girl confesses.

"Do not worry. I understand. Your blood has been mixed."

"I also apologize for the harm we caused under Sihuehuet's servitude," Chilco implores.

"Everyone is forgiven. You were deceived by Sihuehuet. But today you have paid that debt."

"Thank you, my lord. We promise to live only to serve you," Chilco promises.

"I'm sure you will," Tezcatlipoca responds.

"Lord, I have a question about Itzalku," Notchím exclaims.

"What is your question?"

"I have understood that Itzalku was your son. Is that right?"

"Yes, it is. Itzalku was my son. A great warrior, a hero among humankind. Very handsome and powerful, but he stopped being my son when Sihuehuet deceived him. Everything good that was left of him was destroyed by Sihuehuet's spells. My son died long ago."

"Then why did you allow Sihuehuet to free him?" Atlanezi asks.

"With the arrival of the whites and their new gods, our strength has waned. The runes and charms that had been placed on Itzalku's prison were weakening. It was only a matter of time before Itzalku escaped. Had he done so, the world would have suffered his wrath. Sihuehuet was planning to use him at her will, but her power was also waning and we knew she could not control him. The Pipils would have been the first to suffer his wrath, and then the neighboring tribes such as the Mayans and the Lencas."

"What will happen to this place now?" Itzcuauhtzin asks.

"The hill of Cuntetepeque will continue to exist, but its caves have been completely filled with lava. The treasures stored by Sihuehuet have been completely buried."

"And us chaneques? What do we do now?" Chilco asks.

"Return to your native land. You have nothing else to do here."

"How about these weapons? Do we have to give them back?" Xóchitl asks, putting all of her hopes on the god saying no.

"No, of course not. These weapons are bound to you now. They are your reward for the service you have rendered. Your armor will protect you, and the rings are a direct link to the gods. Through them you can use some of our power. No one else other than the two of you can wield them. It is a gift from the gods. You two will do great things, as your ancestors did. But remember, they cannot be used to hurt innocent people." The jaguar god takes two steps back and jumps into the sky running on an invisible path toward the stars in his leopard form.

"Incredible!" Teutli exclaims. "If I had not seen it myself, I would have never believed it."

"Me neither," Acatlel confesses.

"Let's go find the others," Chilco suggests.

"Lead the way," Teutli responds.

Upon reaching the other side of the hill, the warriors see the new volcano still spewing lava and growing, filling its surroundings with ash and magma.

"It's really stunning," Xóchitl exclaims.

"Look. Fires across the river," Acatlel exclaims, taking the lead.

The chaneques' drums and flutes are playing loudly, transforming the tension into a festivity. Shouts of joy from Pipils and chaneques can be heard from atop the hill.

Chilco is the first one to cross the river with Itzcuauhtzin and his body full of leopard patches beside him. His ring is no longer shining, but the patches haven't disappeared since Tezcatlipoca touched his shoulder. The chaneques begin to kneel on one leg when they see their god walking among them.

"What are they doing?" Itzcuauhtzin asks Chilco.

"They kneel before your majesty."

"But I'm not Tezcatlipoca."

"Maybe not, but they don't need to know that. Besides, you have been touched and sent by him. That's enough for me, my king." Chilco guides him through the crowd toward the center of the camp, next to Kompa and the other warriors. Gradually, the people and the children follow the chaneques' example until there is only Elena and Aquetzalli left without kneeling."

"Itzcua?" Elena asks with great doubt.

"By Tlaloc!" Ucatl exclaims. "Is it really Tezcatlipoca?"

"I'm not sure," Ocotlel says, kneeling down.

"Please. Everyone rise," Itzcuauhtzin commands and the crowd slowly start to stand up.

"A few words please, your majesty." Chilco asks.

"A few words? What do you want me to say?" Itzcuauhtzin whispers.

"Whatever you want. We are your servants," Chilco answers.

"But I don't know what to say. Best you speak for me."

"Okay, just follow my example." Chilco turns to his subjects. "Listen up, everyone. Today we fought a great battle and we came out victorious. Sihuehuet no longer has dominion over us and has been destroyed. This is a day to celebrate. Tezcatlipoca has been with us tonight and has commanded us to return to our homeland."

"Yeeeeeeeeeey!" the chaneques shout.

"We will celebrate with our Pipil brothers. Tezcatlipoca is with us. Let the dance begin," the charismatic Chilco shouts.

"Yeeeeeeeeeey!" A loud voice is heard throughout the camp. The chaneques begin to dance around the fire, imitating the rain dance of the natives. Gradually the children begin to join the dance and the festivity begins.

Elena finally comes over to her children. Xóchitl is the first to hold her. "Xóchitl, Itzcua. I'm so happy to see you," Elena exclaims between tears and sobs. Tenoch and the twins also come over and happily embrace them.

"I have several stories for you," Tenoch says to Itzcuauhtzin, showing a pair of ears. Itzcuauhtzin just smiles, very happy to see his brother alive and well.

"Where's Dad?"

"At the Tazumal. Grandma is taking care of him. Where'd you get those patches?"

"Oh, these are a gift from the gods. Tezcatlipoca himself gave them to me."

Chilco invites the Pipil warriors to sit with him in the middle of the camp, and enjoy the dance.

"What are you going to do now?" Itzcuauhtzin asks Chilco.

"Now that My Beloved has been destroyed and with it our home, I think we will return to our land, as Tezcatlipoca suggested."

"And where is your home?" Xóchitl asks.

"In Uxmal. There we have our cities, in the land that you call Mexico, north of Tikal."

"It will be a long journey. How are you going to do it without being discovered?" Teutli asks.

"We have our methods. We've been here for a long time without anyone knowing. After today, we'll have to move quickly, as news of our existence will soon travel throughout the region," Chilco answers.

"Don't worry. We will never say anything about your existence, but we will never forget you," Itzcuauhtzin answers.

"Yes, it's a shame we did not have more time to get to know each other. Thanks for saving my life," Teutli exclaims.

"It was a pleasure," Chilco answers. "But it wasn't me. It was Notchím who healed your wounds."

"A thousand thanks, my friends. I am indebted to you. I'll wear this scar with honor. If you ever need our help, don't hesitate to call us. The Pipils are eternally grateful for all the support you have given us tonight," Teutli exclaims. "We also have our gods in common."

"That's right. Thanks, Pipil. You are a special breed, especially you, Itzcuauhtzin. You possess the power of Tezcatlipoca, and your sister the power of Quetzalcoatl—— the creators of the world. Individually you are invincible, but together you are extremely powerful and untouchable. It's really an honor to have met you."

"Likewise," Itzcuauhtzin answers.

"Isn't Uxmal a Mayan city?" Xóchitl asks.

"Yes, it is," Notchím answers.

"Well, if you are from Uxmal, how is it that you honor the Nahuatl gods and not the Mayans?" the curious girl asks.

"It's a long story, my child. There are a lot of unsolved mysteries about our people. We are a very old race. Our lineage goes all the way back to the creation of heaven and earth, all the way before the construction of Teotihuacán. I'll tell you our story next time we see each other. Besides the Mayan gods are the same as yours with different names, that's all."

"What are we going to do with all these people?" Elena asks.

"I don't know. Let's let the elders take care of that. Many of them will return to their lands, but the majority of children will need a new home," Teutli answers.

"I have no white daughters, I will adopt Chele if we can't find her family, and if she wants to come with us," Aquetzalli exclaims.

A chaneque approaches Kompa with a couple of crowns in his hands. They are made of skunk tail bush leaves, tied with vines and color feathers. "These are for the king and queen," Orszulak, the chaneque who likes candy, explains. A good group of chaneques stand behind him. Kompa takes the crowns and gives them to Notchím.

"My king, if you please." Notchím offers the crowns. "We want to introduce these wreaths in honor of his majesty and his queen." Itzcuauhtzin and Xóchitl turn to look at each other, a little confused.

"Please do not reject them," Chilco whispers. "It is a great honor for the chaneques to have you among us and present you with these crowns."

The Pipil warriors look at each other trying to understand. "Are you sure?" Itzcuauhtzin asks. "I don't think it's necessary."

"It's just a token of appreciation and tradition. It's just for tonight."

"Okay," Xóchitl answers. "I don't see any harm on that."

"My king, my queen." Notchím approaches them and places the crowns on their heads. "The king and queen of the chaneques," Notchím announces.

"Yeeeeeeeeeeeeey!" the chaneques rumble.

"Thank you, my friends. You are all very nice." Itzcuauhtzin thanks, bowing his head in reverence. He takes Xóchitl's hand, and both bow in reverence. "From today on, I declare this day a day of festivities for everyone. It should be celebrated with dances. Let it be remembered as the day when chaneques and Pipils united to defeat the oppressors of our lives, thus uniting men and chaneques in friendship."

"Yeeeeeeeeeeeeey!" All scream cheerfully.

"Let the festivity continue." The very happy chaneques start dancing again until the fire slowly begins to die down and the more tired chaneques retire to sleep among the trees and stones.

The children also look for a place to sleep, and gradually everyone falls asleep. Itzcuauhtzin and Xóchitl finally retire as well and go to sleep next to their family. Xóchitl lulls Felipe, and Elena takes Sebastian. Only Teutli and Ucatl stay up talking to Chilco and Notchím, sharing war stories and mythical legends.

"Chale, Kompa, prepare the people; we leave at the break of dawn," Chilco quietly commands to avoid waking up his new friends.

By dawn, the camp is almost empty. Most chaneques have started their long way back to homeland. Most kids are still asleep, except for Tenoch and Calixta who have risen early and gone to the river to wash their face. Many young people are saying their good-byes and many have already begun their journey home. Most of them have taken the road toward Lake Coatepeque and others the route to the Tazumal, but there are many detours along the way and only they know what their ultimate destination will be.

"Your majesty, it was a pleasure to fight beside you. Hopefully next time we meet, it would be under better circumstances," Chilco exclaims. "If you ever want to visit us, just look for us at Uxmal. We'll be waiting."

"Thank you Chilco. Have a good journey," Itzcuauhtzin answers, giving him a strong handshake. The other warriors say good-bye to each other. Notchím and Narib are the last to say good-bye and then leave heading toward the jungle.

"Do you think we'll see them again, Itzcua?" Xóchitl asks.

"Yes, I have a feeling we will. I'm not sure that they will all go back to their homeland," the young warrior answers.

Behind them, the new volcano continues to drip lava, leaving rivers of obsidian in its wake. During the night, the volcano has grown more than ten times since the boys fell asleep, and it's already at the same height of the Cuntetepeque Hill and is still growing.

EPILOGUE

Mictlantecuhtli's throne is located between the rivers of horror and the bitter ponds, hidden by the dark and misty mountains. That's where all souls come to be tried by the old god of death after they die; by the one who swallows the stars by day and wears their bones.

Mictlantecuhtli could barely hide his excitement. It had been a long time since he had a soul so dark in his claws. Just by thinking about the party he'd have with his wife, Mictecacihuatl, and his subjects, the old owl shivered with excitement.

The woman stared at him in horror. She had never seen him in person, but the human eye necklace around his neck was proof enough to know that this is the lord of darkness—— the god of the dead and ruler of their souls. Being part goddess, she never thought she would end up in this place and did not count on her human side to condemn her to such a cruel punishment.

"My dear husband, what are we going to do with her?" Mictecacihuatl asks.

"Nothing," Tlaloc answers from behind their backs, in the darkest part of the cave.

"Tlaloc! What are you doing here?" Mictlantecuhtli asks, turning around to face the gods that have just appeared out of thin air. "This woman belongs to me," the lord of death declares.

"No. This woman is indebted to me," the god of rain answers. His wife Chalchiuhtlicue and Quetzalcoatl stand beside him.

"Quetzalcoatl! Are you going to allow this? Or are you interested in her as well?"

"You know very well what this woman has done and all the damage she has brought to the realm. Her last attempt almost caused the destruction of the human world. Plus she is part goddess," Quetzalcoatl answers.

"She is also human and has a soul. You can't deprive me of my rights."

"I'm sorry, but you know well enough that you have no right to her deity. She doesn't belong to you." Quetzalcoatl and Tlaloc approach the woman.

"I just wanted to be with my love," Sihuehuet confesses.

"Silence!" Tlaloc commands with his thunder voice. "You have caused a great havoc. Not just to humanity, but to the realm as well. Many people have suffered for your ambitions. You unleashed an ancient monster that you yourself created. So I condemn you to live as a spirit of fear and horror. You will never find your son, and you will only appear to evil men, the liars, and the cheat;

to those who lie to their women, going around breaking young girls' hearts; to the men who travel at night to do their evil deeds. Your dwelling place will be the ravines, rivers, and landfills. Never again will you be known as Sihuehuet. From this day on, I name you Sihuanaba."

GLOSSARY:

Cuachicqueh: a member of the most prestigious warrior society. Cuachicqueh warriors shaved their heads, except for a crest of hair in the center and a braid on the left ear. They painted their faces half blue and the other red or yellow. At initiation, they vowed not to step back during the battle on pain of death at the hands of their comrades.

Calmecac: an Aztec school that prepared the sons of nobles in the duties of priests and chiefs—distinguished from Telpochcalli.

Ichcahuipilli: Quilted cotton armor which was soaked in salt water brine and then hung to dry in shade so that the salt would crystallize inside of it. One or two fingers thick, this material was resistant to obsidian swords and atlatl darts. **(From náhuatl: íchcatl, cotton, and huipilli, shirt)** Mesoamerican military armor similar to European gambeson, and was commonly used by the Mexica and

Tlaxcala. It was built of several layers of twisted cotton and hardened with brine and other substances.

Macuahuitl: Also called the baton. It was a bar or club less than a meter long with sharp obsidian blades embedded (able to kill or seriously injure).

Māhuizzoh Chimalli: a warrior's shield. They were decorated with many different things like feathers, flowers, and even gold. The word translates to shield of great honor.

Niltze: Nahuatl word that means "Hello"

Pila: a washing sink. Mostly used in Central America. All Pilas have a "tub" area to hold water, and one or more "washing" areas/slabs.

Pipil: The Pipils or Cuzcatlecos are an indigenous people who live in western El Salvador which they called Cuzcatlán. Their language is called Nahuat or Pipil, related to Nahuatl.

Quauhololli: a mace or club, typically made from either wood or a combination of wood and stone. The Quauhololli was a melee weapon used by the Aztec and featured a curved handle for ease of striking, and with the mace head, was able to strike foes with.

Tamemes: Carriers, most cadets in the Pipil academy start as carriers then advance to warrior apprentice and finally. A seasoned warrior.

Telpochcalli: From Nahuatl, meaning "house of youth". Noun. **Telpochcalli** (plural telpochcallis). (Historical) A school for the children of Aztec commoners.

Tlacateccatl: In the Aztec military, Tlacateccatl (Pronounced [t'aˈka teˈkkatɬ]) was a title roughly equivalent to General. The Tlacateccatl was in charge of the *tlacatecco*, a military quarter in the center of the Aztec capital, Tenochtitlan. In wartime he was second-in-command to the *Tlahtoani* ("ruler", "king") and the *tlacochcalcatl* ("high General"). The Tlacateccatl was always a member of the military order of the *Cuachicqueh*, "the shorn ones".

Tlahtoani: Is the Nahuatl term for the ruler of an altepetl, a pre-Hispanic state. The word literally means "speaker", but may be translated into English as "king".

Yaoquizqueh: Nobles who had been train for combat. Similar to the modern Army Reserve troops.

Yaotecatl: Nahuatl word that means "warrior".

MESOAMERICAN GODS

Chalchiuhtlicue: Goddess of water, rivers, seas, streams, storms, and baptism, related to another water god, Chalchiuhtlatonal. Reputedly universally revered at the time of the Spanish conquest, she was an important deity figure in the Post classic Aztec realm of central Mexico. Wife of Tlaloc.

Mictlantecuhtli: (Pronounced / ˈmiktaˈntekˈwtˈi, meaning "Lord of Mictlan"), in Aztec mythology, was a god of the dead and the king of Mictlan (Chicunauhmictlan), the lowest and northernmost section of the underworld. He was one of the principal gods of the Aztecs and was the most prominent of several gods and goddesses of death and the underworld.

Mictecacihuatl: (pronounced /miktekasiuatʃ/) is Queen of Mictlan, the underworld, ruling over the afterlife with Mictlantecuhtli, another deity who is her husband. Her role is to watch over the bones of the dead and preside over the ancient festivals of the dead. These festivals evolved from Aztec traditions into the modern **Day of the Dead** after synthesis with Spanish traditions. She now presides over the contemporary festival as well. Mictecacihuatl is known as the *Lady of the Dead*, since it is believed that she was born, then sacrificed as an infant. Mictecacihuatl was represented with a defleshed body and with jaw agape to swallow the stars during the day.

Teotl: The Nahuatl term is often translated as "god", but it may have held more abstract aspects of the numinous or divine, akin to the Polynesian concept of Mana. In Pipil mythology Teotl is known merely as the creator and the father of life.

Tezcatlipoca: One of the four sons of Ometeotl (Also known as Teotl), he is associated with a wide range of concepts, including the night sky, the night winds, hurricanes, the north, the earth, obsidian, enmity, discord, rulership, divination, temptation, jaguars, sorcery, beauty, war and strife. His name in the Nahuatl language is often translated as "Smoking Mirror" and alludes to his connection to obsidian.

Tlaloc: God of rain, fertility, and water. He was a beneficent god who gave life and sustenance, but he was also feared for his ability to send hail, thunder, and lightning, and for being the lord of the powerful element of water.

Xochiquetzal: Also called Ichpochtli Classical Nahuatl: Ichpōchtli, meaning "maiden", was a goddess associated with concepts of fertility, beauty, and female sexual power, serving as a protector of young mothers and a patroness of pregnancy, childbirth, and the crafts practiced by women such as weaving and embroidery. The name *Xōchiquetzal* is a compound of *xōchitl* ("flower") and *quetzalli* ("precious feather; quetzal tail feather"). Wife of Tezcatlipoca.

KOSKATLAN – The Pipil Saga

The Market Place (sample)

●●●

Kozkatlán was smaller than expected. Yeisun had been to Tula when he was a child, and found that place to be very big for human city standards. And the way the people had built their pyramids, was impressive. Kozkatlán in the other hand was too small. The pyramids were not even as big as he had expected they would be. Some were not even finished. Tlaloc had said that it was a new city and that it was starting to grow, but the young god expected that at least it would be half the size of Tikal, but this was too small. He could hardly call this a city. It was more like a glorified village.

There were a lot of people here though; apparently they had come from all over the kingdom. At least that was good. It showed that the people cared for his father's festive day. That was good. With time the city might grow to be as big as Tikal or at least Copán.

The young god resembled a fisherman. He even smelled of fish, which he didn't complain about since he loved the sea creatures. He passed by some merchants who quickly approached him and asked him about his fish. "How much do you want for your fish, boy?" One of the merchants asked.

"Oh, they're not for trading," Yeisun answered.

"Where did you catch such magnificent fish?" He insisted. The fish were bigger than normal. They were fat and about twenty inches long. Tlaloc always brought magnificent sea creatures for trading. It was usually big fish that would catch the merchant's attention though, but sometimes like in the city of Tula, he would bring octopus. People in the north loved to eat Octopus.

"From the lake," The boy responded.

"What lake? Not this lake. This lake doesn't have any fish like that," the man told him.

"We caught them at Ilopango," Tlaloc said, interrupting the conversation and saving his son from talking too much.

"Oh, now that's a fine lake," the merchant responded.

"Tell you what. I'm willing to trade the fish for some fine garments. I have some good garbs made of pure wolf skins. Here, come and take a look." The man grabbed Tlaloc by the arm and pulled him closer to his merchandise. Tlaloc was used to this kind of hustles. Merchant traders were like this everywhere. They always hustle for goods. "I'll give you one good garment like this one for half a dozen of your fish," the man offered.

"No, thank you we don't need clothing. We need those fish for our dinner," politely said Tlaloc.

"You will still have plenty fish left for your dinner. Besides, your lovely wife could use some new cloth," the man said, looking at a not so attractive woman standing next to Yeisun. Chalchiuhtlicue looked like a regular fisherman's wife. She was dirty and her hair was a mess. Her close looked old and torn. Her face was stained, just like every other fisherwoman who spent too much time in the sand and salted water.

"We are okay, really," Tlaloc insisted.

"Come on I insist," the merchant said. I'll give you one garment for your wife and one for your son. It will keep them warm at night."

"You will give us two garments for six of our fish?" Yeisun asked.

"Yes of course. I have some made of cotton as well but those are more expensive," the merchant said and turned back to Tlaloc since he was the man making the decision.

"Why would he do that?" The boy asked his mother in a low voice.

"The fish are from a far land. People love things that are from foreign places. Places that they don't have access to, or are too far to travel. Especially food," Chalchiuhtlicue explained. "He will probably trade the fish for something else later. That's how merchants work."

"What do you say?" The merchant pressed on.

"It sounds like an even trade," Tlaloc finally said and turned to his wife. "Chal, why don't you choose the garments?"

"Really?" Chalchiuhtlicue pretended to be excited about her new garments. It was an act she was used to performing every time she visited the human cities. She hated the feeling of animal pelts in her delicate skin, but they had to sell the act. Trading with the locals was a good way to blend in.

"Chal? What a beautiful name my lady. Please come this way." The merchant guided her into his small lot and showed her some of the nicest garments that his wife and daughters had made from raccoon skin. Chalchiuhtlicue did not want to know how many raccoons had taken to make garments like these.

"So that's why you wanted the fish," Yeisun said to Tlaloc once the merchant was out of earshot.

"It is always good to bring something to trade. You can't pass as an outsider if you don't have anything to trade. If you show up empty handed, you'll attract suspicion and that's not good."

"Suspicion? For what?"

"Spies. They are always spies in cities like this one. They come from all over, some as far as Palenque."

"How does this look?" Chalchiuhtlicue interrupted.

"They look good ma. I like them," the boy answered.

"Here this one is yours," she said handing him out a garment made of cotton fiber. Tlaloc unhooked six fish from his knot and gave them to the merchant. The merchant gladly accepted them and placed them on a basket.

"Thank you my good man. It was good trading with you. Don't forget to stop by before you leave town. I should have some other goodies by then," the merchant said and moved on to look for another client.

The small family of gods kept walking down the market place; Chalchiuhtlicue was always fond of the jewelry the women made of special stones. The most expensive ones were always the jade necklaces. The Jade stone was one of the most rare and most venerated jewels of the region. It was said that it was one of the god's most precious gifts to man.

The market was full of people. There were merchants with food, cloth, jewelry, weapons, pottery, stones and livestock. Yeisun was amazed to see all the people walking around, trading and looking at the merchandise. Yeisun was entertained by the sight of it all, but at the end of the row he saw the most beautiful girl he had ever seen. He hadn't seen such beauty even in Tlalocan. He stared at her for what it seemed an eternity.

The girl was poorly dressed but she carried herself as if she was royalty. Her face structure was round, with high chick bones. Her figure was perfect as his mother's. She was surrounded by three other girls, poorly dressed as her but not as beautiful. While his parents were entertained looking at some pots, he decided to walk over to the girl and talk to her.

"Niltze," the young god said as he approached the girls.

"Niltze," they all replied.

"I'm Yeisun," he said in a very polite manner. The girls giggled and stared at him.

"Are you a fisherman?" One of the girls asked. Yeisun had forgotten that he was carrying the fish and his new clothes.

"Yes I am," he responded. "I come from a small village in Ilopango. We have great fish there," the young god responded using his father's excuse.

"That's nice. Excuse me," the beautiful girl said and moved on to the next jewelry post.

"Aren't you going to tell me your name?" Yeisun asked.

"Why?" Another girl said. "Should we?"

"Well, I gave you mine. It is only proper for you to respond back with yours."

"I'm sorry but we are not allowed to speak to strangers," the younger girl replied.

"Don't listen to them. My name is Sihuehuet and we are from Güija." The beautiful girl introduced herself. "It was nice to meet you Yeisun the fisherman. But we have to go," she said and placed the jade necklace back on the floor cloth.

"Do you like that necklace?" Yeisun asked quickly before the girl could leave.

"Yes I do but I don't have anything to trade for it," Sihuehuet answered.

"I do," Yeisun offered. "I have fish. I can get it for you."

"Thank you, but no. I'm sorry, I can't accept it. Besides you worked hard to get those fish, I'm sure," Sihuehuet replied.

"But it's a gift, from me to you," Yeisun insisted.

"Listen, Yeisun. I'm sure you mean well, but I don't know you and it's not proper for a maiden to accept gifts from strange men. Thank you though, you are very nice." The group of girls turned and left. Yeisun just stood there staring after the girls.

"Who was that?" Chalchiuhtlicue asked.

"Her name is Sihuehuet from Güija."

"She is pretty. Come on we have to go," his mother ordered.

"Did you see the look on his face? He looked like he was about to cry when you refused his gift." Mikal teased and everyone else giggled.

"Leave him alone. He meant well," Sihuehuet said.

"He was going to trade his fish for the necklace. You should have let him."

"Yes, and what was I going to say to my dad? That I found it?"

"No, just tell him the truth— that someone gave it to you," Mikal suggested.

"Are you crazy? That kind of thing only happens for wedding proposals."

"But he is foreign. They do things differently where he comes from. Maybe that's how people from Ilopango are," Oxaly suggested.

"No, it's not proper and you know it," Sihuehuet turned to look back and noticed that the boy was still standing there staring at them. She smiled.

"*HEY!*" The crowd was cheering.

"What's going on?" Oxaly asked a merchant woman.

"Must be the royal family. Everyone that's not from here always gets so excited to see them," the woman said, but the girls did not wait for her to finish. They were already running and trying to make their way through to take a peek.

"I can't see them," Mikal complained.

"Me neither," the rest of the girls answered. By the time they made it to the front, the royal family had already passed. There were only guards marching behind them and they were all blocking the view.

"We missed them," said one sad Oxaly.

"Don't worry you will see them again tomorrow at the inauguration of the Atlcahualo," a familiar voice said from behind.

The group of girls turned around and to their surprise it was Ácatl, the rude brute, but handsome young warrior from last night. "Niltze," he saluted.

"Niltze," the girls answered back, except for Sihuehuet who didn't really like the young man anymore. Sure he was handsome and brave. But just like Balak, he was a bully. A bigger bully than Balak ever was. This was the kind of men that her father always told her to stay away from. The kind that like to play with all the girls but never commit to anything. "*Hummingbirds*" everyone called his type. Sihuehuet was sure that that's exactly what this man was— a hummingbird going from flower to flower tasting their honey.

"What are you girls doing here?"

"We were just leaving," Sihuehuet answered and started to move away.

"No, wait. Don't go," the young man begged. "Let me at least apologize for what happened yesterday."

Sihuehuet turned around and waited. So did the rest of the girls.

"Well…" The man started. "Would you please forgive me? Yesterday was our first day here and we had been drinking Chicha. I was a little drunk, and wasn't thinking right."

"That's not an excuse," Sihuehuet spat back and started to move away.

"No... Please. I really am not a bad person. I just want to get to know you," Ácatl grabbed Sihuehuet by the arm. The beautiful girl span a pushed him away in disgust.

"Look, you are a bully and a brute. I don't want to get to know you. You are just like all the other warriors. You guys think you own the world."

Ácatl just stood there staring at her. He had never seen an angry woman like that. This had never happened to him. All the girls usually threw themselves at him, but not this one. This one was different; she had some kind of inner fire.

"Good bye," Sihuehuet said and left him in the middle of the street staring after the four girls.

Yeisun and Chalchiuhtlicue had decided to go food tasting. They loved the food. Yeisun had tried the Chichimec and the Toltec foods up in the north. The northerners had made good use of the corn. Their tamales were always good. But the Pipil tamales were better. They were juicier. "These tamales are different," he told his mother.

"Yes. The Pipils use banana leaves instead of corn leaves to wrap their tamales. It preserves the corn oils and adds a very distinguish flavor."

"Very exquisite," Yeisun added.

"Yes. They sure are." Chalchiuhtlicue agreed.

"What about this drink?" The young god asked. He was having a bowl of some kind of dark beverage. It was thick and it had black beans and some other kind of green sauce on it.

"That is what they call 'Chuco'."

"Chuco? What is it made of?"

"They make it out of fermented black corn. That's how it gets its bitter taste. The beans are just regular black beans, but the sauce is made out of pumpkin seeds. It's one of my favorite drinks."

"Wow. These Pipils are good cooks." Yeisun took another sip of his Chuco.

"I'm glad you're enjoying yourself," the goddess of water said. Yeisun smiled and continued to enjoy the food. "Calm down, don't eat so fast. Make sure you leave some room for some dessert. You need to taste their pastries. They are really good. I'm going order our cooks to learn to make them."

"I will," the boy muffled with a full mouth.

"How do you like it here?" Chalchiuhtlicue finally asked.

"It's Okay. Kind of small. I like the food though."

"Yeah, that's true it's not as big as Chichen Itza or Tula, but the people are really humble and friendly."

"Kind of small aren't they?"

"Yeah, that's how they got the name Pipil. Cause they kind of resemble big children. Plus the way they talk sounds kind of childish."

"I thought Pipil meant 'Nobles'?"

"Yeah, 'Noble children' or 'Childish Nobles' it doesn't matter," the goddess responded.

"Their cooks are good, but how about their warriors?"

"I don't know much about them. But I'm pretty sure they are fierce, or else they wouldn't be building such a nice city in this area. Tezcatlipoca would know more about that. He is venerated as much as Tlaloc in this region."

"Did someone call my name?" A beggar asked. The poor man looked ill. His skin was dark and his face looked like it had been burned by the sun. He was taller than most Indians here though. Yeisun stared at him for a while; he wasn't sure what to say.

"What do YOU want?" Chalchiuhtlicue sounded annoyed by the beggar. The beggar stared at the boy and then sat down next to her.

"So this is your youngest son. What's his name?" The man asked. Yeisun seemed confused. Why was this beggar asking questions about him? And how did he know he was the youngest?

"Don't be alarmed boy," the beggar said. "You are not the only gods here today." The old beggar smiled.

"What?" Yeisun seemed agape.

"This is Yeisun. My youngest son," the goddess answered. "What are you doing here Tezcatlipoca?"

"Visiting the Pipils. It seems like they have a nice city going on here," Tezcatlipoca answered. Yeisun finally saw the sparkle in the god of discord's eyes. He tapped into his power and then saw the beggar's full face, and he noticed Tezcatlipoca's black stripe across his face and the leopard skin on his shoulders.

"You are planning something," Chalchiuhtlicue accused. Tezcatlipoca was always up to something. And it was never good. He loved to create chaos among the

Indians. It was his favorite pastime. He loved wars and that's why the Toltec and Chichimec people were his favorites. The Pipils were too peaceful, like most Mayans. He usually got bored with them. That's why Chalchiuhtlicue was so surprised to see him here.

"Of course not. Can gods just come down and enjoy some good Chicha?" The sarcastic leopard god asked and drank from an old cup.

"How did you know we were here?" Yeisun asked.

"I saw you at the market. I recognized your father, and then I saw your mother. No one can hide such beauty," the overconfident god exclaimed. Yeisun did not like the way in which Tezcatlipoca said it. Not one bit. And the way Tezcatlipoca was looking at her didn't help either.

"Where are your wives?" Chalchiuhtlicue asked.

"Xochiquetzal is busy and didn't want to come. Chicomecóatl had some other business to attend," Xochiquetzal had been Tlaloc's wife long time ago, but Tezcatlipoca had stolen her. Chalchiuhtlicue didn't care for her at all, she always thought of her as too self-centered. But thanks to Tezcatlipoca, Chalchiuhtlicue was now the queen of Tlalocan and not Xochiquetzal. Chicomecóatl was different though. She was more like Tezcatlipoca, always causing chaos. It wouldn't surprise her if Chicomecóatl was here now trying some kind of prank on the locals. Or at Tula, which was always a good place to start chaos.

"So you came alone?" Chalchiuhtlicue asked.

"No, not alone. My son is here too. He is trying to enjoy the riches of this place. Especially their women." The god of discord winked at Yeisun.

"Which son?" Chalchiuhtlicue asked curiously. None of Tezcatlipoca's sons were good news. They were as mischievous as the war god himself.

"Itzalku."

THE PIPIL SAGA

KOSKATLAN

MILTON MANRIQUE JUAREZ

Coming Soon...

ITZALKU – The Pipil Saga
Also available in Spanish.
Disponisble en Español.

ABOUT THE AUTHOR

Milton Manrique Juarez is of Mayan/Pipil descent. He was born in El Salvador and moved to the USA when he was a pre-teen, but he never lost the passion and the rich culture of his people. He now resides in Southern Nevada where he has pursued his writing career. Milton started as a Christian song writer and has written many plays for his local church youth group. He is now currently working on a prequel to Itzalku among two other long term projects.